MADDIE KOPECKI

Nowhereland

For the best friend I could ever ask for and all the adventures we'll have together. I love you, Sam!

"A dream you dream alone is only a dream. A dream you dream together is reality."

JOHN LENNON

Contents

Acknowledgement

This book would not be possible without all of the people who believed in me before I believed in myself. If I'm being completely candid, I'm a little scared I'll forget someone. If this ends up being ridiculously long, I apologize.

First and Foremost, I need to thank the people who read this book first. When it was still a rough draft and absolutely terrible, others believed in it, and that's how I am where I am today. Thank you to Grammy, Jen, Tater, Ashley, George, and Mrs. Sevick.

Shout out to my family. Specifically, I'm talking about my dad, my moms, my sister, and my brother. I love you all with my entire being, and life without you is nothing.

I also have to thank my friends, especially Sam, who is my real-life River Fields. She's been around for nearly half my life (God help her) and I can't imagine having another best friend.

My eighth grade English teacher has been nagging me about publishing a book since I was in her class, and now I'm doing it. Ms. Romero, you're awesome!

Much love for all the people who have made this dream possible! There isn't enough time to name you all, but I appreciate you regardless.

Signing off,
Mads

1

Chapter One

Then

For sixteen years, what I knew about life and the world was pretty much confined to a town in Louisiana with only two thousand people. If you were determined enough (and bold enough to brave the sweltering humidity outside) you could walk from one side of Nowhereland to the other in a matter of hours, straight down the road that cuts through the middle of it. It was that small.

Everyone knew everyone. Our community was isolated and compact. We didn't even have a Walmart, but somehow had enough spitting, yelling preachers to have more than one church. That's sort of the Bible Belt in a nutshell, though. You tend to get a lot of old guys yapping on about Jesus, but not much capitalism. It's a shame too because whenever the grocery store raised its prices, everyone in town got grumpy about it.

Nowhereland was what River Fields, my partner-in-crime, called our hometown. I thought it was stupid at first, to steal a piece of a lyric from a song by The Beatles and turn it into a name for the place we'd grown up. But that was River, my best friend in the whole world and an avid Beatles fan. As much as I complained about his taste in music at first, I came to love it too.

We had been twelve at the time when he raised a hand in the air, gestured around us, and declared, "We gotta get out of here, Emmy. This is Nowhereland!"

From that moment on, we were in Nowhereland, as far as we were concerned. It stuck, and pretty soon, I could barely remember what this small dot on a map of Louisiana was actually called in the first place.

On my sixteenth birthday, when Riv told me he was taking me on an adventure, I couldn't fight the giant smile that spread across my face. I nodded excitedly, let him drag me by the arm to his rusty, well-loved red convertible, and got in the passenger seat.

It was the season of bug-spray as we counted down the days to summer. By the time we reached March, both of us were anxiously anticipating the end of the school year. We settled for weekends with busy Sundays like this one.

It was a season of downpour and sunshine; the weather couldn't make up its mind through that stormy spring. My legs were tanning again, exposed by a pair of old Levis shredded by kitchen scissors to make shorts fit for the heat and humidity. My curls fell just past my shoulders, framing my narrow face spattered with freckles and wide brown eyes.

He handed me a pair of aviators he probably snagged from some gas station out in the middle of nowhere, grinning wickedly. I wondered what he was planning, knowing it probably couldn't be good and decided not to care either way.

River was almost seventeen, about ten months older than I

was. The only reason we were both juniors was that I skipped fifth grade back in the day. Despite him being the older of the two of us, I would tease him, saying he acted much younger than me. He would pick me up and throw me over his shoulder in response. It was as I hung upside down, his arm curled around my legs, that he would demand an apology. Usually, I would wait until my face got really red before I finally gave him one.

That day, we were sitting side by side as he pulled out onto the main road and sped through the small town we'd known forever. The convertible had been his dad's, but after the old man died a few years back, it was left to River. I couldn't begin to count the hours spent in it.

We rushed past the gas station, the school that every kid in Nowhereland attended K-12, and even the trailer park where he lived. We'd probably loop back, but for now, we skipped on by.

We were a one-street town. The main road connected to a massive highway that was always clogged with traffic. It was terribly cliché.

Considering Riv was ignoring any and all speed limits like a madman, I now had grounds to be more than a little worried, but also excited. In a place like this, you nearly killed yourself to feel alive.

By the time we hit a hundred miles an hour, I was screaming.

My hands danced up in the air, legs propped on the dashboard as he hit the gas and floored it. The poor convertible wheezed from the effort and my dark hair lashed against my cheeks, but all we cared about was how *amazing* this felt.

How reckless, how young, how human we were in that moment.

When we reached the spot where the main road branched off into the highway, he slammed his foot down on the brakes and the car lurched forward. The tires screamed and I did too before my seatbelt slammed into my chest and cut off my oxygen.

We came to a stop at the end of the street, watching cars and big cargo trucks drive by for a few seconds as we caught our breath. He was somehow laughing and I was gaping at how dangerously close we were to oncoming traffic.

After the recklessness and adrenaline left me, I found myself mildly angry at him. If I'm being entirely honest, I never stayed mad at River for too long, but I unclicked my seatbelt and slugged River as hard on the arm as I could anyway.

"When you said we were going on an adventure, this is not what I thought you meant, dumbass!" I clutched my chest. "I'm never gonna grow real boobs now! Your seatbelt compressed my poor breasts. As if I wasn't flat enough!"

"Your boobs are fine." River cackled in his seat, dimples indenting his cheeks. "Christ, Emmy, you've got a mean right hook."

I punched him again. "You could've killed us."

"We didn't die," he retorted, gesturing around us. "The car is stopped and both of us are alive. Ain't that just lovely?"

"I'm gonna kill you and hide the body where no one will ever find it," I grumbled. "I hate you sometimes."

"But you also love me," he reminded me. "And *that* is why your threats are empty."

He isn't wrong there.

I buried my face in my hands. "This is why teenagers die in so many car accidents. They probably act as stupid as you."

River stopped laughing, leaning across the center console to look at me. His familiar hands pried my fingers away from my face and forced me to make eye contact. "Hey, I didn't mean to scare you like that. I'm sorry."

I was stunned by how lucky we were that the junker car's brakes didn't combust and the fact that he was actually apologizing to really respond. River never said sorry. Neither of us did— at least, not genuinely. Since we never set out to hurt each other, there was never a need to feel remorseful.

"Is this really happening?" I gasped. "Is River Fields really apologizing to me?"

The tips of his ears went red. "Shut up."

I gave him a hug and swatted him on the back of the head. "If you do anything like that again, with or without me in the car, I'll give you hell for it. I can't get out of Nowhereland without someone to do it with."

"I can't help that I'm an adrenaline junkie," he said.

"No, you're an idiot. That's what you are."

"It was fun though, wasn't it?"

I wouldn't give him the satisfaction of knowing that, yeah, it kind of was fun.

He reversed the car so that we were no longer at risk of slipping into the path of giant eighteen-wheelers and other vehicles plowing through. A few minutes later, we were outside the city pool, which was locked up and dirty because it hadn't been cleaned after the last storm.

He opened my door for me, and even though I wasn't sold on the idea quite yet, I climbed out.

"You want to swim?" I grimaced. "The water is nasty."

"We've swum in nastier," he said. "Besides, it's your birthday. I have to pull out all the stops."

He pulled a small duffel out of his trunk and heaved it over the fence. When he laced his fingers together and cupped his hands to give me a boost, I didn't argue and just scrambled over the gate. We'd done this a million times and city authorities never seemed to care. Besides, it was going to open for the summer in a month or so anyway. River liked using the pool before then because it got crowded during the hotter months.

My one-piece was getting thin and worn out, but I was grateful to have something to change into. River planned it out, bringing sunscreen, towels, bathing suits for both of us, and messy PB&Js for later. My favorite, naturally.

"By the way, your boobs look fine," he said when I emerged dressed.

I flipped him off and shoved him into the murky water, knowing he was going to grab me and pull me with him. When we broke the surface, I splashed him. "You don't get a free pass to just look at my boobs!"

He just shook his head. "You can't complain about them and expect me not to peek!"

"You're such a boy!" I said lamely.

We bickered like that for a few minutes as the sun dipped low, then climbed out and wrapped ourselves in towels to eat our sandwiches. I chewed on stale white bread and licked the jam off my lips.

We'd grown up together, so I never noticed the changes in him until they were blatantly obvious. Sitting at the pool, it seemed like he got five years older in a couple of days. His jaw was speckled with real stubble, not just fuzz anymore, and his eyes were still green as ever, but more determined. Fiercer. He was still that kid with messy dirty blonde hair and crooked teeth to me, but other girls didn't see him like that. It was like we suddenly stepped into an alternate universe.

I still felt so young, like I hadn't aged at all, while he was a man with real muscle and facial hair and everything. Funny how some things change. Even funnier how some things don't.

"Hey, Emmy?"

I looked over at him and answered with a full mouth, "Yeah?"

"Happy sixteenth birthday."

"Thanks, Riv," I replied. "I'm officially getting old. Pretty soon, I'm gonna have grey hair from all the stress you cause."

He set his sandwich down beside him and stared at me long and hard. "Nope. Not a grey hair in sight. Just a frizzy, brown mess."

I pushed his shoulder playfully. "Shut up."

"I'm kidding, Em. You know, you're actually really pretty,"

I raised my eyebrows. "Thanks? Did you think I was ugly before or something?"

"Oh, shut up, Emmy. Don't be an asshole."

"You love me."

"Unfortunately, yes."

He reached over beside him and pulled out his Walkman, slipping a Beatles CD inside. It was the obvious choice, and I liked the familiar noise.

"So what's next, River Fields?" I leaned my head on his shoulder, his skin hot against my cool cheek. "Should we head back to the trailer and see if we can get any TV channels to come in?"

Before he could answer, the sky above us cracked with thunder, which meant we could expect another sudden rainstorm any time now. He helped me to my feet and got me over the fence before it started coming down. We drove to his place with me huddled up next to him in the convertible, my jacket held above both our heads.

We were still soaked to the bone when we got inside, but that was why I kept dry pajamas in his room anyway. I toweled my hair as he messed with the antenna. It took a while before we concluded the old junker television wasn't going to get reception in weather like this.

Instead, he pulled out a crossword puzzle book I bought him for his birthday that year and let me try and help him answer the questions, even though he knew more than I did.

We didn't really have to talk. We'd been best friends for so long that we could communicate without words. I knew him well enough and he knew me well enough for us to go hours without speaking.

I took the pen from him when I knew an answer and vice-versa. The crosswords were a mess of both of our handwriting; disastrous and sloppy loops for me, straight and neat letters for him.

Around eight, his mom brought home a pizza and a box of chocolate chip cookies from the grocery store where she worked. Because it was late, I texted and told my parents where I'd be for the night. We were always at each other's houses, even as we grew older, so they weren't surprised. All I got was a simple "okay" from my mother.

"I know you probably wanted a Gatsby sort of party," he told me later as we listened to that Beatles CD again. "I'm sorry, but Nowhereland doesn't really have that swanky New York City feel."

"It's okay," I assured him. "It was perfect."

He beamed, and my day got even better.

Days always passed like this. We sought adventures where there weren't any to be found unless we were looking really hard for them. The key was to find little things that excited us

8

and thrive on the feeling. We didn't have Disneyworld near us, but we could push River's car as fast as it could go, and that was close enough.

It didn't stop raining until well after midnight. By that point, it was too late to leave the trailer anyway. The dirt path outside would be blocked by mud and would swallow our legs whole if we tried to cross. Besides, River's tires were so stripped they wouldn't make it through.

River searched for a new CD as I tugged my hair into a braid. We were playing chess on the board his father had splurged on for his tenth birthday. Quite a few of the glass pieces were scratched (and his white knight was missing a head) but he loved that damned board with everything he had, so I never complained about playing chess with him. I was notoriously bad and almost always lost. If I got lucky, or River took pity on me, it would end in a stalemate.

I pushed a bishop diagonally across the board and he closed the Walkman and Green Day filled the silence. "Your move," I called as he skipped ahead to *American Idiot*. It was his favorite track.

He barely gave the board a glance before using a rook to take my queen. I cursed loudly, knowing that no matter how many games we played, I always lost my queen early. I never seemed to learn better.

"Checkmate." He smirked at me.

"Are you ever gonna let me win?" I whined.

"Your victory wouldn't be valuable if I went easy on you." He laid down beside me, his legs on top of mine. "And I wouldn't want to deprive you of a true win against this chess master."

"You just like winning," I huffed, narrowing my eyes at him. I laid my cheek against the material of his worn long-sleeved shirt, listening to his heartbeat. He fell back into the pillows, exhausted.

"Wanna hear something funny?" His eyes were closed as he said it.

"Sure."

"Even tired, I can still beat you at chess," he said smugly.

We were listening to the wind for the next hour, just letting time pass. I lifted my head to see if he was asleep, but his eyes flicked open and met mine.

"You should really go to sleep," I said, glancing at the clock. "We have school today."

"It's already Monday?" He threw an arm over his face. "Let's ditch and sleep in."

"We have a trig test first period," I replied. "As much as I would like to, we can't miss it."

"You should go to sleep." His voice was soft and his words were slow as if he was forcing himself to stay awake and talk to me.

"I'm enjoying the rain."

"You hate it when it storms," he pointed out.

"Only when I'm outside."

He pulled me closer and tugged the blanket over us. A few seconds passed before he conjured up the energy to respond. "I can't sleep until you sleep, Emmy."

"Fine," I conceded.

In the end, he fell asleep first.

His breathing evened out and his heartbeat slowed down. His arm around me fell limp. A few minutes later, I was out too.

* * *

We got up the next morning a few minutes late, which lead to us fighting over the sink in the cramped bathroom to brush our teeth, scrambling to get dressed, and making it to class right on the bell. It was a typical start to the week.

River sat behind me, which meant I had to tolerate him clicking his pen over and over while I took my test. He was done early, not surprising considering he was a genius. I was limping through physics, another class we shared because of how small the student population was. He handled it with ease. He wanted to be a physicist when he grew up, but I thought that career sounded awful.

"What did you get?" asked Riv as he bounced excitedly in his chair and waved his graded answer sheet in my face.

"I got a C minus." I stared down at the page, thanking whatever god was out there I hadn't gotten an F due to my lack of studying. "I assume that you acting like a five-year-old means you got an A?"

He nodded. "I got lucky there. Really thought I would bomb it."

"You're the next Einstein, Riv," I turned around and shoved my paper in my backpack, trying to hide my envy. "You're incapable of failing anything. It's all so easy for you."

"Are you mad at me?" His head tilted left, confusion marking his face. River knew me well, which meant it was near impossible for me to lie to him. He knew something was up oftentimes before I truly grasped what I was feeling. We could read each other all too well.

"No," I quipped as we stepped out into the throng of students on their way to class.

He took hold of my wrist gently, forcing me to stop. We stood against a row of metal lockers, his gentle fingers keeping me from running. "Em?" he prompted. "Talk to me."

"I'm mad at me, not you." I let him take me into his arms for a hug, even though I never liked showing affection in public. It was weird to me. "It's frustrating how smart you are. You've got the world in your hands and you don't even have to try. I want to be better."

"You're great on your own. It's just math. You're way better at history and always ace your English papers." He squeezed me tighter. "We make a good pair. If you put us together, we would have a shared four-point-oh."

He released me and we walked side by side toward our next class. We had history together, then I went to gym and he went to study hall. We would meet at lunch and go to our remaining courses together since we shared them. It was rare that we were ever apart.

This class was Riv's favorite because the teacher liked him best out of all of us. River had managed to sneak into the seat beside mine, so we always shared a textbook and compared notes before every test. We had a routine between the two of us, a comfortable one at that.

There was a shift in the River-Emery universe when a boy tapped me on the shoulder and asked me for a pencil. His name was Keith and I'd gone to school with him since kindergarten. He was shy and still had his top row of braces. I barely knew him, and I never figured we would ever have a conversation.

I handed over a yellow no. 2 and turned around to face the front again. To my surprise, there were no sarcastic comments from River about giving away my good pencils to strangers. In fact, there was nothing from him at all. Period. He was staring hard at his notes, eyes cast away from me, and at the time, I thought he was just looking over them for the quiz we would be having about the Cold War.

I didn't know any better.

2

Chapter Two

Now
Soft Southern California sun has spoiled me. Even in autumn, it's warm and lovely.

I get out of bed every morning and walk down by the beach until I reach my favorite coffee joint. It never gets too hot here and it never seems to rain. I love the weather. It's so unlike Louisiana that it trips me up sometimes. It acts as a reminder that I'm here in Long Beach at twenty-one, excited to get started with the rest of my life and almost done with college.

It's early, which is why even in a city like this most people aren't awake yet. Saturday mornings are the quiet ones. I appreciate them the most.

There's a stark contrast between the likes of Nowhereland and here. For one, California has a wide array of businesses and places to see. Just about everything is a drive away back home. California is so much bigger than Louisiana. The entire population of my hometown could fit inside the first floor of my apartment building.

My accent has faded into the standard dialect of California, but every once in a while, the southern part of me makes an appearance. I don't know why, but I'm grateful that I can blend in, forget where I came from (or escaped from, flip a coin). Admittedly, a small part of me belongs to where I grew up, whether I admit it or not.

I open the door to Cornerside Coffee House and my senses flood with the smell of ground coffee beans and baked muffins. Eyes closed, I inhale, wondering to myself if this is really my life. I made it. I get to have good drinks every day and a quality education far away from the likes of Nowhereland. God, nothing smells better than a fresh brew.

It occurs to me then how sad it is that I had an utter dissatisfaction with my life from the minute I entered high school. But thankfully, it's paid off. Now, I can't imagine being anywhere else.

When I open my eyes, Caroline, the barista I've befriended, beams at me. She's painted her nails red and the color compliments her ebony skin perfectly. Her black ponytail swings behind her as she heads from the espresso machine toward the counter. "The usual, Emery?"

I nod. "Please."

She scribbles on a cup and sets it to her left before reaching for another. "And what about the boyfriend? Does he want one too?"

I look down at my feet, fighting the smile and blush that usually comes with thinking about him. It's funny that even five years into the future, he still makes me feel excited that I got so lucky.

"That would be great, Caroline." I reach for my wallet and pull out a crisp five-dollar bill. As another employee works on the coffee, Caroline counts out my change and slides a receipt across the counter.

"So how's school going?" she inquires. "Are you still studying physics?"

"Of course," I say. "At this point, I can't imagine studying anything else."

"I graduated with a real degree," she says. "And somehow, I'm still a barista. Make sure you get a good job. Make the debt worth it before you become old and withered like me."

"Old?" I can't help but laugh. "You're only twenty-three."

"Don't be so technical," she says dismissively.

We stand in silence for a few minutes as she gets the hot water started. I stifle a yawn and let my mind wander to the homework I have for my quantum mechanics class. It's a tedious set of equations and whatnot, but it shouldn't be too difficult. I'm already doing some of the math in my head when Caroline's voice brings me back to the present.

"Where's your man anyway?" she glances around, shifting her stare back to me when she comes up empty. "Don't you usually come in together?"

"Yeah, the poor guy has the flu. Can't say I'll fondly recall rubbing his back while he puked into the toilet but hey, that's love for you." I vividly recall how disgusting that particular event was, but I didn't mind it. He's always there when I'm sick, and because I have a crappy immune system, that's quite often.

Caroline makes a face. "TMI, Emery."

"You asked," I reply matter-of-factly.

She shrugs. "I didn't want the details. But hey, at least you're comfortable with each other."

"I would hope so," I say. "I mean, we've been together since

I was sixteen."

As she brews the coffee, she sighs longingly. "I'd kill to have a love like that."

"And you'll find it," I assure her, and mean every word. "It's around here somewhere, just waiting for the right moment."

"It better get here soon," she jokes and sets the drinks in front of me on the counter. "Order's up. One iced Americano and a skinny hazelnut latte to go."

I take the cups in each of my hands and turn to leave. "Bye, Caroline, it was nice talking to you."

Caroline waves as I head for the door. "See you later, girl!"

I'm met with the warm sun and a nice breeze when I make it outside. It's only a short walk. My apartment building is so close to the beach that I can always smell the ocean. Even though it's a little pricey, it's well worth it. I lucked out with scholarships, so I don't have to worry about tuition. My job as a secretary takes care of the rest. Between my boyfriend and me, we make it work.

The apartment is quiet when I arrive, which means he's still sleeping. I put the extra cup in the fridge for him to drink later and leave a message on a post-it note I stuck to the lid. One glance at the clock tells me I have to be at work in an hour, so I should probably get going soon.

Don't get me wrong, the job isn't great, but making copies and answering the phone for a few attorneys isn't too demanding. The silver lining is that it pays well, even if it's boring. Besides, on slower days, I can do homework.

I savor my last few moments of freedom in the silence of the apartment by drinking my coffee and doing a crossword puzzle. I'm always surrounded by people, always heading somewhere or doing something. I take moments of peace like this and enjoy them because you never know when you'll have another.

I'm wearing my usual: blazer, button-up, jeans. My headphones are on and my head is low the entire way there. Like always, I take the city bus, which isn't as unpleasant as it might sound; the ride passes quickly and it drops me off right outside the building. A typical morning begins with me expertly navigating the maze of doors until I reach the office, and today is no exception.

I get a phone call five minutes into my shift. There's only time for me to push up my sleeves and keep a pen in my hand, ready to scribble notes.

In my cheeriest voice, I chirp, "You've reached Scruvener and Smith, how may I assist you?"

The hours pass in a blur of answering phones and my pen scratching against yellow sticky notes. During lunch, I do my homework, which consists of writing my paper for the physics portion of my university's academic journal. I'm particularly excited about the outcome of my efforts. The project is dreary, but I'm pushing forward.

Astrophysics is what I'm fixated on, which is surprising considering I hated physics for the longest time. Eventually, I came around and declared it as my major, and I've been studying the subject ever since.

I'm so caught up in my work that I don't hear the heavy footfall of expensive dress shoes.

"How's my favorite physicist?" My boss, Glenn, raps his knuckles against my desk.

"Not a physicist yet," I remind him. "I have to graduate first, then apply for a job at the university."

"Why physics, Miss Leigh?" He cocks his head at me. "It

seems so confusing."

I take a bite of the apple I brought. "It's not really. In actuality, it explains things. All the abstract stuff that seems so confusing can be answered with physics. Like gravity."

It's the answer I've practiced, avoiding the precise reason I chose it. I don't know to this day. I know why it's a reputable field, I know why it's valuable, but I don't know why I picked my major. That's probably an issue, but it's one I'm not willing to address.

He chuckles. "I'm forty years your senior and yet, sometimes, you seem older than me."

"Now you're just flattering me." I glance back down at my computer screen. The cursor blinks at me as if saying *get back to work, Emery.*

Glenn starts walking toward the doors that lead outside, noting the end of our talk. "I better let the genius get back to work. I'll be leaving early, so it's just you and Jerry for the rest of the afternoon."

"Where are you headed?"

He seems so overjoyed as he answers, "It's my anniversary with Moira, and I'm taking her to dinner."

"Have fun!" I call after him as he all but skips away.

Glenn is the nicer of the two attorneys. Jerry barely acknowledges my existence and only speaks to me if he needs notes or something scheduled. I don't mind it much.

This is my life. At times, it can be dull, but I've decided that looking on the bright side is the only way to get around all the stuff that comes with being an adult. I work, I clean, I go on dates, take classes, etcetera. Though admittedly, sometimes I get nostalgic thinking about being sixteen.

There were a lot of firsts that year. New lessons to be learned and all that jazz.

I take the city bus back to the apartment so I don't have to walk in the dark. The way there, I listen to a podcast my upper-level physics teacher records weekly. While I listen, I can't help but wonder what'll happen once I graduate. I wish I could say I had a clear answer, but I don't, not really.

The podcast gets boring. I realize that I've probably sat through one dry lecture too many by this point in my life as I switch to music. The song, of all that could play first on shuffle, is one that catches my attention.

The Beatles.

Instantly, I'm sixteen again, lying in bed next to my best friend in the entire world. The boy I loved more than life itself. The boy who named our tiny town Nowhereland and took me on adventures.

River.

I can't help but smile.

3

Chapter Three

Then
Being a teenager sucked. Between trigonometry giving me hell, the stressful prospect that next year we would be applying to college, and the fact that I was feeling particularly moody that Tuesday following my birthday, I didn't understand the hype.

The second we got back to River's trailer to hang out, I was about to make a beeline for the couch, but I stopped when he said, "Uh, Emmy?"

I turned around and faced him with eyebrows crinkled in confusion.

His face was red and he was rubbing the back of his neck like he couldn't figure out how to phrase what he wanted to say to me. "You, um, you should probably check the back of your jeans."

I'd never seen him so embarrassed before, but when I looked in the mirror and yelped, I'm pretty sure I won the "Most Humiliated" award.

I got my period. And bled all over my jeans.

"How long was I walking around like that?" I demanded. My mind was reeling from the possibility that all day, I was sitting in my own blood and making a complete fool of myself. This was beyond mortifying.

It's not like River and I had boundaries. I knew there was nothing I could say to shock him or throw him off. There was nothing I could do to get rid of him. This wasn't something really groundbreaking, but to my teenage self, it was the end of the world at that moment.

"Not long," he insisted. "I just… I didn't see it before now. I probably would've noticed if it happened earlier."

"You were staring at my ass?" I sputtered. "River Michael Fields!"

He pinched the bridge of his nose and looked away from me. "I'm a guy, I look at asses sometimes."

"You didn't have to look at mine!" I shoved past him to punctuate my statement and found myself searching his drawers for extra clothes.

"Em, I didn't mean to upset you—"

"It's fine," I dismissed him. "Whatever."

Frustrated, I pushed away from his dresser when I came up empty. He sighed deeply and opened a different drawer, handing me a pair of sweats and clean underwear. He must've cleaned them for me after I left my clothes from last week in his hamper. His kindness made me feel ready to cry.

He stopped me before I could rush out again, blocking my path. "Mom has tampons under the sink," he whispered softly. "And the shower is yours. I'll clean your clothes for you too."

I blinked at him, at a loss for what to say.

"Consider it my redemption for staring at your ass." He drew me in for a hug. Instantly, I felt awful for being so harsh to him, burying my face in his chest and inhaling. He smelled like, well, River, and it always comforted me.

When I was in the shower, I washed all the blood off my legs and left my clothes on the floor. He knocked once, and I knew he was lingering outside.

"Can I come and grab your clothes so I can throw them in the wash?" he asked, hesitation obvious in his tone.

"Yeah," I called out, running a bar of soap over my arm. "I guess."

He walked in and I poked my head out of the curtain to peek at him. He glanced up with pink cheeks, staring at my face for a few seconds. His expression softened. "Do you need anything?"

I shook my head.

We were looking at each other as if for the first time. It occurred to me that he really did care, that he only meant well by telling me I had bled through.

"I don't like it when you look at my ass," I told him. "But I get it. I'm sorry for being mean to you. You were just trying to help."

"It's fine," he said.

"No, it's not." I suddenly didn't care I was still standing in the shower. "I'm sorry."

"It's okay." He stepped forward and rested his hand on my wet cheek, pushing the hair out of my eyes. "It really is."

I leaned into his palm and thought about how no one had ever touched me like this. I thought about how much I loved him and considered, maybe for a moment, that this bond between us was more complicated than it used to be. I looked up at him with the shower curtain still pulled over my body and wondered what he was thinking about.

Suddenly, he jerked away. "I should let you finish showering."

The door closed behind him and I was left to wonder what the hell just happened. Letting the curtain fall away, I rinsed off the soap and replayed the exchange over in my mind. My skin was tingling as if his fingers were still resting against it.

I got dressed, took care of the tampon situation, and met him in the living room where I saw he had baked chocolate chip cookies for me.

"Careful," he warned. "They're hot."

I ignored the plate of tempting cookies on the table and sat down next to him on the couch. His arms were at his sides, so instead of tucking myself under one, I took his hand. We always kept our palms clasped together when we did, but this time, I slid my fingers through his and let our hands intertwine completely.

He squeezed.

"You made me cookies," I stated the obvious.

"I did," he said.

"Why?"

I expected him to say *the dough was going to expire* or something, but not what he responded with. Instead, he just earnestly said, "They're your favorite."

I'm pretty sure that's the second I wanted to burst into tears. It was such a small act that spoke volumes. River was the only one who cared that much next to my own mom and dad.

I swallowed hard. "I love you, Riv."

We said *I love you* all the time, but this time it felt different. He was my best friend, so all the times we traded those words, it was natural. I couldn't place why it suddenly felt more meaningful now.

"Love you too, Em." He pulled his hand out of mine and lifted his arm to put it around me. I tucked myself up close, knees to my chest, and felt his lips linger against my temple. I wasn't even sure it happened. It felt like he kissed my forehead.

Holy crap... did he just kiss my forehead?

I glanced up at him. He was staring straight ahead at the TV that was airing a generic sitcom, volume so low he couldn't really be watching it. I had no idea what they were saying. I was hyper-focused on how fast his heart was beating.

I wanted to say something to break the silence but didn't know what. So I kept quiet, nibbling on one of those amazing cookies while we both pretended to pay attention to the TV. My stomach was curled in knots, but I couldn't place why. All I knew was that I needed time to think.

"I should probably get going soon," I announced, glancing at the clock for emphasis. "I wasn't home last night, so..."

River frowned. "It's only four-thirty. Since when do your parents want you home before they're done with work?"

Busted. I chewed my lip and tried to continue the lie, "I dunno. It's probably a late birthday thing. I'll see you later?"

I started for the door and shouldered my backpack, halted by him getting to his feet. "Want me to drive you?"

"I can walk," I insisted.

I knew he was probably aware that I was avoiding him. He didn't let on. He just moved out of my way and let me leave in a hurry.

When I reached the end of the driveway, I heard the screen door creak as River stepped outside. I pretended not to notice, continuing on with my head low. Soon enough, he was walking alongside me silently, long strides slowed to match my pace.

"You don't have to do this," I told him.

"I know," he said. "What kind of man would I be if I let a lady walk home alone?"

I didn't say anything, so he kept going, "Did I do something wrong?"

I shook my head. "Just drop it."

"No." He reached out and grabbed my hand, but it wasn't like before. It was just palm against palm, fingers separate. I already missed his being threaded through mine.

"It's just my period," I said smoothly. "It's really embarrassing and gross."

He believed it, rolling his eyes as he told me, "Why would it be embarrassing? It's a natural thing. It's not gross."

He knew my excuse was complete and utter BS but he didn't push further than that. We kept walking and somewhere in the middle, he laced our fingers together. Oblivious, I dismissed it as platonic, my mind preoccupied with other matters.

When we got to my apartment, I fumbled for my key as he leaned against the wall beside the door. He'd only been in my house a handful of times. We'd never stayed there together for too long. His place was warmer and always felt more like a home, which is why it was our main spot.

I felt a bit guilty for practically avoiding him, so I figured I should cut it out. Besides, nothing had changed. All of it was just in my head, hormones or something like that. Or at least that's what I forced myself to believe.

Think about it like this— when your best friend has been your only companion since the dawn of time, you don't want to do anything that could possibly jeopardize that. As far as I was concerned, we were only friends and we were supposed to stay that way.

I unlocked the door and walked in, leaving it open so that he could come in.

Riv followed me to my room, which was down the hall and to the left. It occurred to me that he'd never seen it before as I flicked on the light and kicked my sneakers off. They hit the wall with a dull thud and landed on the carpet.

He looked around at the walls covered in magazine cutouts, pictures, and all the normal fixings of a teenager's room. My bookshelf sat in the corner by my tiny twin-sized bed, the mattress covered by a quilt my grandmother had made me. It was a simple space, but it was comfortable and familiar to me.

"You kept the Barbie?" He nodded his head at the blonde doll that sat on the shelf beside *To Kill A Mockingbird*. He'd got it for my eighth birthday with his allowance that he'd saved up. Because I knew how much he'd worked for it, I kept it all these years.

"Of course," I said.

"And the chessboard?" He pointed at the top of my dresser where the box was.

"I keep all the birthday presents you buy me," I replied like it should've been obvious. He didn't get me a gift every year, but sometimes he surprised me with little things, like the aforementioned presents or the unraveling friendship bracelet he'd made me in middle school.

"That reminds me," he said and withdrew a small wrapped parcel from the pocket of his worn-out jeans. "Look, we established I'm broke, so I got you something small and forgot to give it to you yesterday. Happy late birthday, Emmy."

I unwrapped it slowly and lit up instantly when I saw what he'd bought me. It was a charm bracelet, a golden *E* dangling from it. He knew me well enough to get me something meaningful without being too fussy. Immediately, I clasped it around my wrist and threw my arms around him.

He chuckled, relieved. "You like it? Thank goodness."

"Of course I do, idiot, it's from you."

River was probably the only person aside from my parents who made a place like Nowhereland remotely bearable. Sometimes, I wasn't sure he realized that.

After I let go, I sat down on the bed with the chessboard and began to set up the pieces. "Shall we, Fields?"

He grinned before he moved a bishop to the correct position on the board. "Of course, but you really need to learn the right placement for your knights and bishops. Otherwise, we're going to have a serious problem."

I rolled my eyes but allowed him to fix my mistake. He always let me have the first move, just to give me an advantage that never seemed to work in my favor anyway. This time, we ended in a stalemate, but at least it seemed to be genuine, rather than him just going easy on me.

After another match that he won, I gave up and accepted that I'd been defeated.

River put the board back on my dresser and lay down beside me, staring up at my unfamiliar ceiling with the same fascination he'd gazed at my walls with. It was marked by old pictures that I'd run out of space for. I had stood on my dresser to reach it, so a few were crooked, but I didn't mind.

Everything had died down. We were both exhausted. He seemed eerily calm as if someone had flicked a switch in him and turned off the River Fields I was so used to.

"That's us in kindergarten." He pointed at one of the pictures on the roof. "You keep all of these things, but you also try to tell me you're not sentimental."

"Okay, maybe I'm a bit sentimental," I conceded. "But this is my life, you know? I just figured I should turn the adventures we have into documented memories."

"There aren't real adventures in Nowhereland," River said dryly. He threw an arm over his eyes and sighed deeply. "Isn't it sad that I feel like I'm wasting my life at sixteen?"

"Sort of." I propped myself up on my elbows. "But I feel the same way, so I understand it. It's like we have so much potential and we waste it in small-town Louisiana."

"Exactly why I call this place Nowhereland," he told me. "Because this is the place where life ends, not where it begins. Ever notice how no one here is really happy?"

He wasn't wrong. My parents were always bearing hunched shoulders, looking as if the weight of lost dreams was pushing down on them. The teachers at school seemed to be waiting for something more too. Not everyone was planning to escape like we were, but the people we encountered didn't seem particularly content to be here either.

"We have the rest of our long lives to do great things," I said to him, as much as to myself. "This is just the starting point. It teaches us what we don't want and what we won't have. We won't be like them."

I was promising him, and me, in the same breath.

4

Chapter Four

Then
     "You're insane, River!" I exclaimed, a few days later while we were driving home from school. When *All You Need Is Love* started playing on the radio, he pulled the convertible over immediately before cranking up the volume and jumping out of the car.

He was currently standing by the passenger side with the door open, his hands holding mine. "Please dance with me."

"This isn't a dancing song."

"You can always dance to The Beatles," he insisted. "Dance with me."

I looked up at him, prepared to give him a stubborn glare. Instead, I found him staring at me with those wide eyes of his and found myself unable to say no. I rolled my eyes, getting out of the car against my better judgment.

He grinned so wide I decided it was worth it.

He took my hands and spun me around slowly. We danced on the side of the road, swaying to the music the entire length of the song, even if it seemed a little silly. Near the end, he held onto my hips and dipped me dramatically. Even if he was goofing around, when he pulled me back up, the mood was different. Our faces were agonizingly close together, and at that moment, I knew there was something different about us, even if his lips never met mine.

He let me go, kissing my cheek before we broke apart completely. "Thanks, Emmy, for dancing with me."

"Who else would humor your craziness, Riv?"

Long after we got back in the car and drove back to his trailer, I held onto the memory. Being friends with Riv was weird, sure, but I wouldn't trade it for the world.

* * *

Considering the great afternoon we'd had the day before, I knew something was wrong when the bell rang in trig that following day and River was nowhere to be found. The seat behind me remained empty, absent of the familiar face I loved.

He was almost never absent, even though he could probably ace his classes without bothering to show up. The last time he'd missed a day was freshman year when both of us had the flu and could barely make it from our beds to the bathroom to vomit.

To say it was out of character would be an understatement. I checked my phone for texts off and on throughout the class period and pretended to pay attention until the bell finally rang.

Mom and Dad weren't super attentive when it came to matters like attendance, so I decided the risk of getting caught ditching was worth it. The walk from the school to River's trailer was a short one, but then again a walk anywhere in a place like this was short.

I trudged through what felt like endless dust in Louisiana heat. The weather was so temperamental; first, it was so hot you wanted to strip down and peel your skin off, then, it was raining so hard you couldn't see two feet in front of you. I was wearing shorts and a tank top that stuck to my back with sweat.

It was almost April, a few weeks away from summer, and a little over a year until graduation. Whenever I was doing something tedious, or something that reminded me how thoroughly shitty Nowhereland was, I occupied my time by thinking about how close I was to breaking free.

I tried calling River, but I knew he wasn't going to answer even before I got the automated message. When I got to the trailer, I stood outside and knocked for a few minutes as I waited for him to answer. Nothing.

My hand wiggled the knob and the door swung open. The fact he left it unlocked was worrisome. I wondered if he knew I was coming; he knew me well enough to know I would come by.

"River?" I called, scanning the living room. "Riv?"

It seemed his mother, Carly, wasn't home. He was alone.

I wandered forward a bit and stopped outside his door, watching him. He was under the blankets with his back turned to me, curled in on himself. I knew he wasn't asleep; his breathing wasn't even enough.

"Hey," he said quietly.

I sat down on the end of his bed and stole a glance at him. He looked ready to burst into tears, which I knew wasn't a common occurrence. Something was wrong here. "Are you okay?"

He shook his head.

I climbed up beside him, our faces close together, and I rested a hand on his cheek before I could stop myself. "Is it a bad day?"

The bad days came every once in a while. The change in River was subtle, but there. They usually occurred after periods of limitless happiness, when he felt untouchable and seemed like he could taste the stars and the infinite possibilities of life, but it had never been this bad before.

He closed his eyes. A silent yes.

"I'm here," I whispered. "I'm here for you."

"Can you get under the blanket?" he murmured.

I obliged, sliding closer to him under the heavy quilt. His hand came up to rest on my thigh. As we lay there, I noticed my thumb brushed the corner of his mouth, and since he had yet to tell me to take my hand away, I left it there.

He kept his eyes closed but smiled. "Don't you have a class to be in?"

"Don't you?" I countered.

He shrugged indifferently. "Mom called the attendance office for me. As for you... Well, I figured you'd wind up here at some point."

He wasn't wrong. Part of me wondered if he deliberately ignored my calls so I would be concerned enough to stop by.

I dismissed the thought. *He knows if he asked I would be there in a second.*

River was uncharacteristically quiet. It was unnerving.

Slowly, I took my hand away from his face and let it fall on the mattress between us. I half-expected him to take it, but his hand remained on my thigh. Normally the contact would feel intimate and borderline uncomfortable, but it didn't this time.

Probably because he wasn't himself, because it wasn't really River whose fingers squeezed the soft skin gently.

When I froze, he must've noticed, because his hand fell away and found mine.

"Sorry," he said.

"It's fine. Do you want to be alone?"

"No."

"What can I do?"

He was silent. All he did was squeeze my fingers as if that would make me feel better. It was strange how he was comforting me when he needed it.

"You scared me," I said sharply. "I hope you know that."

"I'm sorry," he apologized again. Both of us opened our eyes, gazes meeting. He looked at me as he continued talking, "I can't get out of bed, Emmy. It's like the world is on fire and I'm left to burn with it. It hurts. It hurts so much."

That was never a good sign.

I intended to touch his face again, so I slowly began to pull my hand free of his. My fingers slid up a few inches along his wrist. When I reached his bicep, I found the soft skin along the inside of his arm was ragged. Immediately, I pulled the blankets back, choking back a sob when I saw horizontal lines dancing across the skin, freshly scabbed over. Four of them. He'd cut himself four times.

River bowed his head in shame, unable to look at me.

"When?" I demanded, my voice cracking. "When did you do this?"

Silence.

"Answer me!"

"Last night," he confessed.

"Why would you do something like that?" I asked through

my tears. "Why would you hurt yourself?"

I didn't know who moved closer to who, just that soon, his face was buried in my chest and his fingers were grasping my shirt tightly in his hands. Warm tears dripped down my skin along the collar of my shirt. His. Mine. A mixture of the two.

"I just wanted to feel something," he whispered. "That's all."

"That's not the way to do it, River," I blubbered incomprehensibly. "You could've come to me."

"It's fine," he said. "I'm okay."

"With what?" I asked sharply. "What did you use and where did you get it?"

"Razorblade." He kept his eyes screwed shut, afraid to look at me. "I took it out of my pencil sharpener."

My breath caught in my throat. I was angry and upset and above all, I was hurt. I was hurt that he decided to turn to self-mutilation instead of his best friend.

"Promise me," I ordered, my hands clasping his cheeks. "Promise me you'll never do this again."

He nodded, chin bobbing up and down against my palms.

"Say it," I insisted. "*Please*, River, say it."

"I promise," he said.

From that point on, I held him. It was all I could do.

Eventually, we fell asleep like that, tangled up in each other. It wasn't terribly uncommon for us to sleep curled up against one another. Frankly, I liked it better than sleeping alone.

When I was startled awake a couple of hours later, I found that his side of the bed was empty. My fingers stretched out across the sheet, finding that it was still warm. An irrational part of me worried about him wandering off in his current state of mind, but two minutes later he came back with wet hair from a shower and my worries subsided. He was shirtless,

I noticed, but I wasn't too focused on that. More or less, I was relieved.

And angry.

I was pissed that I had to worry about him. It felt wrong to be so concerned about his well-being. I wanted to feel like I had the assurance of knowing he would be okay, but I didn't. It scared me.

I got up wordlessly and pushed past him. Considering I hadn't thought up a destination, I realized I was stupidly standing in the living room, trying to decide if I felt comfortable just leaving him here to do God knows what.

He came out of his room in a long-sleeved shirt, no doubt trying to hide the evidence of what he'd done. His gaze found mine. "You're mad at me."

I rolled my eyes. "No shit, Sherlock."

I glanced away from him and out the window, where I could see the sun was starting to set. If I was going to leave, I had to do it soon.

River crossed the room and took my hand. I yanked it away from him reflexively.

"Emmy." My name rolled off his tongue in a pleading voice. "Please talk to me."

"It hurts me too, you know!" I screamed, the dam inside me breaking. "When you hurt yourself it hurts me too, River. That's why I'm mad at you!"

He clenched his jaw. "I'm sorry."

"You don't get to be sorry," I said sharply. "You don't get to just apologize like that'll make it okay."

He turned away from me. I knew he wasn't a crier, so my walls tumbled down when his lower lip trembled. It was an emotional day all around.

"I didn't want to tell you," he said.

"Why?"

"Because I knew you'd freak out." His eyes were locked on the floor.

I came closer to him, no longer angry, just sad, and hugged him around the middle. "You can always tell me things. Even if I freak out."

"I won't do it anymore," he said. "I never want to hurt you again. I can't believe I could be so stupid."

"Riv—" I started.

"I hurt you, Emmy," he went on. "And I'll never forgive myself for it."

After we broke apart, we opened our wallets and scrounged up the cash for a pizza. It was easier to change our focus than to address the problem. I called in the order, he slid a Beatles CD into the Walkman, and we pretended to be okay.

His fingers fell across the buttons until he stopped on a track I'd probably heard but couldn't recall. When I heard the first few lyrics, Deja Vu hit.

"He's a real nowhere man sitting in his nowhere land."

I quirked a smile. "So that's where you got it from."

"I'm not very original."

I sat down on the edge of his couch and leaned my head against the arm of it, my cheek resting against the upholstery. My hands sat idly in my lap as seconds passed.

Eventually, the pizza arrived and we sat with our thighs pressed together, balancing the box on our laps. As we ate, we tried to get a signal on the TV. No matter how many times River's greasy fingers punched at the button on the remote, it wouldn't budge. Outside, thunder cracked across the sky and rain began to fall.

"Gotta love Nowhereland and it's goddamn rain," River said with a smirk.

I chuckled as it pounded against the roof of the trailer, wondering when the stormy season would finally pass.

The pizza was greasy and kind of gross, but since it was the only place in a twenty-mile radius, we bought it regularly. Beggars can't be choosers. In the end, I ate two slices, he ate four and put what was left in the fridge.

For the rest of the evening, River was quiet, even as he beat me at chess, even as we finished a crossword puzzle. We didn't talk about his scars, his depression, any of it.

It was just a normal week after that. It took a day or so, but we got back to normal. Almost as if it never happened. *Almost.*

5

Chapter Five

Now
Considering it hasn't been that long since I've listened to *I Will*, it's strange that Paul McCartney's voice sounds unfamiliar, borderline foreign. I almost don't recognize it... until I do.

I never liked The Beatles nearly as much as River. To this day I wish I was just as enamored with them. Even still, I don't skip the song, I listen. It's a nostalgic thing, bringing me back to the times I had forgotten. It's strange how time in Nowhereland passes differently than it does here. In California, in my new life, I blink and everything is different so fast.

Through the memories that play while I lose myself in the song, I almost feel Louisiana sun, almost feel the sweat on the back of my neck. I'm almost there again until reality reminds me that I'm older now and far away.

Before I'm back at the apartment, I get a text from Caroline that brings me out of my reverie. She just got off work, much like me, and wants to hang out.

Caroline: Drinks tonight? My treat!

Caroline: Don't let the boyfriend keep you homebound. I need company. I can't spend the evening with my houseplants again. Besides, I heard this pub has the best tater tots.

Caroline: Don't even try to pretend you don't like tater tots, I know better.

I laugh and send a text letting "the boyfriend" know I will be home late before I reply to her.

Me: Okay. But you're buying the tots too

I hop off the bus at the next stop and spend a few minutes waiting for her to pick me up. She drives a nice Jeep, a newer one she bought after saving her tips from the cafe, and she's listening to the radio when I hop in the passenger seat.

"Hey," I greet. "How was work?"

She looks totally annoyed when she says, "I made thirty-two caramel lattes today. Thirty. Two. Why the hell are white girls so insistent on ordering the same damn drinks as each other?"

"Could be genetic," I suggest.

"Sounds like it," she agrees. "Or it's a conspiracy and they're all in a cult."

"I can see the headline now: coffee conspiracy." I gasp theatrically.

She ignores the joke and just shakes her head. "Anyway, enough about me and my shitty job. How's lover boy doing?"

I roll my eyes. "He's fine, thanks for asking. It's just that time of year where he seems to get sick. The flu has been going around anyhow. I love him, so I sit there through the puking and all the nasty things that come with it."

"I don't know if this is weird for me to say, but I wish I had someone like that in my life," Caroline muses.

"I think it would be cheesy for me to promise you will find that person, but it's true. Maybe during our tater-tot adventures, I can be your wing-woman?" I suggest.

We've stopped at a light, so there's nothing deterring Caroline from throwing her head back as she laughs wildly. "Dude, Em, every time we go out somewhere for you to play wing woman, the guys give *you* their numbers."

"That is so untrue," I reply. "That one guy was just being friendly."

"And what about the one who grabbed your ass while he was flirting?"

I blush. "He was an exception. Besides, you intervened."

She cackles. "I intervened? By me, you mean Fields, who literally hauled him off the stool and practically choked him with his own t-shirt. Your boyfriend is protective of what's his."

"Okay, first of all, don't refer to my boyfriend by his last name. And secondly, I'm not his. I'm a person, not a piece of property," I say.

"Don't go all feminist on me," she says, raising a hand in surrender. "I don't have the energy for that debate again. I think it's kind of cute actually. He shouldn't be insecure about your relationship, you've been in love with him since you were in high school."

"Boys are weird."

"I'll drink to that. Quite literally. While eating tater-tots too."

The rest of the drive we rock out to the radio, which plays a consistent selection of the trending pop hits for the month. We've learned the tracklist almost by heart, which means the two of us can sing Taylor Swift's newest single at the top of our lungs word for word.

The pub is a place I don't mind being at. It isn't Caroline's usual scene; it's quieter and more relaxed. A local artist, an older fellow, sings a Bob Dylan song in the corner as he plucks an ancient acoustic guitar. The voices here are more hushed, the lights dimmer than the harsh glow of a club.

Caroline relaxes as we settle in beside the bar. She orders the tater-tots and I order a glass of whiskey. She goes for wine, which is ironically pretentious in a place like this. As she sips from her glass, I swallow the burning Jack and remember what it felt like to taste it for the first time in Nowhereland. It's almost funny how bad I was at drinking. River was always taking jabs at me every time I coughed or spit-up.

"You look like you're thinking." She nudges my shoulder. "Earth to Em."

"Sorry," I apologize. "Long day. The physics thesis is getting really hard and I can honestly say that I wish I had picked an easier field of study."

"But easy is so boring," Caroline points out. "At least you're passionate. There aren't enough people like you. It's like you've got it together. You always know it's going to be okay and that you can work it out."

"Are you kidding?" I guffaw. "I'm probably the least put together out of everyone I know. Sometimes, I have to remind myself that college is worth it, even when it's hard. Besides, part of being an adult is mastering the art of pretending to have your shit together when really your shit has hit the fan and rained down on your life in a fiery explosion."

"You must be a good actress. It's kind of hard to hide a fiery explosion," she says and takes another gulp of red wine. Her lips are stained with it as it dribbles down her chin. Instinctively, she reaches up and wipes it away. This turns into a self-deprecating punchline. Much of everything she says does. "See? I haven't learned how to drink without spilling. You're still better off than me."

"I recommend whiskey. It's easier to clean if you spill it." I take a sip for emphasis, remembering to pace myself. Whiskey is easy to get caught up in, which is never good for me. I hate being drunk, but a buzz doesn't hurt every once in a while.

Caroline sets her glass down to pull her hair back. A quizzical look crosses her face as she scans my eyes a few seconds. "How come we never talk about your hometown? Or even you in general? It feels like you're just so private."

"Isn't it normal to be private?" I raise my eyebrows. "We don't talk about you that much either."

She gives me a pointed look. "That's untrue. I can prove you know more about me than I do you. What's my mom's name?"

"Kelley," I reply, wondering where she's going with this.

"Who was my last boyfriend?" she asks.

"I want to say his name was Greg. You met him at the coffee shop, right?"

"Yep. Remember why I dumped him?"

I think for a second before answering. "Because he was a pothead and never sober?"

"Right again." As she finishes her glass, she looks satisfied. "See? This is a clear demonstration that you know a lot about me. I can't answer either of those questions if you asked me."

"I guess I'm just more of a listener." I shrug.

"But it's weird that I know so little. I don't like babbling all the time, I want to hear all the crazy details of your life. For all I know, your real name is Leonardo and you're a secret serial killer with a new identity."

While her comment is funny, there's an underlying truth to it. I know so many details about Caroline, about her life and the people in it and even the small things she offhandedly mentions. It's true I'm a listener, but it's also true that I deliberately don't talk about much more than surface-level things. She knows I'm in a committed relationship, I study physics, want to get a job for my university's academic journal, and I presently work as a secretary. But that's about it.

I can't help but smile. "I assure you, my name is not Leonardo. What is it you want to know then? Since you're so interested."

I'm trying to be casual about it. I want to pretend that I'm not opening the door to something that scares me. Maybe if I play it cool, I can redirect the conversation before it opens a door to parts of my life I don't want to talk about.

"Mom's name?" she asks.

"Miriam," I say. "I'm sure you're riveted."

"Not quite." Her smile is wicked. "Now, let's get to the fun stuff. Who was your first kiss?"

His name comes out automatically. "River, of course."

"Any ex-boyfriends?"

"I've only had one."

She looks surprised. "No kidding. Most people have had at least two by twenty-one. I've had four."

"There aren't a ton of choices in Louisiana, let alone in a town like mine," I reply. "You know, Nowhereland was the sort of place they write about in a movie. There really was only one street. It ran through the center of town and fed into the highway you had to take to escape city limits for a bit."

"Dude, was it actually called Nowhereland?" She seems fascinated with the name alone. Normally, I call our town by its actual name, but sometimes the little nickname we had for it slips out instead. I think I've called it Nowhereland more than anything else.

When I shake my head, she thinks for a second before saying, "Let me guess; it was River's idea."

"Of course it was. He got it from a Beatles song."

Dimples indent her cheeks. "That's too cute. I love him already and I barely know anything outside of what you tell me about him."

"It's impossible not to love people like him. They really are one of a kind."

Luckily before she can ask more about Nowhereland, a plate of crispy tater tots is set down on the counter in front of us and cuts off anymore talking. With a mouthful, Caroline asks me about losing my virginity.

I scoff. "Really? It's not that exciting of a story."

"What was it like?" she asks, voice muffled by her food as she chews.

"It was… simple," I finally admit, the memory of the awkwardness and the newness of it all coming back. My cheeks heat. "I mean, it was a nice night and he was really sweet and understanding. Nothing big."

"So Fields is your only? Damn. I'm jealous. My first and I weren't even dating. It never went anywhere."

"Then he's a douche," I say as I'm finishing off the first glass of whiskey. Sex is something that seems important to her, and I can see that it bothers her that her first time was spent on someone who doesn't share the same sentiment toward the act.

"She," Caroline corrects me. Her cheeks pinken, which is something I haven't seen from her. She's always unapologetically confident, which is partially what surprises me about that detail. As open as she is about her personal life, this is

45

definitely news to me.

I'm admittedly caught off guard. "Oh, yeah?"

"I've had two girlfriends along the way," she says. "Discovering your sexuality is something every teenager goes through, but yeah. I haven't really told my parents about it, so I've been hesitant to openly date a girl."

"I think you should do what makes you happy," I say sincerely. "Your love life is your business and whoever you choose to tell about it is up to you."

"Well, there is a girl I work with…" A slow smile spreads across her lips. "Her name is Rosemary and she's really great."

Thankful that the subject has shifted away from me, I take a few tater tots of my own and listen to her tell me about this beautiful coworker she has. It's obvious Caroline really likes her, so I make an active effort to persuade her into asking her out.

"Aren't you going to tell me being gay is a sin?" she asks cautiously.

"Just because I'm from the Bible belt doesn't mean I'm religious," I drawl. "Besides, I've lived in liberal California for some time now and I'm unbothered by it. You're my friend, why would this make you any different to me?"

Admittedly, most people who were different for any sort of reason were hiding in the shadows of Nowhereland. The town was one shade of grey, and people who stood out, whether they thought differently like River, loved differently like Caroline, or even *looked* different, brought hues of unwelcome color to the portrait. Maybe it's how I grew up and my refusal to conform to that mindset that makes me feel as if nothing's changed between Caroline and me.

"Where were you when I was growing up?" she wonders

aloud. "I needed to hear that. When I told my friend Tallie I was bisexual during senior year, she told me that being bi wasn't even a real thing."

"Tallie sounds like a bitch."

"She was."

After that, the conversation grows lighter and we fall back into our usual routine of teasing, sarcasm, and just enjoying the company. The rest of the night is spent in a comfortable banter and the occasional drink. Neither of us gets overly hammered and by the time we're parting ways, Caroline promises to talk to Rosemary. Overall, it's a good night, one for the books.

When we say goodbye, I give her a chaste hug and head in the opposite direction for the last bus back to my apartment. I'm smiling because it's really nice to be good friends with someone I met here, as opposed to a friendship formed back in the day. It's a change of pace and a welcomed new experience for me.

Even though I'm caught up in who I am now, I can't help myself from listening to *I Will* on the way home, just one more time. Okay, maybe more like two times.

The past is never gone— it's captured and frozen forever in a box, and, sometimes, taken out to explore for old times' sake.

6

Chapter Six

Then
  Come next week, everything had gone back to normal. River's scars were shallow flesh wounds that healed quickly, fading back into his skin as if they'd never existed. He took to holding my hand more, keeping me close as if I was slowly slipping away by the second.

I didn't tell him that I knew he was faking the recovery. There was something behind his eyes, you see. This flicker of pain erupting through his irises occasionally interrupted the steady flow of nothingness.

His shoulders were more slouched, his body looking defeated. His symptoms were so... obvious. Pronounced. He could go without making a sound but, inside, he was screaming.

I wondered how long he had been hiding this from me. I wondered why it wasn't going away. I was walking on eggshells for the week following the day he hurt himself. I did most of the talking like our roles had been completely switched.

Thursday marked the day he shifted, like the revolving door that had been stuck in place for so long finally started turning again.

It was a normal day and I was tired of being patient. I walked to school alone that morning instead of waiting for River to drive me there. He always picked me up, but I didn't want to sit in silence with him for another day. I couldn't take it.

What they don't tell you about being close to someone who is sick is how exhausting it is. I could only describe what was happening in River as being sick. He wasn't himself. He was missing everything that made him who he was, and it terrified me. He'd barely spoken to me, mostly responding in short answers or nods. He tried to play it off like this was normal, but I missed his chatter, his lack of filter, his excitement.

That day, I was pushed too far.

I trudged through the puddles of mud as it rained until I reached the high school. It wasn't very far, but it felt like an eternity as my feet sank into the ground. I constantly had to yank my sneakers free. By the time I got there, my shoes were caked in mud and my clothes were plastered to me, but I kept going.

I was standing at my locker wringing out my hair when he approached me. I knew it was him just by his footsteps, as crazy as that sounds. I had memorized him, just like he did with me.

"Emmy?"

I didn't turn around. I just swallowed the lump in my throat and said, "Yes?"

"You didn't let me drive you."

It was the most he'd spoken in days. My resentment threatened to boil over as I slammed the door shut and shouldered my bag. I still wasn't looking at him. "I wanted to walk."

Before he could say anything else, if he was going to say anything else, I left him standing there and went to trigonometry early. He tried to get my attention in that class too, but I wasn't in the mood. In retrospect, I was being kind of bitchy, but I just couldn't take it anymore.

History class was where it got bad.

Usually, I'm better than giving someone the silent treatment. I knew how to use words, I knew how to speak and communicate how I felt. Except at that moment, all I could think was that I felt like I failed River as a best friend, and I didn't know how to express that. I felt like I had failed as a person in general because I didn't know how to help him and that was all I wanted to do. I would feel more useful that way.

In history, he took his seat beside me and stole a glance. His hand reached for mine, but I yanked it away under the desk and his fingers landed on my thigh. My bare thigh. My skin suddenly felt really hot, but he didn't move yet.

"Emmy?"

I looked away and shrugged him off, my legs sticking to the chair. They were still damp from the rain, but I stubbornly refused to wear jeans after February, no matter the weather. Besides, it wasn't cold or anything, just raining all the damn time.

I buried my fists in the pocket of my hoodie and stared straight ahead at the board. River gave up his futile attempts to speak to me, looking more hurt than anything else. Guilt tugged at my heart, but I ignored it. I was upset. And when I was upset, I wasn't always a pleasant person.

Keith took his seat and gave me a smile that I returned,

probably a little too wide for River. I made it a point to make a big show of laughing at his jokes as I turned around to speak with him.

Keith said, "So are you going to that dance next week?"

"Are you?" I shot back.

His response was clever, smooth for a high school boy. "Only if you're going with me."

River froze beside me and a twisted part of my brain liked his discontent.

Spring formal was our school's failed attempt at trying to attract teenagers away from parties to a safe environment. They had these lame events a couple of times a year, but I never paid them any attention.

The whole affair consisted of a throng of teenagers standing in a humid gymnasium. We would be listening to loud, outdated music (something River would probably enjoy if they had The Beatles) and wearing nice church clothes. They would probably have sour punch and stale cookies from the bakery down the block laid out on a table. It wasn't my scene, not even close.

River and I had never been to a dance. We preferred drinking whiskey on the roof of his trailer.

I didn't know why I wanted to accept Keith's offer. It was like another girl was opening my mouth and saying "yes" instead of rejecting him.

Keith grinned and showed off his braces. "Great!"

It was then that the bell rang and interrupted any conversation. Keith took his seat and I took time to process. I thought he was cute, nowhere near Zac Efron or anything, but not unbearable either. I definitely felt a little bad about leading him on because I wasn't interested in him like that, but the damage had been done.

The teacher announced a partner project, a research paper to be done with the person sitting beside us. River and I spent the entire period ignoring each other until after class when I stopped him in the hall. The silence was deafening, thick with tension, and I knew I had made a mistake.

"Riv?"

He clenched his jaw. "So *now* you want to talk to me?"

"Don't be like that," I pleaded, even though I deserved it.

"Go bother your boyfriend about it," he said dismissively. Something different flashed across his face... anger? At least he was responsive.

"Keith isn't my boyfriend!" I spat. "He's just a guy I'm going to a dance with."

"Yeah, whatever." River scoffed and started to walk away.

"You've been shutting me out!" I quipped. "You can't expect me to just ignore everything and pretend it's okay when you won't even *talk* to me."

He didn't turn around. His back was to me as he disappeared down the hall and left me standing there. A single tear slipped down my cheek. I furiously wiped it away and went to my next class.

My ill-placed anger didn't have a long shelf life. By the end of the day, I was waiting for him by his convertible, just sitting on the hood. It was raining again, but not as hard as it had been before. It sprinkled down and dampened my hair as I mentally formed my apology.

When River got to the car, he dropped his backpack in the back seat and stared at me. A silent understanding was traded between us as he leaned in, grabbed me around the knees, and gently pulled me forward. Then I was off the hood and on my feet for a few milliseconds before he hauled me into his arms. I buried my face into his chest and inhaled the smell of him. *River*. God, River.

"I'm sorry," I whimpered, promptly bursting into sobs.

River didn't say anything. Silent River was the elephant in the room as of late, but even on his bad days he was still my best friend and I didn't want him any other way. I knew that better now.

He held me until I stopped crying and a little bit after.

We drove back to his trailer holding hands. I wasn't distraught anymore, but I was still beyond worn out from the events of the day. I laid down on his bed shortly after we arrived, expecting him to follow, but he shook his head and covered me with his blankets.

"I'm gonna take a shower." That was all he said before he left me alone in his room wrapped in his covers. I tried to stay awake for him when he came back, but I was so exhausted I just crashed.

When I woke up an hour later, I heard the familiar sound of *I Will* coming from the kitchen.

My first thought was that I hadn't heard The Beatles in a while. It was like the bad days had taken away the part of River that loved music.

My second thought was that River hadn't said more than a few words in a little over a week, but right now, he was somehow singing at the top of his lungs.

I crawled out of bed and rubbed my sleepy eyes, blinking in confusion. He was in the kitchen cracking an egg against the counter, wiggling with energy.

He lit up when he saw me. "Emmy!"

I cocked my head in confusion.

"I was digging through the fridge and I found some chocolate chip cookie dough," he said excitedly. "So I'm currently baking, want to help?"

I didn't say anything. I was so confused. It was like all of a sudden a switch had been flipped inside of him, as if he could be okay again at the drop of a hat.

"What's wrong?" He crossed the room and turned down the music. "Emmy? You look like you've seen a ghost."

I thought you were gone, I didn't say.

He kissed my forehead and hugged me. "Are you having a rough day? I know we fought earlier and I'm sorry. I'll finish the cookies."

"You're back," I whispered.

"I never left," he said, clearly confused.

But you did.

I sat on top of the counter and watched him hum along with his music before he put the cookies in the oven. He seemed so happy, chattering to me about how his cousin was going to visit that summer and how we were almost out of school for vacation. He didn't talk about the cuts, or the depressive episode, or any of it. We just went back to the normal River and Emery dynamic.

"Are you okay?" he asked me as he scraped the cookies off the pan with a spatula.

I nodded, forcing a smile. "Never better."

We sat down at the table and played chess while we ate. I lost my queen relatively early in the game, so he won. Of course.

I decided not to question his sudden change. I was just grateful I had him back.

I left before the sun went down and he drove me home in the rain. We made sure the cover was on the convertible so as not to get drenched on the way there. I held him to say goodbye and his hands squeezed my waist comfortingly. This was home. He was home.

When I walked in the front door, my father had his sweaty feet propped up on the coffee table and grunted at me. This was his version of 'hello'. Mom was in the kitchen making a casserole and smiling like always. She seemed like a better conversation partner.

"Hey, sweetie," she said brightly.

"Hi," I said.

She was still in her scrubs with an apron tied over them as she fussed over dinner. Her days were spent as a dental assistant in an office in the next town over.

Dad wasn't so lucky. He didn't get to escape every day to a place that wasn't here. Instead, he was a tired pharmacist with long shifts. In all honesty, he hated his job with a passion and did nothing to hide it.

After she slid the dish into the oven, Mom gave me a quick kiss on the cheek. "How's River doing?"

"He's great," I lied. "We've been great."

"That's great," she chirped. "Hey, how about you get started on your homework before dinner?"

I had already finished my assignments at River's as we routinely made time between games of chess to get it done. My mom hadn't cared about my grades in years and I doubted she would start anytime soon. This was just her way of getting some alone time.

As I walked to my room, I wondered if she and dad had spoken much today. It wasn't that they were unhappy, just that they didn't seem to be super in love either. They got home around the same time every day and had a good half hour before I usually got back from River's. Though it wasn't like they did much with those minutes. Dad would likely be on the couch until ten and mom would be asleep by nine-thirty. Just like always.

I hid out in my room for most of the night, only making an appearance for dinner, and then I went back inside. The day itself was so overwhelming between everything that had happened, and I needed time to slow down and process.

I was going to the dance with Keith.

I got into a fight with River, but he came back.

I had Riv by my side again. That alone was comforting enough for me.

Even so, I left my phone turned up and close to my head as I fell asleep so I knew he could get ahold of me if he needed to. Part of me was on edge, wondering if this would be the last string of bad days River would have. Naively, I wanted to believe so, but the better part of me knew this wasn't a one-time thing. It had happened before, albeit not the same extent, and all signs pointed to it getting worse.

But I didn't want to think about that. I *couldn't* think about that.

7

Chapter Seven

Then
The rest of the week passed by quickly. After a few hours with River back to his old self, I found myself settling back into a comfortable routine. You can imagine how happy I was to find that he had a surprise for me after school that Friday. It wasn't that I was excited about the surprise, but rather that I was excited to see him recovering.

We met outside in the parking lot under an overcast sky. The air was warm and the climate felt thick with humidity. My hair was disastrously frizzy and needed a trim soon. My shirt stuck to my back with sweat. Yet, despite all the little things I normally would've complained about, I couldn't have cared less. River was there and I was so unbelievably grateful that it outweighed everything else.

He covered my eyes with his warm hands from behind, my back pressed against his hard chest. I could hear his nervous breath in my ear. "You ready?"

"Should I be worried you're gonna murder me?"

He shushed me. "Okay, keep your eyes shut until I get the

trunk open."

"What's in the trunk?" I asked immediately.

"It's not a surprise if I tell you." A few seconds passed before he finally gave me his blessing to look at its contents. My eyes snapped open to a bag with snacks, some warm Coca-Cola, a tent, sleeping bags, and a bunch of... fireworks?

I turned to look at him with a silent question.

"I'm going to drive you down to the creek," he said. "And then we're going to light some fireworks and camp out overnight."

"In *March*?" I laughed. "You could wait a couple of months for July. Why would we bring out the sparklers now?"

It wasn't so much that the camping was the issue; we did this kind of thing all the time. The fireworks were what confused me, but I put that aside. I took the smile on his face and the genuine look in his eyes as a sign he was trying to make up for the lost time.

"You love them," he replied. "And it's not just sparklers, I brought a few that we can shoot in the air too. Besides, I found them in the shed last night and thought we could kick off the weekend right. We can buy new ones for the Fourth of July."

"With what money?"

"That's a future River problem." My logical question was met with his indifferent shrug and his persistent belief that everything could just simply work out. Riv was impulsive as hell, especially in those days.

He took my hand and tugged me toward the car. I slid into the passenger seat beside him and watched him struggle to get the engine to work. After a few seconds, the car started up and he pulled out into the main road. I shot my mom a text to let her know I'd be with River overnight. She didn't respond immediately, but I knew she wouldn't have a problem with it.

We got to the creek in a matter of minutes and parked under an overgrown oak tree. It was a spot that we frequented, often climbing into the long branches no matter how old we got.

He got out first and spread out the picnic blanket for me. I sat and watched him pitch the tent, absently drinking coke and giving him the occasional sip from my bottle. We didn't care about sharing germs, so most of the time we didn't have our own drinks.

We still had a couple of hours until sundown, so he unpacked the trunk and showed me the entertainment he would be providing. Of course, the Walkman made an appearance with his CD collection. There was also our crossword book, some pens, and the chessboard.

"Is there anything you didn't bring?" I wondered as I surveyed what he had.

"I forgot toothbrushes," he admitted. "But at least there's an actual bathroom around here."

By that, he meant the nasty outhouse type building that had been installed for recreational purposes a while back. Nowadays, the hiking trails were overgrown and the "bathroom" was just as neglected as everything else here. Still, beggars can't be choosers.

"Please tell me you have gum."

He pulled his typical pack out of his back pocket and tossed it to me. I could always count on River to carry gum with him. He liked chewing it when he had a quiz or a test, and since we'd done a small exam in history, today was no exception.

I set it down beside me and reached for the snack bag.

"Peanut butter and jelly." I pulled out a few sandwiches in little bags smeared with the strawberry jam. "You know me so well."

59

He tossed the rest of our stuff into the tent and unceremoniously dropped down to the ground beside me. "I even brought the rest of our cookies."

Sure enough, the leftover chocolate chip cookies from a few days earlier were at the bottom of the bag next to the chips. I had wondered why he insisted on saving a couple at the time, but now I knew.

"Why, Riv?" I turned to face him.

It was a vague question, but he probably understood what I was really asking. I'd only said two words, but I'd thought so many more. I hoped that he got it.

He looked down at his folded hands and bit his lip.

"Well?" I prompted, nudging him with my shoulder.

"Because I felt bad about what happened and I guess I…" He paused for a second. "I'm sorry for how I was acting and I wanted to make it up to you."

I looked over at him and watched him clench his jaw. "You don't have to make it up to me." *You're with me now. That's all I need.*

"I feel like I have to," he replied stubbornly. "So please, just let me."

I squeezed his hand. "Okay."

He maintained the silence for a few seconds before clearing his throat. "Alright. Are you hungry? I think we need sandwiches. Yeah, we totally need sandwiches."

He reached forward and handed me one of the baggies first. It was pretty obvious he was trying to change the subject, so I just took a bite and leaned against him. He and I sat like that for a while before finally finishing a crossword we'd been working on for weeks. I provided the missing word, which made me feel pretty smug up until he beat me at chess again.

After sunset, he handed me a sparkler and withdrew a lighter from his pocket. It took a few tries and he burned his thumb in the process, but pretty soon we were drawing pictures in the air with glittering sparks. Out there, it was quiet except for our laughter and the crickets.

Eventually, he set a firework down by the bank of the creek, aimed it for the sky, and handed me the lighter. "Want to do the honors?"

I nodded and lit up, watching as it soared into the night and exploded in a shower of color. We stood under the blackness glittering with stars and watched the display of beautiful lights one by one.

He set another off, and another, and another, until we decided it was probably wise not to light anymore. We saved a couple for July at my request.

As Riv zipped us into the tent and picked at a second sandwich, he looked over at me meaningfully. I knew what he wanted to ask before he did, so I answered. "Yes, I've had a great day. Thank you."

He looked so relieved. "Thank Jesus."

I twisted the bracelet he'd bought for me around my wrist. "You seem surprised. You know I love doing things with you."

The corners of his lips tilted up before he looked away, busying himself by opening our crossword book to a new puzzle, a new page. He clicked the pen and handed it to me, stiffening when our fingers brushed in the handoff. My breath caught, but I recovered.

"So, uh, you're letting me start it off?"

"Yeah," he said, gesturing at the blank page. "And the first one down is easy anyway. You know the sixteenth president right?"

61

"I'm not stupid." I poked him with my pen. "Considering you memorized the entire Gettysburg address in fifth grade and performed it non-stop, it's impossible for me *not* to know who Lincoln is."

He chuckled, fondly remembering the times I chased him around because he was getting on my nerves. He would make his voice deep and presidential and recite lines from it until I was certain my ears would explode. "You know you love that speech."

"Not after hearing it a million times." I passed him the book and watched him fill out a few questions. We traded off every so often until I fell asleep with my fingers loosely closed around a ballpoint pen.

I don't know what time it was when it started raining.

My eyes opened when I felt the water running down my face. River, who slept like a rock, was oblivious as it transitioned from a drizzle into a downpour. I swore and shook his shoulder, resisting the urge to laugh when he gave me a bewildered look.

"Is it raining?" he wondered sleepily.

"I don't know. You tell me," I drawled sarcastically.

He narrowed his eyes. "Whatever, Emmy. Just help me get our stuff. We can sleep in the convertible."

We were already pretty soaked and the rain was coming down harder by the second. I shivered and tugged at the shirt that clung to my torso as he grabbed what he could. After we got the tent unzipped, I trudged after him in the mud— barefoot, might I add— and crawled into the car as he struggled to get the top on. After that, he thanked the universe that there weren't any leaks coming through the roof.

My teeth chattered. He noticed.

"Are you cold?" he asked.

We were both on the wide bench that made up his backseat, me freezing with my arms around myself, him just watching me. Coming to his senses, River leaned forward and fumbled around on the floor until he pulled out an old red hoodie.

I took it gratefully, using it as a makeshift blanket as I curled up into a ball.

"It's raining." He said, almost bewildered. "It's actually pouring."

Both of us glanced at each other and started laughing hysterically. I clamped a cold hand over my mouth to suppress my giggles.

"This is just our luck," I pointed out.

"I swear the forecast didn't call for a storm," he insisted. "I checked it, like, five times."

"Riv, it's fine," I assured him.

"Says the girl who looks like a drowned rat."

"Hey!"

"Tell me I'm wrong."

"You're a jerk," I said maturely.

The smirk on his face widened.

"Quit looking at me like that!" I said. "Don't be smug."

"I'm not," he lied.

"Whatever, River." I pushed him lightly.

Above our heads, lightning cracked across the sky ominously. The rumble of thunder didn't make me feel any better about our chances of the rain clearing up. I peeked out the window, attempting to peer through the beads of water cluttering the window. I could barely see anything, which definitely meant this wasn't going to stop anytime soon.

"It's too cold for this," River remarked, his teeth chattering.

"Want to go back to the trailer?"

"What about our stuff?"

"We'll get it tomorrow," he said. "I don't know about you, but I sure as hell don't want to sleep in my car."

I rubbed my hands together to try to warm them up. "I agree, let's get out of here."

He climbed over the center console to get in the driver's seat and started the engine. When the convertible started, the clock on the dashboard revealed it was after two o'clock in the morning. No wonder we were so tired.

The windshield wipers had recently been replaced, so at least the front window had more visibility as we drove. We had to run from the car to his house, our feet sinking into the mud as we raced up the path leading to his front door.

Both of us formed puddles on the tile as we peeled off our soggy shoes in the living room. He got us some towels out of the closet and passed me one. I immediately began wringing my tangled hair out, cringing at how matted it was. His was spiking in every direction, but somehow, it was so unapologetically River that he made it work.

Since Carly was asleep, I kept my voice down as I whispered, "Can I borrow something of yours to wear?"

"You don't have to ask. Take whatever you want."

I swiped a pair of his old sweats that didn't fit him anymore and rolled them so they'd stay around my waist. His t-shirt was oversized too, but the clothes were warm and dry and for that I was grateful.

We snuck into his room after changing, staring at the rainy world outside through his window. In the mobile home, we could hear the sound of the storm clearly. Every drop that hit the roof reverberated through the house. It just added to the

64

charm of the Fields residence.

"You know what's insane?" he wondered aloud.

"Ted Bundy?" I guessed playfully, rolling over to face him.

"I said what, not who," he retorted, clearly annoyed.

"What then?" I questioned.

"One day we won't be doing this anymore," he said. "No more sleepovers. No more Nowhereland. Isn't that crazy? It's like one day you're in middle school and you're just a kid dreaming up this big escape plan. And then all of a sudden, you actually get to go through with it. You actually get to go free because you're older now and ready to take on the world."

"That is insane," I finally agreed, unsure of what else to say.

Another bolt of lightning crashed, making his face glow. "You're my best friend, Emmy."

"No duh," I said. I meant to say it with a half-joking tone, but it came out serious.

"There's no one I'd rather solve crosswords with," he told me. "Even though you suck at them."

"I do not!"

"Yeah, you do, but it's okay."

I had stayed over at his house so many times before that sleepover, but as we lay there on top of the blankets talking to fill the silence, it occurred to me that we had changed so much between now and the first one.

Growing up terrified me, and as we spoke, I realized that maybe it terrified him too.

8

Chapter Eight

Then

When we woke up the next morning, it wasn't raining anymore and the sun was filtering in through the blinds. I sat up and scrubbed my face with the heels of my hands. It was probably an ungodly hour, but my brain was always waking me up early regardless of how late I'd gone to sleep. It was the blessing and curse of a morning person.

River immediately threw an arm over his face. "God, it's too early."

"So go back to sleep, you big baby."

"Only if you do too."

I rolled my eyes and tucked myself under the covers beside him. I wasn't going to fall back asleep now that I was up for the day, but River was already dozing off again. I spent the time reading while he stayed passed out beside me. Occasionally, I would steal glances at him as he snored softly.

He slept on his back with an arm resting under his head. I watched his chest steadily rise and fall, seeing his expressions twist as if he were making a face in his dreams.

The detail that caught my eye made me feel cold.

His sleeve had slid down to reveal those thin lines on his bicep. The evidence of a dark time we had only just put behind us haunted me.

I reached out and felt the skin underneath my fingertips. It was still uneven, mostly healed and pinkening, but still damaged. My eyes welled with hot tears and my throat closed thinking about it, about how helpless I felt, and imagining how much worse it was for him. I could see it in my mind, the haunting scene where River Fields stood in the bathroom with the shower on so no one would hear the sound he made as he took a blade to his skin.

I was still running my fingers over them when his eyes opened slowly.

"Hi," he murmured.

I pulled my hand away slowly and tried to pretend I wasn't about to cry.

Realizing I could see the scars, he yanked his sleeve down and reached for my hand. "Emmy?"

"I'm sorry!" I exclaimed, almost hysterical over something so small. "I just— I need a shower!"

It was such a random thing to blurt, but it popped into my head and it was the quickest way to avoid the subject at hand.

His eyebrows raised. "Okay?"

I got up out of bed and all but ran into his small bathroom. It was noon, which meant Carly had left for her shift about an hour before. It was just us left to our own devices. I shut myself inside and turned the water on, trying to calm down. The last thing I needed was for River to start his day with me freaking out.

It was hard for me not to look at River's razor and want to

take it from him. Even if it wasn't the type of blade he would use to cut himself, it was still a blade. I felt like I couldn't trust him with any sharp objects anymore.

When I got out of the shower, he was eating a Pop-Tart in the kitchen. Despite my best efforts to act natural, I made a scene.

I tried to sound casual. "Hey."

"Want me to get you something?" he offered. "Are you hungry?"

I shook my head. My voice felt broken like I'd lost the ability to talk and think coherently. I didn't know why I felt that way. I figured it was irrational since he was *fine*. He was back to being the same River I loved and knew better than I knew myself. We had an amazing time with our camping endeavor, even with the rain, and we'd been doing well for the past few days, but somehow, I still felt like I was walking on broken glass.

I sat down on the counter and folded my hands in my lap, trying to get it together. River watched me a few seconds before setting the pastry in his hands down on the wrapper beside him.

"Are you mad at me?" He sounded crushed when he asked it, afraid I'd say yes.

My head snapped up. "What?"

"Are you mad at me?" he repeated.

"No," I said.

He came closer and rested his palms on my knees so that our faces were close. My breath caught in my throat, but unlike me, he seemed unaffected by our proximity. Just inches from my mouth, he whispered, "What did I do?"

I closed my eyes. "Riv, I'm fine. Really. I'm just PMSing is

68

all."

He didn't buy it. "It's about the cuts, right?"

I didn't say anything.

"I'm sorry," he apologized sincerely. "How many times do I have to say I'm sorry to you?"

I inhaled before I started babbling, firing my thoughts out of my mouth without filtering them. My rambling was pretty incoherent, but it didn't deter me.

"I saw the scars and they made me think about how angry I was about your hurting yourself," I explained. "I'm your best friend and I'm supposed to be there for you and help you through the bad stuff. I failed you and I'm never gonna forgive myself for it. How could I? I keep wondering if maybe I could've stopped you or said the right words to make you feel better."

"Stop, Em," he urged.

I didn't, I kept talking. "I just keep wondering if it's the last time. I keep wondering if the next time a bad day comes, you'll go deeper. It scares me in a way I can't describe. I feel like I'm not doing enough for you. I feel like a shit friend because I wasn't there when you needed me."

"Em, stop." He was pleading now. "Please stop blaming yourself."

I took his face in my hands and I made sure my eyes were locked on his. "River Michael Fields, I need you to listen to what I'm saying to you. Whatever you do, don't hurt yourself like that again. It's been eating me up for days."

His lower lip trembled for a second. My stomach sank. "I hurt you. And I'm so sorry, Emery. Please forgive me."

I knew he was serious because he said my name. River never called me Emery. I was always Em or Emmy, never Emery, never to him. He saved it for special occasions, which made this moment all the more emotional.

"I don't need to forgive you, River." I gave him a watery smile. "It's not you that I'm upset with."

"Then forgive yourself for me," he requested. "Please."

My hands slid up to the back of his neck and my fingers knotted in his chestnut hair. This time, he held his breath, gazing at me with adoration. His lips parted. His breath smelled like strawberry Pop-Tart, but it wasn't in the slightest bit unappealing. Between the beginning of stubble and his deep emerald eyes, he was unmistakably, undeniably River.

For me, there wasn't life without him. For every single one of my best moments, there was always him. Through thick and thin, there was always River. I think that's why the dark days scared me the most. It was like a glimpse of what life without him would look like.

"I will," I promised.

Then, he hugged me tightly, burying his face into the space between my shoulder and neck. I felt his mouth on my cheek before he pulled away.

As we were sitting down on the couch, Carly walked in, carrying a few bags of groceries. Naturally, Riv immediately hopped up to help her carry them to the kitchen and began unpacking out of habit. I trailed behind him, idling by the fridge.

"How was camping out?" Carly asked.

"It was fun, Mom," River said, before helping me lift a box of cereal onto the top shelf.

I wasn't tall enough to reach and had been standing on the balls of my feet with my arm outstretched. It always drove me crazy that he was so much taller, but at least he could get to the cupboards when I couldn't.

"That's good to hear. Now that I'm thinking of it, how'd y'all deal with the rain?" she wondered. "It was pouring last night."

"We came back after the rain woke us up. It ended up being a plain old sleepover in my room," River reported, almost sounding sad.

"There's nothing wrong with that," said Carly. "Remember that time you guys camped out in your closet? You didn't mind a sleepover in your room then."

I could recall that adventure easily, and by the grin on River's face, he could too. We'd spent the night elbowing each other and fighting over blankets before we finally called it quits and moved back to his bed. We were nine at the time, but even now I could see us doing something like that.

"You know, I think I have pictures," she said. "Let me find it."

"Oh God," River said. "Memory lane. I'm not sure I'll be able to handle that awful haircut you had back in the day."

"You're the one with crooked teeth," I pointed out.

"They're what gives me such a charming smile," he retorted. "Now shut up and work on unpacking."

"You're the one who interrupted!"

Carly came back a few moments later and ended our squabbling, holding a stack of photos in an envelope. We finished with the task and sat with our legs pressed together as we flipped through the photos. There were a lot of toothy grins, scraped knees, and other evidence of our adventures.

My heart swelled with more love for River than I think I'd ever felt in a long time. They always say you can't choose your family, and there's truth in that, but I think the same goes for other people sometimes. I don't think I really chose for River to be my best friend. It was more like the universe let our paths collide.

I turned to him to say something but realized I didn't have to. When he kissed the top of my head, I realized he probably knew all the things that had yet to be said.

"Love you, Emmy," he said.

"Love you too."

He turned back to the stack of photos. "Hey, this was a good year!"

He held up a picture of us standing by the sign for the elementary school on our first day of fifth grade. He had an arm around me in the picture, but he wasn't looking at the camera, he was looking at me and I was looking at him. We were both cracking up. Even if I can't remember the joke, I can remember how it made me feel.

"What made it so great?" I asked.

"I got my first kiss," he bragged.

I rolled my eyes. "Elementary school kisses don't count."

He chuckled. "You're just bitter because you never got kissed in elementary school."

I sighed. There was some truth to that, even if I was reluctant to admit it.

"Or ever for that matter," I grumbled.

River's eyes widened. "Wait... what?"

"You heard me," I deadpanned. "I've never been kissed. Big deal."

"Seriously?"

"Yes, now stop reminding me."

I started to shift away from him on the couch, but he grabbed my arm. "Wait, Emmy, how come you never told me?"

I shrugged. "It's not really your business anyway."

"It kind of is."

"Why?"

He looked at me as if it was obvious. "I'm your best friend, for starters."

It wasn't like never being kissed was a bad thing, it was just kind of awkward to talk about it with my male best friend. Especially when he'd kissed plenty of other people.

Especially when I kind of wanted to kiss him.

"Do you want to have your first kiss?" he asked.

I cocked my head at him. "Well, yeah."

"Let me rephrase." One of his fingers gently tilted my chin up. "Can I kiss you?"

Carly had left the room a few minutes ago, meaning it was just the two of us in the living room. As far as places for a first kiss went, it wasn't as romantic as something you'd see in a movie, but I didn't care. With River, it was kind of perfect.

Like a dream.

I nodded frantically.

He leaned forward and pressed his lips to my jaw, just next to my ear. He kissed my neck too, letting his mouth linger a few seconds before he pulled away. His smirk indicated he knew exactly what he was doing to me.

"Your heart's beating really fast," he pointed out.

"You didn't kiss me." I sounded pathetic, honestly.

His hand went to the small of my back, pulling me closer. "Yes, I did."

"You know what I mean." I scowled.

He kissed my nose next. "Happy?"

"Really, River?" I deadpanned.

He chuckled. "You know, for someone who has never been kissed before, you're really eager."

I started to wiggle out of his grasp, but he held me tight. His gaze was intense and I liked it.

"You'll have to be more specific, Em," he murmured, in a way that made my heart race. "I'm just a stupid boy, as you've reminded me countless times."

He wasn't. River was basically a genius, both book smart and street smart. He knew exactly what I wanted and was just screwing with me like he always did. We were perpetually in a constant state of teasing; it was never-ending.

"Kiss me," I demanded.

His lips met my forehead.

"River!"

"Yes?"

"Kiss me."

"Where?"

"You're so difficult, you asshole."

"You shouldn't be kissing assholes, that can't be sanitary."

"RIVER!"

"Yes?" he said, eyes twinkling with amusement.

"Please, just…" I gave up trying to put it into words and finally bit the bullet. I closed the gap between us and had my mouth pressed against his for all of a second before the phone started ringing.

"You've got to be kidding me." He swore and let go of me, stalking over to the landline. "Hello? No, she's not available. I'll have her call you back later, Aunt Lisa. Love you too. Bye."

I hopped down from the counter and cocked my head at him. "Aunt Lisa?"

"My dad's sister-in-law," he explained. "We're not super close but she wanted to call my mom about something. No idea why. Lisa and Mom barely interacted much outside of a few reunions."

He shoved his fists into his pockets and turned away from me. It was then that I realized the tension had subsided and we probably wouldn't be kissing anytime soon.

Moment over.

"What's she like?" I asked as we sat down on the couch.

"She's tall?" he answered, not one for details. "She's got a boy our age and she's a caterer, but that's basically the extent of my knowledge. I haven't talked to her or Silas or even Uncle Rich in years. They got especially distant after Dad—"

He cut himself off. His father was always a touchy subject in any conversation. He'd died three years ago, but the wound still felt fresh. River and his dad, Rob, had been really close, which is probably why he loved that stupid junker car so much. Once Riv had gotten old enough to drive, he'd spent almost the entirety of winter break our sophomore year fixing the convertible up.

"I'm sorry," I said sincerely.

"It's fine." He shrugged. "I have you and Mom and that's all I need."

"And Greta Stacy too," I reminded him. "She's definitely into you."

The week before, she'd asked him on a date. We've been going to school with her forever, but Riv and I rarely spoke to her. He'd shot her down, and she'd stomped away dramatically. It was the story of the day for the junior class.

He groaned. "Christ, don't remind me. That girl is so obnoxious."

I laughed. He wasn't wrong there. Greta was a terrible gossip whose nasally voice was like nails on a chalkboard. When she started talking, both of us cringed instinctively. She was another part of Nowhereland we were excited to leave behind.

After a few seconds, our amusement died and his face grew a bit more serious. My stomach plunged as I wondered if what he was about to say was going to hurt.

"Hey, Em, about earlier," he began, cheeks red. "I think what I was doing was kind of out of line. I know that we're friends. I never want to do anything that might mess with that. You deserve a better first kiss with someone you're actually interested in."

I shouldn't kiss you, he meant. *We can't be like that.*

I think I flinched. I swear I flinched.

We're just friends, I thought. *That's how it's supposed to be.*

Even if I tried to convince myself of that, I knew I didn't believe it for even a second.

"Oh," I said, sounding more hurt than I wanted to. "Okay. Yeah. You know, I should probably head home. Mom wanted to spend time with me this weekend anyway."

An emotion I couldn't identify flickered across his features. "Okay. Bye, Emmy, I love you."

"Ditto," I said. I couldn't form the words *I love you* without them holding more meaning than they should've, so I didn't say them. "Don't forget the tent... and stuff."

It was such a stupid thing to say. He probably didn't need to be reminded, but I was trying to get past the discomfort.

"I won't," he said flatly.

He didn't offer to drive me home. Both of us probably wanted space, and a car ride with him would have been maddening at that moment. A stiff hug was exchanged, and that was our goodbye.

I grabbed my things and trudged away, wondering how

many times we could go back and forth before we both got tired of it. Things were better when there was no attraction, like when we were just children who never thought about being together.

What the hell was I thinking?

Needless to say, I was feeling both mortified and stupid. Most of that night was spent hiding under the covers with my phone silenced, hoping he wouldn't text me and simultaneously hoping he would.

Later, as I struggled to go to sleep, I twirled the bracelet he gave me around my wrist over and over, until the metal left behind small red marks on my skin. I scrutinized every detail of it as if I could figure out what was going on between us if I stared hard enough at it.

River and I hadn't changed much. The dynamic we'd had since childhood was consistent, and I liked it that way. Whatever was happening now had my head spinning, and I was overcome with the sudden realization that we were heading straight into the unknown.

9

Chapter Nine

Now I make it through the rest of the week in a blur of long physics equations, homework, and answering the perpetual stream of phone calls to the legal firm. By the time the weekend comes, I'm exhausted.

Normal people sleep in, but it seems I'm chronically incapable of doing that. I wake up bright and early like always, untangle myself from the blankets, and leave my blanket hog of a boyfriend to sleep the day away.

I'm greeted this fine Saturday morning by a text message that interrupts me in the middle of getting ready.

Caroline: Please tell me you're getting coffee, I need a break from all the caramel lattes.

Me: Now that you mention it, a caramel latte sounds good.

Caroline: I will spit in your latte if you force me to make one.

Me: Gross. Please don't.

Caroline: So... the usual?

Me: Always. See you in a few.

It takes me a few minutes to do my makeup and comb out

my hair, but once I'm presentable, I head out the door with a banana for breakfast and my purse. My usual walk is beautiful and serene like it always is.

When I get to the cafe, Caroline greets me with a grin. "Hey, chica."

Behind her stands a tall, curvy woman with bright red hair. She lights up when she sees me too. "Is this Emery?"

Caroline nods. "Rosemary, this is my best friend, Emery. Emery, Rosemary."

"It's really great to meet you!" Rosemary exclaims sweetly. "Care has told me so much."

When Rosemary turns to take an order at the drive-thru, I mouth *Care?* at Caroline and stifle a giggle when she blushes profusely. She's obviously got it bad for this girl, who is as sweet as I thought she'd be.

I stand by the counter while Caroline finishes brewing my standard drink, inhaling the sweet smell of fresh coffee and listening to soft music that plays from the speakers behind the counter. Since she's a manager, Caroline has control over what music gets streamed. It's usually hers, but I don't mind because she has good taste.

"So I'm moving into a new place," Caroline starts, handing me my coffee and the muffin I ordered. "I was wondering if you and Fields might be able to help me unpack. I could use a couple of extra hands."

"He's still a little under the weather," I say, wanting to make sure he rests up. "But I can do it."

"And I can too!" Rosemary volunteers. "Just give me a time and I'm sure Emery and I could help out."

Caroline's cheeks pinken again as she stammers out, "Sure. Yeah. Could you guys come by after work?"

"Absolutely!" I tell her. "Hey, want me to run by the Thai place we like before I come over?"

"Would you?" Caroline looks relieved. "I haven't done any shopping yet."

"We can help with that too," Rosemary chimes in. "Or at least I can."

She looks at Caroline with sincerity in her deep green eyes, and I nearly fall in love with her on the spot. Part of me wants to shake my friend and tell her to go for it, but I stand by my subtle glances and smirk wryly instead.

"We'll cross that bridge later," Caroline says as she fusses over a new drive-thru order. "For now, I just have to figure out where I'm gonna put all my junk."

Considering she helped me decorate the apartment a few months prior, I figure it couldn't hurt for me to help her out in the same way, all things considered. Before I head out, I confirm to meet up at seven-thirty and spend the rest of the morning reading in my living room.

* * *

That evening, I walk through the door with a bottle of wine and the Thai food I promised. The apartment is an utter disaster and the whole place is lost in a sea of cardboard and dismantled furniture.

Laughing, I set the food down on the counter and glance around. "Jeez, Caroline, it's stuffy in here!"

Caroline emerges from the back room in nothing but a sports bra and running shorts. Her dark skin is glistening with sweat and the thin layer of the hair escaping her ponytail is plastered to her neck. "Tell me about it. They haven't done much about the thermostat, so I've resorted to rotating fans."

She points at a tiny one in the corner that barely spits out enough warm air to cool the room off for emphasis.

"We're calling maintenance after we handle this disaster you call home," I decide. "Where's Rosemary?"

She shrugs. "She texted to say she was on her way a few minutes ago."

"So what's the deal there?" I asked.

"No idea," she answers. "I don't know her well enough to hit on her and I feel like it would be a little weird for me to outright ask if she's into chicks."

"You'll never know if you don't try." I put my hand on her shoulder. "I'm here for you either way."

"I know," she says. "Now let's get started on these boxes before the guest of honor arrives."

We end up sitting on the floor passing a box cutter back and forth so we can get the kitchen unpacked. By the time Rosemary arrives, we're almost finished, so she helps us with the last of the utensils before we eat using the empty boxes as a table.

"Thai food is amazing!" Rosemary exclaims halfway through the meal.

"Haven't you had Thai before?" Caroline asks with raised eyebrows.

"Never," she confirms.

"You're joking!" Caroline and I say in perfect unison.

She smiles apologetically. "What can I say? My parents weren't really into trying new things. But it's good. I should eat Thai food more often."

"Hell yeah you do," Caroline replies, still chewing.

After we eat, the three of us roam around the living room,

stuffing trash bags full of boxes as we try to make sense of the clutter. Because she was moving out of her childhood home, Caroline has enough knick-knacks to last a lifetime.

"Shit!" I exclaim when I slice my finger open on the corner of a box. "This is the second time that's happened!"

I've already gotten a papercut, but this time, I'm bleeding a little, so I grab a napkin from dinner to wipe it up before I get back to work.

"Has anyone ever told you that you have a filthy mouth?" Caroline teases.

"Like you're a saint," I shoot back.

Rosemary chuckles. "You two are like sisters. Always bickering."

"Lovingly," I say. "It's all out of love."

"Yeah, sure," Caroline rolls her eyes.

So far all she has for her living room is a couch and a coffee table that I laid a few framed pictures on earlier. She's got countless photos of her friends and family, which reminds me a lot of myself. I'm sentimental too, even though I try to hide it.

The succulents that she has on the windowsill are wilting, so I pour some water into their individual pots and roll my eyes. "You're going to kill your plants before they even have a chance to see the finished place."

She whacks me on the shoulder as she walks by. "Shut up, I watered the ones in the other room before work today. I just missed those."

"You're such a neglectful mother," I chastise, laying on the sarcasm. "Shame on you."

"It's why I have plants and not pets or actual kids," she explains. "The children would probably starve to death if

I did."

Our conversations for the rest of the evening are playful and infrequent as we focus on getting the task at hand accomplished. Rosemary is helpful as ever and talks to Caroline here and there to fill the silence. Their banter is adorable and I can't help but think about how great they'd be together.

It's a nice night. Even if it's simple, it's still enjoyable nonetheless. Time flies by.

Around eleven, Rosemary yawns and tries to stifle it with her hand, but Caroline sees right through her and says, "You know you can go home right?"

"And leave you two to finish the job?" Rosemary looks horrified. "Absolutely not."

"We should call it a night then," I chime in. "I better go soon so I can get some rest. I have homework I need to get a head start on tomorrow."

Caroline pushes the box she's working on away, clearly relieved. "Thank God. I'm so done with this. It's going to take forever."

"How about we come back tomorrow night then?" I suggest.

"Sounds like a plan," Rosemary affirms. "Anyway, it was lovely hanging out with you guys. Thanks for dinner."

She gives Caroline a long hug before she goes, which definitely catches my attention.

After she's long gone, I arch an eyebrow at Caroline. "Okay, you have to ask her out, dude. You two would be the cutest thing in the world."

"Not all of us have a high school sweetheart like Fields," she replies. "It's not so easy."

"Maybe it doesn't have to be complicated," I say. "Just a little food for thought."

Caroline straightens out the pillows before collapsing on the sofa in a heap. "I forgot how exhausting moving into a new place can be."

"I get that." I lay back on the carpet and take a breath. "I didn't peg you for the kind of person who keeps the little things. Like that bag of birthday cards."

"I feel like it's bad for your karma to throw that kind of thing away," she says. "Besides, there's a lot of thought behind them. I respect that. What about you?"

"I'm a sap too," I admit. "I have an entire box under my bed for all my high school memories."

"No kidding." She sits up. "What's in it?"

"Pictures mostly. I have a few other things in there. For example, River's old chessboard, a Barbie he bought me for my birthday when we were kids, our crossword puzzles, etcetera. I like remembering those days."

"What was it like?" she asks.

"What was what like?"

"Growing up with a best friend like that," she elaborates. "What was it like?"

I thought about it for a second before I answered. "Well, it's sort of like being naked."

"What?" She cackles.

"Being naked is being vulnerable," I begin. "You're exposed, you can't hide anything. It's just you: raw, unfiltered you. With River, I felt like he saw me better than anyone else did. We'd been friends for as long as I could remember. In a place like Nowhereland, you know everyone there from the moment you're born to the day you either leave or die. We met in school and were stuck together from then on."

"Awe," Caroline says. "That's too cute."

My voice holds only fondness. "It really is. He could read my mind. There wasn't anything we wouldn't do for each other. It was like we only got closer as time went on. All of it was so effortlessly perfect. I couldn't imagine spending every day with anyone else. I really loved him with everything I had. He was amazing. You know those people who just light up a room? That was River. He was enigmatic, reckless, and brave. He was so many things, but above all, he was my best friend in the entire universe. You don't get anyone like him more than once in a lifetime."

She frowns slightly. "You said was."

I pause for a second. "What do you mean?"

"You say he *was* like he isn't that person anymore," she points out. "What's the deal there? Why do you talk about him past tense?"

My chest tightens as I correct myself quickly. "I mean he *is* amazing."

It seems stupid to be rewriting the narrative for Caroline, but a twisted part of me feels like I have to, as if I owe it to River to give us a better story. I've read plenty of stories, and he's told me more than a few of his own, but if anything, all stories have taught me is that life never works out like you want it to. It's messy, flawed, imperfect too.

It's a blur of horrible truths, grim realities, dark pasts and emotions you don't want to process. All of it hurts to imagine, so I try to gloss over them.

Caroline pours us each another glass of wine and eyes me skeptically. "What happened, Emery?"

I swallow hard. My mouth feels dry and the room is suddenly too small.

"I think…" I pause to collect myself. "I think the better question is, what didn't happen?"

She knows me well enough to gather that I don't feel like talking about River anymore and lets me go in a hurry. I practically run to my car, trying as hard as I can to stop thinking about it, to forget.

After the door shuts, I run the engine and struggle to hold back the sob bubbling in my throat. Even though Nowhereland is behind me, I can never truly get away from it. I see that now more than ever.

When The Beatles start playing on the oldies station during the drive home, it takes everything in me not to scream.

10

Chapter Ten

hen

T One misconception about growing up in a small town wedged deeply in the Bible belt is that everyone you encounter is ready to drill the holy spirit in you. Quite a few of us aren't like that. When I woke up on Sunday morning, I knew the majority of Nowhereland's population was ready to hit the chapels, but I wouldn't be among the masses. Dad was working and Mom would be catching up on her rest, so I was on my own for the day.

Part of me wanted to call River and ask him to spend the day with me. It was as I had the phone lifted to my ear and ringing that I remembered the dreaded almost-kiss and found myself hanging up before he could say "hello" to me.

I felt stupid.

Of course, you feel stupid, Emery, I thought. *You almost kissed your best friend.*

I got up out of bed, dressed in a t-shirt and shorts, and began a long trek with no set destination. Even at eleven am, it was already humid and warm out. As unpleasant as the weather was, at least it wasn't raining.

The streets were uncharacteristically quiet, but then again, they always were on Sundays. Normally, there were people walking around, trading gossip or carrying conversations, but for the next couple hours, the majority of civilians would be crammed shoulder to shoulder in the pews for their weekly dose of Jesus.

I trudged on past the pharmacy where my father had undoubtedly begun his day, past the school, and past one of the two churches we had in town. Even considering how immersed in my thoughts I was, it was surprising how long it took me to realize I was on autopilot and walking to the trailer park I had visited thousands of times. I hadn't set out to see River, it just seemed to be where I naturally gravitated.

The mobile homes were dusty, like everything else in this God-forsaken town, and lined up like perfect soldiers along that one road that ran through the middle of Nowhereland. From here you could see the highway on the horizon, the expanse of a clear sky, and maybe even your future if you daydreamed enough.

I realized where I was when I had already knocked against the screen door and brought myself out of my head and into reality. Seconds later, the door swung open to reveal a sleepy River Fields.

"Emmy?" he murmured, blinking his green eyes at me a couple of times. It was almost like he didn't believe I was there, standing in front of him.

"Hi," I whispered. "I'm sorry, I should probably get going. I didn't mean to wake you and you probably want to go back to sleep—"

"Stay," he interrupted me. "Please stay."

I swallowed, chin bobbing. "Okay."

I followed him to his bedroom, trying not to focus on the fact that he was shirtless and I could see the muscles in his back and shoulders from doing push-ups in PE every single day. My cheeks flamed as I tried to shake off this unfamiliar attraction I felt.

You didn't kiss him because you aren't meant to see each other that way, I pointedly reminded myself.

He was half-asleep as he laid down beside me. One of his hands came to rest on the curve of my waist. His pinky brushed my bare hip where my t-shirt rode up, and a shiver rolled through me.

"I missed you," he told me earnestly.

"I missed you too." I meant it, but I wasn't sure if I meant it in the same way. I was still replaying the way his lips had brushed mine before we were interrupted. Almost kisses were the worst— they were a taste of what could happen if only one of you had been brave enough to move.

"I'm sorry about yesterday," he apologized. "I've been apologizing so much lately because I just keep screwing up with you. I just... Emmy, there's so much I haven't said and done. I can't keep pretending I'm making the right choice when what I want and what I think I should want are different things."

My breath caught in my throat. Hope surged through my chest.

Is he saying what I think he is?

"What are you saying Riv?" I asked, trying not to overthink anything. I didn't know what he was insinuating, and I didn't want to jump to any conclusions.

"I'm saying I screwed up yesterday. I'm saying..." he trailed off. Words had failed him.

Suddenly, he was cupping my cheeks in his hands and sliding nearer until we were as close as we had been yesterday. We were close enough to kiss.

His thumb ran across my chapped bottom lip. I silently begged him to kiss me, looking him in the eyes with the questions I was holding back.

Kiss me, River, kiss me.

In the back of my mind, I was wondering if he would gather the courage to close the gap and change us forever, change everything forever. I was worried about my inexperience, wondering a million and one things like *does my breath still smell like toothpaste?* and *what do I do with my tongue?* I lost my doubts when my name came out of his mouth in a desperate groan.

And then he did it.

River Fields, my best friend in the entire world, kissed me.

I responded to his lips against mine immediately, the foreign taste of his mouth against mine intoxicating and wonderful. My head spun deliriously as he claimed me with his kisses, lips moving against mine perfectly. His mouth was hot and wet, and with a nibble of my bottom lip, I was gasping and his tongue was roaming over mine.

For the record, you don't really think about what you do with your tongue when you're kissing, you just sort of go along with it and figure it out.

He rolled me over onto my back until he was hovering over me with his legs on either side of my hips. My hands were in his hair, on his face, wandering down his chest. His hands were on my waist, sliding under my shirt as he kissed me senseless.

He pulled away slowly, still above me, eyes searching mine as we caught our breath. I smiled at him reflexively, my whole face dominated by a massive grin. He kissed me again just seconds later, a quick peck.

"You taste amazing, Emmy," he said. "Are you wearing chapstick?"

I giggled. "What?"

He pressed his lips to mine, lingering. "Let me guess: strawberry?"

"Of course. It's my favorite."

"Mine too." His smirk was wicked as he said it.

"I'll have to wear it more often then." I shocked myself with my own flirting.

After a few seconds, he rolled off of me and I almost sighed in disappointment. His fingers threaded through mine and gave my hand a squeeze. "So, was that a good first kiss?"

I stared at him in disbelief. "Are you seriously asking me that?"

"Yeah."

"It was absolutely a good first kiss."

"The best ever?" he asked.

"Maybe," I teased.

"You need a refresher," he declared, laying one on me right then. We kissed like we'd never be able to do it again. We kissed like we didn't have lives ahead of us to spend kissing and talking and being River and Emery.

When we broke apart again, he yawned before saying, "Are you sure you've never kissed anyone before?"

I raised my eyebrows at him. "I'm pretty damn sure I'd never been kissed prior to this."

"Just asking," he said defensively. "I'm only wondering

because you're pretty good at it. So either I'm terrible or you catch on quick."

"It's obviously because you're terrible," I replied, barely holding a straight face.

"Is that why you let me kiss you about seven times in the past ten minutes?"

"I just felt bad for you."

"Yeah. Sure."

My whole body was warm, from my mouth down to my toes as they curled inside my socks. This was what first kisses should be like. The majority of the time they were hasty things, done in a hurry for the sake of bragging rights. This was worth the wait. I was buzzing with enthusiasm, blushing all over.

"You're so beautiful," River whispered. "Holy shit, I get to say these things now and it isn't weird. You're beautiful, Em, you're so beautiful it makes my chest feel like it's going to explode. And Jesus, I really like kissing you. Can I do it again before I go back to sleep?"

I nodded excitedly, so fast I worried my head might fly right off my shoulders. It didn't, somehow.

He kept a firm hold on my cheeks as he claimed my mouth with every inch of his. He smelled like River, he tasted like River, and I am pretty sure I fell in love with kissing in those minutes we spent tangled up in his bed making out.

I finally understood the hype.

Eventually, we passed out curled up like a couple would. One of his legs was tucked between mine, his chest was pressed against my back, his breath was a steady hum in my ear as he inhaled and exhaled. He was so warm, bare skin searing through the thin material of my t-shirt. I fell asleep listening to him, the beat of his heart and his breaths. *River.*

When he woke me up a couple of hours later, he did so by caressing my cheek and pushing my curls behind my ear. I smiled and pretended to be asleep just so he would keep touching me. It took everything in me not to open my eyes when he nibbled on my earlobe. He didn't stop there; his palm, which was splayed across my stomach, slid up to my chest, and that's when my eyes finally snapped open.

He pulled away chuckling.

"Asshole!" I exclaimed.

"Faker!" he shot back. "You were totally awake."

"Maybe I liked what you were doing up until you felt me up." I narrowed my eyes at him.

"I'm sure you enjoyed that part too," he said cheekily. "I definitely did."

I pushed him off the bed forcefully, genuinely surprised that it actually worked. When River got to his feet, he gave me a look of mischief. "Oh, you're going to regret that one, Emmy."

The next thing I knew, I was on my back again and he was on top of me, one of his hands pinning mine above my head, his other tickling me fiercely. His fingers skirted up my sides, across my ribs, along my lower stomach, down my neck, everywhere he could reach. I laughed and swore and writhed under him, entirely at his mercy.

"Stop!" I gasped. "Oh my God, River, please! Okay! You win! Okay!"

He tickled me just a little bit longer before relenting. I caught my breath and searched his face, taking in that delighted expression of his, those green eyes ablaze with endless affection, and wanted so desperately for him to kiss me again.

Jesus, Emery, you two have only been kissing for a few hours and you're already an addict.

He was still holding my arms down above my head as he bent down and pressed his mouth against mine, feather-light and slowly. This time, it wasn't rushed because we were taking our time with things, memorizing each other.

"I could definitely get used to that," he confessed. "Now if you'll excuse me, I'm gonna hop in the shower real quick. Give me five minutes?"

"Okay," I said. "Now are you going to let go of me?"

"I'm tempted to hold onto you and take you into the shower with me."

"Maybe another day," I replied, only half-kidding.

He gave an exaggerated sigh and let go of my hands before he headed off. I watched him go and waited until I heard the water running to squeal into a pillow as loud as I could muster. I was so happy in a way I'd never been before.

For five minutes I waited. Then ten minutes. Worry spiked my heart rate.

He's just taking a shower, I reminded myself. *Don't be irrational.*

After fifteen minutes had passed, I got up and knocked on the bathroom door. "Riv?"

When he didn't reply, I opened the door and peeked inside. "River?"

"Yeah?" he finally said. I exhaled in relief.

"I'm sorry," I apologized. "I didn't mean to be a nag, I was just a little worried for a second."

"I'm fine, Emmy," he said lifelessly.

He didn't sound fine. His voice was emotionless. The absence of joy in his tone was one I recognized, one I wanted to ignore and gloss over and pretend I hadn't heard it before. It was his bad day voice.

94

He can't have a bad day now, not when we've spent the morning smiling and kissing.

"Are you gonna get out soon?" I asked.

He shut the water off in response and fumbled for a towel. When he came out from behind the curtain, it was tied loosely around his hips, revealing his bare skin and hard lines of muscle. I wasn't focused on that, partially because I had spent a good amount of time today with River shirtless anyway.

"Riv?" I whispered. "Look at me."

He did, but his green eyes seemed vacant. It was like he wasn't here with me.

I wrapped my arms around him, my cheek pressed against his damp chest. "Please tell me you're okay. I can't lose you again."

"I'm okay," he said, but I still felt like he was lying to me.

I stood on my tiptoes and kissed his cheek, apprehension striking me when I saw his eyes were staring off past me at the medicine cabinet. When I let go of him and opened it, I saw a pencil sharpener with a loose blade sitting next to his toothpaste.

"No." I grabbed the damn thing and listened to it rattle as I pitched it into the trash. "You promised me, River."

He clenched his jaw. "I know."

I reached out and grabbed his arm, my index finger wandering over his scars. "This won't happen again. Do you hear me, River? I won't let you hurt yourself again because I can't take it if anything happens to you."

He hugged me tightly to his chest, neither of us having any regard for the fact he was basically naked as we did so. His nose brushed my collarbone as he tucked his face up close to my neck. He pressed his soft lips to the skin there and told me he was sorry for the millionth time in the span of a couple weeks.

"I love you, Emmy," he reminded me.

"I know," I said.

After he was dressed and we were playing chess out in the living room, he opened up to me a little bit.

Before pushing his rook across the board to take one of my knights, he said, "I'm so happy with you. I got to kiss you and touch you and finally got to let you know how I feel about you. I should be over the moon. When I got in the shower, I was."

I took his rook with my bishop and returned his gaze to let him know I was still listening.

"It's like a switch. All of a sudden I shut off inside and everything feels like it takes so much energy out of me. My whole body hurts like I'm forcing it to keep going. It's like being a zombie, like being dead and watching everyone else keep on living. I don't know what it is. I'm trying to keep this day from becoming a bad day. I'm trying really hard, Emmy."

Judging by the way he described it, it wasn't too far off from how I viewed it. I knew him well enough to know his emotions controlled him rather than the other way around. It didn't seem like River really had a choice when it came to how his brain worked. He shifted back and forth like a swinging pendulum.

This was big for us, though. By talking about it, his problems finally became real. It wasn't like I saw him any differently because of it. He was still River, the same one I'd grown up with and loved for a lifetime. This time, he was River moving forward. He was River trying not to give in to the impending bad day.

I reached over and put my hand on top of his. "We're gonna

have a good day."

"We are," he agreed. "Got any ideas?"

I smirked deviously. "Actually, I might."

11

Chapter Eleven

Then

We were at the gas station out on the highway, barely past city limits. It was a place we'd visited a hundred times. We picked this convenience shop when we wanted to get away for a bit, but knew we couldn't go too far. It wasn't in Nowhereland, which automatically made it a trip to somewhere else. I liked to think of it as a taste of hope.

River adjusted his mirror in the convertible and gave my outfit another once-over.

"As much as I love the outfit, Emmy," he began. "I'm not sure you need to give the cashier a cleavage shot for me to successfully smuggle out a bottle of Jack. We've shoplifted plenty of times without it."

"But this time I know for a fact that Keith is the one working," I explained as I adjusted my bra. "I can keep him distracted while you grab the whiskey."

River sighed. "Fine. Have it your way."

"Jealous?"

"Damn right I am," he replied. "You're parading around in

booty shorts and a low-cut top for some kid who has the hots for you."

"Two kids if you count yourself," I corrected him as I hopped out of the convertible. "Ready to steal some alcohol?"

"I guess." He shrugged.

I could see that he was struggling to be the River I knew and loved, but that it was hard for him. Inside, I was begging him to snap out of it, pleading for his brain to start working right. I wanted him in a sound state of mind for a few minutes longer.

Before we walked inside, I reached up and rested my hand against his scruffy cheek. "This is a good day, remember? We're gonna have a good day, Riv."

"Yeah," he mumbled.

It was something. It was more than silence. I could work with that.

With that, he followed me into the convenience store. He headed straight for the drinks without glancing at the cashier. Meanwhile, I went to the counter and smiled at Keith.

"Hey!" I chirped.

"Hi, Emery," he said, blushing. "So how are you?"

"I'm doing great." I was practically gushing as I picked out a few candy bars to buy. "How about you?"

I leaned forward with my elbows propped up, making sure he had a good view. If he was looking at me, he wasn't looking at the monitor playing live security footage. I watched River shove the whiskey into his backpack and handed Keith money to pay for my candy.

"It's been a slow day," Keith replied, cheeks bright red as he glanced at my chest. "Uh, here's your change."

I kissed him on the cheek, making sure I was the picture of

perfect innocence as I turned to leave with River. "Thanks, Keith!"

"No problem," he said. "Hey, are we still on for that dance?"

"Totally," I called over my shoulder.

When we got back to the convertible, River handed me his backpack with a smuggled bottle of Jack Daniels (the only whiskey he ever wanted to drink) and scowled. "Did you have to kiss him?"

"It was on the cheek!" I scoffed. "Friends kiss each other on the face all the time. You used to kiss my forehead quite a bit."

"It wasn't friendly when I did it," River said pointedly.

"At least we got chocolate and booze out of it." I turned one of the bottles over in my hands. "You know, I used to think this stuff was disgusting, but it's less gross when you're drinking with a buddy."

"We're going to be alcoholics one day," he mused.

"I reject that wholeheartedly! Alcoholism is like staying in Nowhereland forever: not in the cards." I shoved his shoulder playfully as he pulled out onto the road.

By the time we were back at the trailer park, the sun was starting to set. As for us, our day was only beginning. Even though we had school the next morning, we would probably order a pizza and be up on the roof of his mobile home until late.

He had to give me a boost so I could reach the storm gutter to pull myself up. Since he was tall, he never had any trouble. Back in the early days, we had to stack chairs to climb up here, but now it was much easier. There was nothing like sitting high up, waiting for the stars to peek through the veil of piercing night.

As I laid out our usual checkered quilt, River called in our order and told me it would be delivered in a half-hour. He handed me a solo cup and filled it with warm whiskey, then took some of his own straight from the bottle.

"That's disgusting, River!" I exclaimed. "I can't drink any from that one because you got your slobber all over it."

"I had my tongue in your mouth earlier and *now* you're worried about germs?" He gave me a pointed look. Maturely, I flipped him off. He held onto my middle finger and pressed a small kiss to my hand before he went for my mouth.

We didn't talk for the next few minutes, kissing away.

Carly was home from work and inside watching *Judge Judy*. She wasn't the type to check on us, and part of me wondered if she had any idea we were always up to no good. Like now for instance, when we were drinking illegally and making out right above her head.

When the pizza came, River jumped down and gave the delivery boy a heart attack before he paid him. Shenanigans were our forte.

"That was mean," I said, but I was glad to see him joking around.

"I'm mean," Riv retorted.

"You better have given him a good tip," I chastised.

"Yes, *dear*," he said with a snort.

We ate over the box and flicked pepperoni at each other until we were too full to eat anymore. We kept the half-empty bottle of liquor and the leftover pizza at our feet as we curled up next to each other and stared up at the sky.

I liked listening to him breathe, as silly as it sounds. For me, it was a reminder that I wasn't alone, even if I felt a little small and isolated at times. Hours passed as we talked and laughed about everything and nothing all the same.

"What are you going to be when you grow up?" he asked randomly.

"I have no idea," I admitted. "Whatever it is, I won't be doing it here."

"You could be a stripper," River suggested.

"Oh shut up. I don't have the boobs for that anyway."

"I think your boobs are fine."

"You're such a boy."

"Well duh."

After a pause, he had a legitimate suggestion. "You could become a physicist."

I crinkled my nose in disgust. "I hate physics and I'm terrible at math. That sounds more like a River job."

"But physics is cool!" he protested. "Think about it! One day, you could prove the theory of parallel universes or something awesome like that."

As cute as his enthusiasm was, I knew that sort of thing wasn't for me, or at least I thought so then. "You would be a brilliant physicist. That can be your calling, but it's not mine. I'll find something to love and be passionate about. Don't worry."

He grew quiet, so my head perked up.

"What are you thinking about? Your amazing future in physics?"

"Actually, I have a theory about that," he said.

"About what? Physics? The whole point of science is to prove those, you know."

"No," he mumbled. "I mean about the future. I've started to think that maybe… maybe I'm destined not to have one."

I think it was at that moment that my heart learned how to skip a beat. One second it was moving along, calm and orderly.

It quickened when I noticed his shift in mood, then halted altogether once those awful words emerged. I wondered what breathing properly felt like as I choked out a "What?"

"I think I'm gonna die young, Emmy," he went on. "I just feel like I'm not gonna live to be ninety and have kids and see the world like you are."

"How could you say something like that?" I spat. "What the hell, River? You have the choice to live long and happy. You're young and you're healthy and I need you to stop talking like that because, when you do, it sounds like you're talking about suicide."

"I'm—" He searched for the right words. "I'm sorry. Let's just not talk about it anymore."

I swallowed the lump in my throat and blinked back the tears threatening to spill.

Why have I been crying so much lately?

"We said we were going to have a good day," I choked out. I wanted to kick myself when my voice broke a little bit. One look into my glassy eyes could tell him exactly how I was feeling.

"I know." He took me into his arms. "Hey, please don't cry. Please, Emmy, just smile. Don't cry. I didn't want to make you cry."

He kissed one of my cheeks, catching my escaped tears in his lips, and then he kissed the other. He wandered to my forehead, tracing my closed eyelids, and then met me in the middle. We kissed fervently, wild and borderline animalistic. He pressed me down against the blanket with his knee between my thighs. As his mouth left mine and slid down my neck, I gasped and arched my back so that we were pressed against each other.

I didn't know I could sound like this, feel like this.

I liked the burn of his touch. I liked the way we moved together in synchronization. Everything River and I did always felt well-coordinated because we knew each other so well that it was easy to work together.

It was when he started to take my shirt off that I decided we were going too far.

"River," I said against his mouth.

He groaned, obviously not hearing the urgency in my tone. My shirt came up further and my stomach became exposed. His fingers brushed my bra.

"Riv, stop," I told him, pushing him away.

He pulled away immediately, eyes wide and pupils dilated with lust. His blonde hair was a mess, no doubt at my hands, and his lips were pink and swollen. He caught his breath, raggedly inhaling. "What's wrong, Emmy?"

"We can't…" I shook my head, wondering how to put it into words. "We can't fool around. Not so soon and not out here. It doesn't feel right. It feels like you're trying to avoid your problems."

He frowned. "What do you mean? I'm fine."

"Are you though?"

"What do you want me to say?" he snapped. "All day I've been trying to be happy for you. I want *you* to have a good day, so I kiss you and drink nasty ass liquor with you and buy you pizza and make you feel loved. I'm not okay, Emmy! Is that what you want me to tell you?"

"I just want you to talk to me instead of pretending," I whispered, stunned because he almost never used such a harsh tone with me. "You're having a bad day and it's okay because we can make it better."

"Yeah, okay," he said dismissively. "It's not that easy. You can't just make a bad day go away because you want it to."

I looked down at my watch. "Riv, it's almost eleven, maybe we should just go inside and get some rest. You'll feel better in the morning—"

"You don't know that!" he yelled. "It's so easy for someone like you to say it's going to get better because you're not the one going through it. It's so easy for you to just act like everything is gonna be okay because it always is for you. You have it so easy, Em, and you take it for granted every single day!"

Despite bursting into tears, I somehow managed to reason with him, feeling more hurt than anything else. "You really think it doesn't affect me to see you like this? I've watched you cut yourself and tear yourself to pieces inside instead of telling me what's happening to you. I can see it, River! I can feel it too. If you really think I don't get it, tell me how I can understand. Make me understand!"

He buried his face in his hands and took a breath. His whole body shook as he said, "My mind is a train and I'm not the conductor. My head is a revolving door and my hands aren't pushing it. One minute I'm fine and in a second it hurts to breathe. Everything hurts. My whole body is dragging itself along. All I can think about is how *easy* it would be to just roll over and give up."

I flinched at the thought of him being so close to the end of his rope. Desperately, deliriously, I whimpered out words of denial. "Riv, it's okay. It's gonna be okay. We can still have a good day. We can still have a good day. We can still have—"

"Oh, Emery," he said with venom. "Can't you see that it's a very, very bad day?"

I felt as if I'd been doused with ice-cold water. All I could do was helplessly watch him climb down, telling myself that he was fine, that he was going to be fine, that it would all just be *fine*. It had to be, right?

It can be a good day. It can be a good day.

I didn't want to believe that his switch had been flipped again. I didn't want to think that he wasn't my River right now. I wanted to play make-believe and act like it would all be okay. He was right; I really did take the simplicity of my life for granted. I had no idea what he was going through because I had never felt anything so horrible before.

It wasn't until a few hours later that I would know what it feels like to have your spirit utterly broken.

Immediately, I was following him, abandoning our trash for the rain, insects, or whatever got to it first. On the way down, I accidentally kicked the whiskey bottle off the roof, and it shattered against the porch before my feet hit the ground.

"River, where are you going?"

He didn't answer. He stalked away wordlessly.

Before I could get to the convertible, he peeled out of the driveway so fast there was no way I could chase after him. The wheels screeched as he barrelled down the road, far away from me.

"River!" I hollered, trying to jog after the car. There was no way I could catch up, but I still chased him to the end of the street before I gave up. Hands on my knees, feet covered in dirt, I heaved in an uneven breath of defeat.

He was angry and hurt, and I was too, but above all, I was scared. I was scared to let him be alone when he was like this.

It all went wrong so fast.

He had become unpredictable.

"Please don't leave," I murmured into the wind before

collapsing into a fit of hysterics.

When I finally got inside the trailer, I found Carly dead asleep on the couch, snoring and out for the night. She and River were both heavy sleepers. They were so alike it was scary sometimes, down to the way their matching green eyes crinkled when they smiled. He got his height and sense of humor from his father, but he and Carly were almost carbon copies of each other.

I covered her with a blanket, wiped my nose with a tissue, and sat in River's bed to wait for him. Surely all he needed was time to cool off, right? He just needed time to catch his breath and blow off some steam.

Tomorrow we could sort things out, get him a therapist, and find some way of helping him with his mood swings so he didn't feel this out of control. He just had to come home so I could make it all happen.

Please come back, River, please let me help you.

I need you, Riv.

I need you.

12

Chapter Twelve

Now I'm an emotional wreck when I get home from Caroline's.

I walk through the door crying. I head to my room as tears stream down my cheeks. I don't speak, I *can't* speak. My head is so caught up in remembering River, remembering the night he left. I'm trying not to think about it and I'm failing. He's a ghost. He's haunting me.

I throw my keys down on the counter and try not to think about Beatles CDs, about *I Will* being played as River sang along. I try not to think about games of chess and crossword puzzles and whiskey and cuddling.

Stop thinking, Emery, stop thinking.

When I get inside my room, all I can think about is how much I need my boyfriend's comfort. The first thing I do is kick my shoes off and slide into bed beside him. Immediately, he stirs and reaches out to me sleepily in the darkness. I'm pulled into his strong, bare chest, his warm hands holding me steady as we curl up against one another.

"I missed you, darlin," he murmurs.

With the way the words slip out of his mouth and wrap around my heart, there's no way for me to hide the fact I'm dangerously close to breaking down. My salty tears fall straight down into the pillow, and when I try to take a breath and collect myself, it comes out as a sob.

"What's wrong?" He sits up immediately and takes my face into my hands. Dark brown eyes meet mine as his worry grows more and more evident. "Emery, talk to me. What happened?"

"River," I whimper. "C-Caroline asked about R-River."

"Shit," he swears. "Darlin, it's okay. It's okay."

"I let him go," I cry out. "I let him go that night and I shouldn't have—"

"It's not your fault," he insists. "Listen to me, it's not your fault. It's not. You couldn't have done anything to stop it."

"What if—"

I don't get to finish my question, he doesn't let me. He kisses me on the tip of my nose and whispers, "Don't get caught up in that. Stay with me where we are right now. I'm here. I'm here and I'm not going anywhere."

He holds me in his arms for a few long minutes, letting me cry into his chest. When I finally calm down a bit, he says, "I love you. More than anything else in this world."

"I love you too," I say quietly. "I love you so much, Silas."

"I'll never stop either," he promised me. "Take a deep breath for me, darlin. In and out. Breathe with me."

When he inhales, so do I. We breathe together until my cheeks are dry and my eyes are falling shut.

"Don't fall asleep on me yet, you can't wear jeans to bed," he says with a smile.

"You just want to undress me," I mumble.

"That too," he agrees.

I end up in one of his shirts and my underwear, which isn't terribly uncommon for us. I know that he would normally make an innuendo about it, but he doesn't this time. We stay silent, lying in bed tangled up in each other for a few minutes. At first, I wonder if he's sleeping, but his voice dismisses that notion.

"Are you asleep?" he whispers.

I shake my head.

"You need to sleep, darlin." He sighs, running his fingers up and down my arm. I curl up closer to him and feel his lips press against the side of my neck. "Tomorrow we can spend the day together. Let me take care of you."

"You don't have to," I say. "Really. I'm fine. It's rough talking about him sometimes."

"You didn't have to take care of me when I was sick," he replied. "You did anyway."

"Touche." My words are more slurred now, coming out slowly because I'm so exhausted.

"Goodnight, sleepy girl." His grip on my waist tightens as if to remind me that he's there. "I love you."

"I love you, Si," I say back.

* * *

The best thing about Silas is that he knows how to cook. It's definitely not my strong suit, so he handles most of the meal preparation. I love that about him. Since I had such a long night, I wake up a little later than normal. My heart is immediately warmed by the fact he got up early to make me breakfast. I'm almost always up before him.

I come up behind him as he's flipping a pancake and wrap my arms around his torso.

"Good morning, gorgeous," he says cheerfully. "I picked up some blueberry syrup. I know it's your favorite and we were out."

"You didn't—" I start.

"I know I didn't *have* to," he cuts me off. "I wanted to. I also went for a run and picked up some coffee. Caroline made yours iced so it didn't need to be reheated. She's sorry about yesterday, by the way."

"It's okay," I murmur, my face still pressed against his back. "Sounds like you had an eventful morning. What time did you wake up?"

"Eight-thirty," he says. "It's only ten, so I would say I handled everything in record timing."

"You're a superhero," I tell him.

"Only for you," he replies. "Now sit down and let me finish making you breakfast."

"So bossy." I roll my eyes and hop up onto the counter with my coffee in hand. I watch as he finishes cooking with disbelief.

This is *my* boyfriend. This amazing man is *mine*. Sometimes, I can't wrap my head around it.

We eat at the kitchen table and drink orange juice out of the nicer glasses in our cabinet. I'm surprised he used them considering he's always complaining about having to wash them by hand. When I give him a questioning look, he shrugs his shoulders as if to say it isn't a big deal. I know it is.

"This is too much, Si," I say after I finish my pancakes. "Really, you didn't have to do all this."

"I love you," he responds matter-of-factly. "So I made you breakfast and bought expensive coffee and your favorite syrup. And now I'm gonna do the dishes, including these stupid cups, and I'm gonna take you to dinner tonight."

"Are you sure you're not overreacting?" I question. "I appreciate it, but I'm good. I needed some time to cool off, but I'm better now."

"I wanted to remind you that I love you," he responds.

I get up from my spot at the table and wander over to where he's sitting. When I climb onto his lap, he doesn't protest. Instead, he holds me like he always does: right around the waist to stabilize me. Silas would never let me fall.

"I have definitely been reminded," I say.

"Good," he says.

A moment passes. I wrap my arms around his neck and kiss his jawline, right in the spot that drives him crazy. I feel his fingers slide down from my hips to brace my thighs instead.

He swallows hard. "You're not wearing pants, darlin."

"I know." I rock my hips forward against him, and he shivers.

"I can't do the dishes if you're distracting me."

"So how about you let me distract you for a while?" I suggest, knowing how close he is to losing his self-control.

"Forget it. The chores can wait."

Silas stands, lifting me up with him. My legs fall around his waist as he grips them tightly. For a second, he just looks at me, breathing quickly, and then he closes the gap between us. We kiss hungrily as he carries me back to bed.

The dishes end up being abandoned for quite some time before we finally make our way back to the table to clean up. He scrubs our plates in nothing but his boxers, which hang low on his hips and reveal the dimples in his muscular back. I

112

would be lying if I said I didn't find it absolutely sexy.

He won't let me help him and even goes so far as to swat my hands away when I reach for a dish. Instead of assisting, I occupy myself by pushing my hands through his thick, black hair because I know it annoys him.

When he's done cleaning up, he pins me against the fridge and kisses me again.

I break away first, gasping as I say, "I need to get started on my homework."

"We could shower and *then* do homework," he says as he kisses my neck.

"You know we'll never get homework done if we do that." I laugh and step away.

"You're no fun."

"Sorry, but physics papers don't write themselves." I sit down on the couch and reach for my laptop, but Silas snatches it away playfully.

"But this is your third draft," he argues.

"It has to be perfect," I retort, trying to tug my computer away from him.

"Fine, you can do your boring homework. But I'm gonna keep procrastinating mine."

"Really, Fields?" I scoff. "More procrastination?"

He sighs in exasperation. "It's bad enough that Caroline only refers to me by my surname, but now you're doing it too?"

"Seems so."

"Speaking of, how did the move-in go?" he asks, genuinely interested.

One of the many things I've come to love about him is his thoughtfulness. He pays attention to detail and makes an effort with everyone he meets. I'm sure Caroline would appreciate him asking about her, especially because I only mentioned her new place offhandedly to him.

"Pretty good, but there's still work to be done. I have to help out with the last of it tonight." I make a mental note to text Caroline and confirm a specific time for me to be there.

"Do you guys need an extra hand? I can be there," he offers.

"She wanted you to help yesterday, but I didn't think you'd be up for it considering how sick you've been lately."

He smiles. "Your concern for me is adorable, but I'm doing just fine, darlin. I can unpack a few boxes."

"I'll let her know," I say, powering on my laptop. "Now stop talking so I can finish this damn thesis."

He collapses beside me on the couch and turns the TV on while I get to work. We spend the rest of the morning tangled up, and I almost forget what had me so upset the night before. Almost.

13

Chapter Thirteen

Then

I woke up to loud pounding at the door hours later. When my eyes opened, it took me a few seconds to adjust to the darkness of the room. At first, I was confused about why I wasn't in my bed, then after a few seconds, I realized I was in River's. My first instinct was to reach for him and hold his hand, but all I found were cold sheets.

He's not here?

The knocking continued persistently.

I rolled out of bed and rubbed the sleep from my eyes, searching the trailer for any sign of River. I was so groggy that I couldn't recall what time he'd left. He should've been back, but it didn't seem like a big deal in my current state. I only had an acute awareness of my surroundings.

"Is River here?" Carly asked me.

I shook my head as the memories flooded back to me. I could practically hear the phantom roar of his engine as he sped away from his house, from me.

Another knock came. Louder.

"Did he forget his damn keys or something?" she muttered under her breath.

I lingered in the hallway by his room as Carly opened the door with half-closed eyes. I watched her flick the porch light on, revealing a tall man standing in the doorway with his hand closed around a badge.

A badge? Why are the police here?

"Are you Carly Fields?" The officer wore an unreadable expression as he posed the question.

My heart quickened inside my chest, ready to run and hide like I wanted to. It all felt like a bad dream. I knew it couldn't be good before the cop said anything.

She narrowed her eyes. "Who wants to know?"

"I'm Officer Lancey. I work for the highway patrol," he explained. "Am I speaking with Carly Fields?"

She nodded slowly. "What's this about? Is River in trouble? If you've got him in custody, I need to know."

"Ma'am, I'm going to need you to take a seat." Lancey's head bowed as he slipped his badge back into his pocket. The air grew thick with the unsaid words. It was then that I realized my world was about to change forever.

"Why the hell would I do that?" Carly's voice broke a little then, and at that moment, both of us knew exactly why he wanted her to sit down.

"I'm afraid there's been an accident," he said gravely. "Around one am, River sped out into oncoming traffic. There was a collision between his vehicle and an eighteen-wheeler. I'm afraid the damage was extensive…"

"Is my son okay?" she interrupted him. "Where is my son?"

"He received blunt force trauma to the head from the steering wheel," Lancey went on, somber and understanding as he spoke. "When the paramedics arrived, there was nothing they could do. I'm very sorry for your loss."

"You're lying!" Carly wailed, pointing a finger at him. "You listen to me. My son is okay! He was just here a few hours ago. You ask her. Ask Emery. She'll tell you he was here and he just went out for a bit. You have the wrong boy! Not my River! He's all I have!"

She broke down and collapsed in a heap on the couch, holding herself as she said it over and over again. "He's all I have. He's all I have."

I emerged from hiding and met the officer's eyes. It hadn't hit me yet, the loss of him. It was something waiting in the darkness to pounce on me. But for now, I was calm as I spoke, numb to it all. "What do you need from Carly?"

"I was instructed to bring her down to the station to ID the— to make sure it's the right kid." Lancey's eyes glanced at Carly sympathetically. His pity, so clear, made my stomach churn. "She can come in tomorrow morning if she must, but it's necessary for the case that we get the verification as soon as possible."

"I'll do it," I volunteered before I could think it through. "I'm his best friend. I'll do it."

He put his hand on my shoulder. "Miss…"

"Leigh," I supplied. "Emery Leigh."

"Miss Leigh," he said. "It's not an easy sight. I don't think it's wise for you to see him like this."

"I'm his *best friend*," I repeated. "She can't do it, but I can. I need to do this."

My ferocity must've been what persuaded him. He wisely chose not to argue with me, sensing the urgency in my tone. I was stubborn, and I wasn't about to believe River was gone, not unless I saw it for myself.

"Alright," he agreed. "Alright, then."

I promised Carly I would be back soon, but she didn't hear me. She remained in a heap on the sofa, crying her eyes out and praying to God it wouldn't be him in the coroner's office. The Fields family wasn't religious, but she must've felt there was no other hope for her. Desperation does something funny to people, and the more desperate she became, the more she began to pray.

It occurred to me as I rode in the back of the cruiser that I should be crying. My best friend in the entire world was probably dead. I should've cried and screamed and punched something. I should've felt something.

But I didn't.

I later learned that phenomenon was called shock.

The morgue was cold and full of metal. Metal cabinets. Metal autopsy tools. Even a little bit of the metallic smell of blood. There was metal everywhere. Life was replaced with industrial items.

Like a sci-fi movie, Riv would remark.

When the coroner pulled back the sheet, everything inside of me broke.

River.

There he was, pale and lifeless on a metal table. There was a long gash around his hairline where his head must've met the steering wheel. His beautiful green eyes were closed, no longer able to crinkle when he smiled, no longer able to meet mine. The veins in his skin stood out against the backdrop of translucent white flesh. He was a corpse. My best friend had gone from larger than life to a dead man.

"That's him," I said, just before my voice cracked and the

tears started to pour. "That's River."

Before they could move the sheet back, I ran forward and took his ice-cold face into my hands. Even though I had just confirmed the dead body right in front of me was him, I wasn't ready to believe it. In my mind, I figured might be able to wake him up if I had enough willpower.

I clasped his cheeks and talked to him, absolutely hysterical, "Riv, it's me. Dammit, you're such a heavy sleeper sometimes. Wake up, River. It's me, Emmy. I'm here. I'm here now. We're gonna make it better, you hear me? It's just a bad day, but we can have a good day tomorrow. And we can have a good day after that. River, wake up. Wake up, River, *please*."

"We need to get her out of here," the coroner said, but it was all just background noise to me.

"River?" I whispered. "Officer! Officer, he's not breathing. We need someone to help him breathe! He can't be alive if he isn't breathing!"

"He's gone." Officer Lancey put his hand on my arm. "Miss Leigh, he's gone."

"No, he's not!" I yelled, throwing myself over his limp body. "You don't understand! He's okay! He just had a bad day and he's only sleeping. It's only a bad day, but he's okay. He has to be okay—"

A different officer who must've heard the commotion pulled me away from River, trying to comfort me as the medical examiner pulled the cover back over him.

"River!" I screamed. "River, wake up! Wake up and tell them you're okay, tell me you're okay. River!"

Someone started to yank me away as I kicked and screamed and fought against them. The door to the morgue closed and locked, leaving me in the hall with a bunch of strange people and without River Fields.

I didn't say goodbye. I didn't get to say goodbye. He can't be dead because I didn't get to say goodbye to him.

They sat me down with a female cop in a new room, one that was warmer and probably meant to be more welcoming. I couldn't have cared less about the setting. The cheesy motivational posters meant nothing to me without Riv being there to make fun of them.

"I need to contact your parents and have them come get you," the nice lady said. "How about you tell me your mom's number and you can go home?"

"I don't need to go home," I told her, still as unhinged as I was a few moments before. "I need to go back to the trailer. River is gonna be back soon."

She sighed deeply and took my hands in hers. Then, she gave me a look I would come to see often. It was one grown-ups had whenever they heard I was the girl whose friend killed himself. They all felt bad for me, and every crease in their faces made sure I knew.

Softly, she said, "Honey, I'm afraid River isn't coming back."

"Don't say that," I snapped. "That's not true. He promised we would get out of Nowhereland together."

"What's Nowhereland?" she asked.

I scowled at the wall.

"Emery?"

"Here!" I raised my voice. "Here is Nowhereland! And he promised me!"

She held me in her arms and tried to get me to calm down as I babbled on and on about how he was supposed to come back. I insisted that we were supposed to escape together until I finally stopped talking.

Eventually, I cooperated enough to let them call Mom and have her pick me up. As she hugged me, I told her the same thing I told the cop lady; *"River promised we would get out of Nowhereland together."*

The truth of the matter was that River escaped Nowhereland, but he didn't take me with him. Two weeks after my sixteenth birthday, I lost the most important person in my life.

He left me too soon.

* * *

I didn't go to school the next day. I didn't eat either.

I occupied my time by laying in bed and moving pieces across my chessboard as if I were playing the game with somebody else. I tried to think what River would do as if I could simulate him beating me one last time. There was a hollowness in my chest that wouldn't go away, a lingering impression he left behind.

"I need you, Riv," I said in the silence of my bedroom. *"Dammit!* I need you."

I punctuated my statement by throwing one of my knights across the room. It smacked against the wall and hit the carpet, but the sound was lost to my ears. All I could hear was my ragged breaths as they faded into sobs.

My mother eventually gave up on trying to speak with me. I kept my door shut and locked as if that could keep reality away from me. Every time her fist came to knock, I imagined it was River's. I wanted so desperately for it to be River's.

I was surprised when it was Greta who showed up to drop some make-up assignments off for me. She'd only come over to my place once for a birthday party in elementary school, but in a town like this, it was always easy to find addresses. She probably asked someone, which was more effort than I ever thought she'd give something related to me.

The whole time she was there, she didn't say anything, probably because she knew that her tiny crush on River amounted to nothing now. I was glad she didn't pretend to mourn. She didn't know him enough to do it.

I managed to thank her, so I didn't feel like an utter asshole when she went home.

Mom forced me to choke down some leftover pasta from a couple of nights before. After that, she left me alone to cry and feel sorry for myself. Part of me felt nothing but self-loathing because I could've fought harder. If I had made him stay—

If I had made him stay he would still be here right now.

It hurt to think about, but I knew that I had to accept it. I messed up. My mistake was the reason my best friend was dead.

Breathing felt like a chore, even though biology had taught me it was a function the body did automatically. I couldn't fall asleep, partially because I wouldn't allow myself the sweet release it would give me, but also because I didn't want to close my eyes and see him.

If he were there, he would've reached over and kissed my forehead. He would've said he was sorry he made me cry, but that he was there to make it better. There were a million things he would have done if he were there. But he wasn't. And he would never be again.

I think, at one point, I started trashing my room, but it's all a blur. One second I was on my bed, the next my dad was pulling me away from the wreckage I had made of my drawers, of my bookshelf, of the wall where I punched clean through it.

"Emery," Dad whispered over and over. "Emery, honey, calm down. Calm down."

"He's gone!" I screamed. "He's gone and it's my fault!"

I proceeded to bawl my eyes out for the fifth time that day. My dad simply took me by the hand and led me away from my mess. He let me climb into bed with him and Mom like I was a little kid again.

I slept in the middle of their mattress for the next week. It was a tight fit, but my parents made the sacrifice without complaining.

Days passed like this, like I was stuck at a standstill as I tried (and failed) to recover.

The untimely deaths are the worst kind. They assign blame because of their injustice. They make you think of all the things you could've done differently in order to prevent it.

The worst thing about them is that they make you wish that you had died too.

14

Chapter Fourteen

Then
I hadn't spoken more than two words since the night I effectively demolished my bedroom. I communicated to Mom and Dad almost exclusively in nods or shaking my head. Sometimes, I threw in a hand gesture.

I went back to school a few days after shit hit the fan, but the second I sat down in trig and River didn't come in behind me, I had a full-blown breakdown. After that, I was moved to an indefinite independent study.

Two weeks later, Carly gained enough of her emotional stability back to plan a memorial service. It was hosted at the church by the trailer park, a place River would never visit on his own accord, and I was expected to speak on his behalf.

I didn't know what I was supposed to say, but when Carly came to my mother with red-rimmed eyes and asked her to get me started on a eulogy, I knew there was no getting out of this one.

I dressed in one of River's sweaters, a baggy black thing that I wore over leggings, and walked alone in my battered sneakers to the church that Friday afternoon. Mom was working and so was Dad, so it was just me left to grieve the boy they'd known just as long as I had. I imagined River complaining about the entire affair as I trudged along.

"Churches are depressing," he would've grumbled. *"Sinning is the best part of life."*

"You heathen," I would've said back.

I remember reading somewhere that suicide was a sin, and River might've found it poetic.

It was hot and stuffy in the sanctuary. At the door, they had folded programs outlining the formal service, along with his school picture and the years he was alive. His birthday and his death date were all I could focus on. *April 2nd.* There was a very real chance he could've died on April fool's day, a grand cosmic punchline, but since his death had occurred roughly an hour into April 2nd, the opportunity for humor had been lost. It was morbid sure, but just the sort of thing he would've cracked a joke about.

I took a seat near the front and stuffed my shaking hands under my thighs to hide them. Carly was fanning herself with the eulogy she had prepared, which was neatly written on lined paper. I wondered if she'd taken a notebook out of his bag, one he would never use again. At first, I wanted to scream at her for tearing a page out of his composition book, but I realized how irrational that was and bit the inside of my cheek instead.

We sang *Amazing Grace.* Or rather, everyone else did. I sat there silently and sang nothing. I wanted to leave, but I knew that would look bad, so I stayed in my chair and counted down the seconds to when I was expected to speak.

Carly gave the first speech, somehow keeping her composure through most of it.

"River was always so funny," she began, wiping her eyes on the sleeve of her black dress. Black. What an utterly depressing color. "When he was only eight, he came home from school one day and he asked me why I named him River. It was his dad's idea actually. Rob had so many Rs on his side of the family that he felt like he had to continue the tradition. He thought River sounded just unique enough to stand out in a small town like this. Even before he was born, we all knew River was meant to be unique. He was so much more than your average kid."

He really was, I thought. *He burned so brightly that he went out too soon.*

"River said he wanted to change his name because the kids at school had made fun of him for it." She eyed me wryly with a watery smile. "But the next day, he told me that his friend, Emery, had called all those boys some 'not so nice' words so they wouldn't do it anymore. He loved her from that point on."

I couldn't remember that story, but it sounded so much like us that I believed it.

"He was a good son. He took so much on after Robbie died. And he was an even better friend. There aren't too many people like that in this world. I loved him with all my heart, and I pray to God he's up there watching over us. All I want is for my baby boy to be happy."

I knew she would probably be at Sunday services more often, praying as she sought comfort. If that made her feel closer to Riv, I supported it, but that wouldn't be how I coped. I didn't believe in all that because in my mind, God was a dick. What kind of god would kill a kid before he even turned seventeen?

We sang another hymn at Carly's request. It was awkward and tearful and I was barely hanging onto my own sanity.

Don't cry. Dammit, don't cry.

Standing up was so much more difficult than I imagined. My legs turned to stone and sank into the floor below me. My lungs deflated and turned to metal. Oxygen stopped flowing. My eyes fell on the giant ass Jesus statue hanging above the stained glass windows. It was almost like I was asking the man upstairs himself to climb down and carry me out of there. I could barely move, but luckily, I got up to the podium.

I stared out at the small crowd. Some kids from school had made an appearance as if they actually cared enough to be there. His family members, strangers I'd only seen once or twice over the years, sat in the pews expectantly.

They were waiting for me to talk. Waiting for the curly-haired girl to stop hugging herself, to open her mouth and say something about her best friend in the entire world. But she couldn't speak. *I couldn't speak.* I knew that if I did, I would start crying again.

It was in this very church that we had our first whiskey night. It occurred to me as I stood there that I was only inches away from where I spat up my first ever drink of alcohol.

River had noticed the window was open when we were wandering around one night. He was fourteen, newly so, and still missing his father more deeply than I could imagine. It was a heart attack, a spontaneous one at that, and it was so sudden that River couldn't have seen it coming. Even in his death, Rob was unpredictable.

A few months had passed, but even though Riv pretended he was fine, I knew better. I was thirteen and he wasn't much older, so we weren't exactly emotionally mature enough to

127

discuss how we felt.

River had been cleaning out the kitchen earlier that day when he found his dad's old liquor stash. We were walking down the road with a mostly empty bottle of Jack when he spotted the open window. After convincing me to come with him, he gave me a boost into the building.

The church was dark and dreary, having returned to silence after a Sunday full of Bible time and preaching. Standing in it gave me goosebumps. It felt both wrong and creepy.

"We broke into a church," River said proudly. His green eyes crinkled with amusement.

"We didn't break so much as enter without permission," I corrected him. Back then, I had a thing for telling him he was wrong about something, even if he wasn't. It was a wonder we managed to tolerate each other.

"Whatever," he replied. "Trespassing isn't as cool when you put it that way."

He wrenched the bottle open and took the first sip unceremoniously. With a wince and a hard swallow, he downed it. His lips curled to reveal his crooked teeth as he groaned. "That stuff is nasty."

"It can't be that bad." I took a sip of my own and marveled at how utterly right he was. The whiskey was warm and stale and burned the entire way down. My body rejected it mid-swallow, which meant I was coughing it up all over myself in seconds. He laughed, but still drank more.

"Why?" I wondered aloud. "Why keep drinking?"

"Because I like the way it makes me feel." He punctuated the statement with a third swig.

From someone so young with a bright future ahead of him, the words were jarring. They should have set off alarms in my brain, but for some reason, they didn't. I didn't think anything of it.

He got a little drunk and I managed to keep down a second sip. There wasn't much, to begin with, so the bottle wouldn't go very far. It didn't matter since we'd never had alcohol before and were probably lightweights.

Our history of whiskey nights never extended to the church again. It was a bit sacrilegious and, besides, after that night, there never seemed to be open windows. But hey, it made for an interesting part of our history.

As I pulled myself from the memory, I realized I was standing there deep in my thoughts for several minutes while they waited for a eulogy. I could've told them the story of the first whiskey night, even if it was a little messed up on a moral level. Middle schoolers drinking in a closed church wasn't exactly a great image to have, but it was better than nothing. I could've said a million things about River, but at that moment, my mind went blank, as if it disconnected itself.

As I stood there with my mouth ajar, struggling to make a sound, I realized my legs were working again. I bolted, racing down the aisle as people began to chatter in surprise. Carly called my name, but I knew it would make me feel guilty if I had to face her, so I didn't look back.

I didn't stop running until I was under a tree at the top of a grassy hill out back. Tears flowed easily. I felt utterly pathetic sitting out there sobbing my heart out. All I seemed to do was cry, and I hated it.

River would've known what to say, but thinking that only made me miss him more. I pressed my head between my knees, gasping for breath. It was there, when I could barely stay grounded, that I finally mustered words.

"River Fields is…" I whimpered upon realizing my mistake. I hated having to correct myself. I hated that River had become past-tense. "River Fields *was* the best friend you could ever have. He was smart. Really smart. And kind and sweet. And yeah, he was also an asshole sometimes but every sixteen-year-old can be. He didn't get to turn seventeen, which makes me sad because he'll never get to buy his own ticket for an R-rated movie or see the world. He deserved so much more."

That was all I said, realizing how futile it was to mutter aimlessly into the universe. At the time, I believed the tree I sat under was my only audience member. That notion was dismissed as soon as a throat cleared and a boy sat down in the grass next to me.

I knew his face. He was one of Riv's many cousins I'd encountered at a reunion a long time ago. From what I could tell, he was the same age as me, which made me question why I hadn't seen him more. I barely recognized him, but he seemed to know who I was.

He stretched his long legs out in front of him and leaned into the grass, studying me.

"He's dead," I observed, as if we weren't dressed for the funeral we were supposed to be attending.

"So they tell me," he replied in a deep voice that left goosebumps on my arms. He didn't have the same thick drawl the rest of us did, meaning he was probably far from home. His dark eyes were bowed to the ground, and his black hair was a wavy mess in the wind. His knuckles were white from clenching the lawn and he held onto the strands for dear life.

"I can't even eulogize him. What kind of best friend am I?"

"The kind who's grieving," he answered. "No one will fault you for that, Emery."

I blinked at him in disbelief. "How do you know my name?"

"Everyone knows your name," he said matter-of-factly. "Aunt Carly introduced you."

"I hoped no one would be paying attention to me," I admitted. "God, I went and blew it up there. I'm probably gonna be the talk of the town."

"Nah. They've already moved on with the service," he told me. "Don't worry about it, darlin'."

Darlin, I repeated. *Who is this guy?*

"Did you know him well?" I asked.

"Not as well as I should've," he replied. "I never really spent enough time with River. Now I don't really get a do-over."

"I could use one of those," I stated grimly.

"I think there isn't a single person in there who wouldn't take the chance to do something differently. I also think you're the only one who doesn't need to change a thing. I'd be willing to bet you gave him all the love anyone could ask for."

"Maybe you have too much faith in me."

"Maybe you need more of it," he countered.

His hand came to rest on top of mine and I let him hold it. Even though his hands were different than Riv's, bigger and warmer, I could almost pretend it was River touching me.

"I almost feel like I'm dreaming," I said after some time had passed. "But then I remember that dreams don't hurt this much."

I stopped talking after that, wondering why I was telling a complete stranger how I felt. Talking wasn't helping. If anything, it was just making me sadder, and I didn't know why. I never even got his name, but I don't think either of us wanted a formal introduction.

He got up to leave once people started coming out of the

131

church, but I stayed. I only budged when I realized I probably should head home before my mom assumed I'd offed myself too.

Between the random guy comforting me when I didn't deserve it and the fact the entire experience was emotionally draining, I was ready to sleep for a long time. My head pounded and my feet dragged as I walked back to my apartment. Mom gave me a hug when I walked through the door and made me eat something before I was allowed to go back to my room.

Admittedly, I puked it up in my trashcan the second I was alone. It wasn't intentional, but my stomach was uneasy and I made no effort to keep the meal down. I just held back my hair and vomited until my stomach was as empty as I felt.

My room had been mostly restored. Everything I'd broken was either at Goodwill or in the trash, but I hadn't wrecked it all entirely. I spent most of that night on the floor sifting through plastic bags stuffed full of pictures.

The photos didn't do him justice. Riv's eyes weren't as bright when printed. His blonde hair didn't reflect the hours we spent in the sun. His teeth matched his asymmetrical smile, but it didn't look the same as I remembered it. There was no life in it. In the photos I found of us laughing, I had no idea what the joke was. I hated myself for it. I wanted to drown in endless punchlines and inside jokes and moments of us. There wouldn't be more of them coming, so I needed to savor the ones I had.

I ended up googling factors that lead to suicidal behavior. Among them, I found a few that rang true, ranging from a history of mental illness to a death in the family. Ever since we covered mood disorders in health class, I knew something was off about how hot and cold River could be.

Could he have been bipolar? It seemed likely.

Maybe if I had just spoken up about it, I started to think. *Maybe he'd still be here.*

After I went through the usual list of everything I might've done differently, I realized that Nowhereland wouldn't have provided what River needed. Here, mental illness didn't exist. Everything that wasn't a physical problem was a reflection of a spiritual crisis. The only help anyone would've offered was God, but they couldn't pray the struggles out of River.

In the weeks following the funeral, I stayed awake for many nights, wondering what the hell I was doing with my life, wondering if it would ever feel better. I didn't do much of anything productive. Mourning was all I was good for, but after a bit, I decided that was okay. I needed to work through it, and I needed to do it soon before I became a shell forever.

Gradually, the pain faded. It was still there, but leaving slowly. I felt as if I had been deposited on the beach after years at sea spent drowning, and the tide was finally receding.

15

Chapter Fifteen

Now Silas drives to Caroline's place with one of his hands holding mine tightly and the other on the wheel. We're silent, listening to the music I'm streaming from my phone. When *Nowhere Man* starts playing, I immediately skip the song. Si knows me well enough to suspect something is up.

"Do you want to talk about it?" he asks.

I shake my head. "There's nothing to talk about. I'm fine."

"You've been acting weird since Caroline asked about River," he points out. "And now you won't even listen to The Beatles without freaking out. You can talk to me about this."

"I said I'm *fine*, Si," I snap.

His jaw tightens. "Yeah, sure. You can say that all you want, but I know better, Emery. I know you better."

Somehow, even though I'm the one treating him unfairly and he has every right to be mad at me, I feel hurt by the fact he called me by my name instead of *darlin*. "You never call me Emery," I whisper.

"I'm sorry," he says, softening. "That sounded harsh. I didn't mean for it to come out like that."

Since we're on Caroline's street, it isn't long before he can cut the engine and take me in his embrace. His apology is in his body too, in the way he holds me.

I bury my face in his chest. "I miss him, Silas."

"I know you do." He runs a hand through my hair. "It's okay to miss him."

I'm not sure that it is. It almost feels like I'm caught in the past when I start letting myself dwell on it. I have to remind myself constantly that if River hadn't died, I wouldn't have gotten close to Silas. Good things came out of the tragedy, but sometimes, I lose sight of that.

"You know that I love you, right?" he says.

I nod. "I love you too."

"If they ask about him, I'll just shut it down, okay?" he assures me. "We don't have to talk about it."

"If they ask questions, I'll answer them," I say. "I owe it to Caroline. She knows enough about River to deserve the whole story, even if I hate talking about that awful town and all the stuff that happened in it."

"Hey," he teases. "I liked Nowhereland because it was honest. You can't have secrets in a town like that."

"Unfortunately, you aren't wrong," I say with a laugh.

As we linger outside, I'm reminded that he can always cheer me up, even when it seems impossible.

Silas holds my gaze to make sure I'm genuinely brightening up. His dark eyes, brown streaked with gold, read my face. He likes to be certain of my reactions. It's almost as if he commits every smile, every movement, every crease to memory.

"Darlin," he says softly. "If you need to talk about it, you can talk to me. I'm here."

"I know that." I lean forward and gently kiss him on the mouth.

He puts an arm over my shoulders after we break away. "Now, let's get a move on."

When we get to the door, Caroline has it propped open with a cardboard box. She's blasting some loud rock music and sweating right through her t-shirt. I already regret wearing long-sleeves and know that, at some point, I'll be parading around in my sports bra. Not that Silas would mind.

"Still no AC?" I ask upon feeling how hot it is.

"Sadly," she confirms. "Hey, Fields."

"Hi?" he says with a chuckle. "I have a first name, you know."

"About that," Caroline begins. "I've been having trouble pronouncing it. I've only ever seen it typed out over text."

"It's pronounced like sigh-liss," he explains.

"Okay, Silas," she tests it out with a smirk. "I guess it works, but I like calling you Fields more."

He shrugs. "I've given up on this fight. You've even got Em saying my last name now."

"It'll be her last name eventually," Caroline says. "May as well get her used to hearing it."

"Damn straight," Silas agrees.

I blush from my face down to my feet. "Uh, I mean…"

"Don't worry, darlin, I'm not proposing right now." He hugs me from behind and presses his mouth to my temple. "You can even hyphenate your last name when the day comes."

"How do you know I'll say yes?" I challenge.

He and Caroline both narrow their eyes at me as if to say *really?*

"Emery Fields does have a nice ring to it," I concede.

"I agree," Silas says smugly.

Caroline clears her throat and gestures to the remaining boxes. "Not that this isn't adorable, but my apartment is a huge mess right now. We need to get working."

I untangle myself from him and follow her to the bedroom. She's putting her bed frame together, albeit clumsily. While Silas helps set up her furniture, I start hanging her clothes up in the closet.

About halfway into the job, Rosemary shows up, sitting in Caroline's beanbag and scrolling through Twitter while she watches us work. It takes a while to get the bed constructed, with no shortage of cursing from Silas. I bite back several giggles while they struggle, happy I'm organizing shirts instead.

"I need water," Caroline says when it's done, her face red from the effort. "Anyone else want one?"

"We'll take two," Silas replies on my behalf.

"Sounds good," she calls on her way to the kitchen.

When I bend over to grab one of her sweaters, I feel Silas give my ass a pinch and turn around instantly to glare at him. "Was that necessary?"

"I would say so," he states smugly. "Those pants fit *really* well."

"He's not wrong," Rosemary chimes in, looking up from her phone.

"You aren't helping," I tell her.

"I think she is," Silas argues.

I reach for a hoodie and, naturally, he does it again.

"I can't get anything done if you keep touching me!" I quip.

He rolls his eyes. "Fine. Have it your way. You know you can hand me some stuff so it'll go faster."

"You're terrible with laundry," I say. "All of your shirts end

137

up with creases in them because you either hang or fold them wrong."

"Not true." He crosses his arms defensively, and I gesture to the rumpled fabric of his sleeve to prove my point.

He ends up leaning against the wall while I get everything situated. By the time I start on the box full of shoes, Caroline and Rosemary have moved on to a different room and it's just the two of us.

I try to reach the top of the closet to set the first pair of boots up there, but I can't get it. I know Silas is fighting the urge to laugh without looking at him. Being short has its perks, but sometimes it can be really inconvenient. Like now, for instance.

He chuckles. "Do you need me now?"

"Shut up."

His hands slip under my shirt and tighten around my hips, which makes me shiver. "Silas, what are you doing?"

"Brace yourself," he warns.

Before I can ask what he means by that, he yanks me off my feet and lifts me onto his shoulders as if I weigh nothing. He likes to pick me up just because he can, even when I protest. Despite my annoyance, I don't try to climb down. Instead, I take advantage of my new height. Now that I can reach the top of the closet, the job is much easier to accomplish.

"Hey, Em, are you almost—" Caroline stops when she sees where I'm sitting. A laugh bursts from her lips as she lifts her phone for a picture. "That's just hilarious. Were you too short to do it without help?"

Silas lowers me to the ground and I cross my arms in frustration. "I could've done it myself."

"That's a lie," he interjects.

"The technicalities don't matter," Caroline says dismissively. "I ordered pizza if you guys are hungry."

Silas immediately perks up when he hears the mention of food. He's the first one in the kitchen helping himself to a slice.

"Really, Si?" I laugh. "You're like a human garbage disposal."

He grins at me as he wolfs it down. "You love me anyway."

We end up congregated in the living room watching a rerun of *Friends*. Rosemary picked up a pack of beers on the way over, and everyone except Silas takes one. It doesn't surprise me. He's never been a drinker in all the time I've known him, but he doesn't question when I have one, or even when I drain a second. It's when I grab a third can of Budweiser that he takes it out of my hand.

"Em," he mutters quietly enough that Caroline and Rosemary don't hear him. "I think you've had enough."

I raise my eyebrows at him. "Are you serious, Si? I'm fine. I can drink. I'm an adult and there's barely any alcohol in these."

Rosemary turns to look at us and my cheeks heat in embarrassment.

"I bought them so you guys could have some," she says, clearly confused.

"She's had two already," Silas says. "While the offer is sweet, I just don't want Em to get carried away. She's got a math test tomorrow. Right, darlin?"

I shouldn't have mentioned the exam. "Whatever. I won't have another beer."

I push off the couch to excuse myself, but before I can stalk past Si, he grabs my wrist gently and gets to his feet.

Great, I think. *This is about to become a fight.*

"What's wrong with you, girlie?" Caroline asks, muting the

TV.

"Nothing," I reply. "You guys are just overthinking this. All I wanted was a beer, not an interrogation."

Rosemary, who can obviously see that I'm upset, tries to intervene. "I think Silas means well and only wants to make sure you aren't hungover for your test tomorrow."

"I think Silas is reading too much into something simple," I huff, crossing my arms defiantly.

Silas holds out my beer. "Fine. I'll give it back when you tell them why I think this is about River."

"River?" Caroline's brows furrow as she processes the name. It takes her a few seconds to piece it all together, but once she does, she freezes.

"Who's River?" Rosemary asks.

"He was my best friend." My voice cracks as I realize there's no way I'm getting out of this. I'm about to cry and I'm acting like a child about it. It's terribly, painfully awkward.

"Was," Caroline repeats slowly. Her face pales. "You said *was*. Is that why you left yesterday when I brought him up?"

Yes.

"I'm sorry for your loss," Rosemary says. The sentiment is sweet, but it's gotten old.

Sorry doesn't bring him back.

I'm grieving, plain and simple, somehow even years into the future.

Silas tries to speak up too, but his words are lost. As much as I'd like to pretend I wasn't rattled talking about what happened to Riv, it's so obvious that I am. I can't hide the reality, and it only makes it worse that Caroline feels sorry for me. I open my mouth to tell her it isn't her fault, that she didn't know better, but all that comes out is a sob.

When I make a break for the bathroom, no one stops me. I end up on the floor with my face pressed into my knees.

From where I am, I vaguely hear Silas telling them what happened. All I catch is, *"When Emery was sixteen, River got into a car accident and died. It's really hard for her to talk about it sometimes."*

I can't make out most of the conversation through the door, but it seems like Silas covers everything with his explanation.

"I think we've done enough tonight," Caroline says. "All I really have left is a few extra boxes in storage, but other than that I'm all set. Thank you so much for your help."

Silas probably smiles, but I can't see it. "It's no problem."

"You're all awesome," she says, then lowers her voice. "Hey, can you please tell Emery I'm sorry for asking about River? I'll try to be more careful next time."

"It's okay," he tells her. "She'll get through it. She's tough."

I hear a new set of footsteps approach, followed by Rosemary's kind voice as she says, "This is my number. Let her know she can always come to me if she needs someone to talk to."

The deja vu flashes through my mind when I realize that history is almost repeating itself. After River passed away, people spoke to my mother about anything that concerned me. Everything went through her first, from my homework to the apologies that never stopped coming.

Now, Silas is my buffer. I didn't mean for him to step into that role, but it seemed to happen by default. Maybe because he loves me. Maybe because he feels bad too. I'm not sure, at this point.

I'm angry at myself for becoming that girl again: that girl who let her voice be stifled by loss.

Five years, Em. It's been five years.

There's no timestamp on this sort of thing. I'm still struggling when I hear a funny joke and expect River to be at my side to laugh with me. I struggled every day in my undergraduate psychology class when we covered bipolar disorder. All I could think was that, if he had a diagnosis and therapy, he would be here with me. You never stop reeling when you lose such a substantial part of your life. It's never the same.

I take a few moments to collect myself and splash some cold water on my face. When I emerge from the restroom, I know that the worst of the hysterics have passed.

"I'm sorry for how I reacted," I apologize. "It's been a rough couple of days, but I'll get through it. Thank you, guys."

"My door is always open if you need it." Caroline reaches out and squeezes my shoulder reassuringly.

"And the same goes for me," Rosemary adds.

I give them both a hug for good measure, grateful that I have friends like them to keep me sane. I know River would've loved them, especially Caroline.

Before we go, Caroline asks Rosemary if she plans to head out yet and Rosemary tells her she'll stay a little longer. I cross my fingers for Caroline on the way to the car. She deserves someone as gentle and earnest as Rosemary in her life, and I'm hoping for the best for both of them.

I keep my fingers crossed until Silas takes my hand. He kisses me under the streetlights, and even though I should feel elated by it, I feel like I did at sixteen: sad and scared for what comes next.

I expect the kiss to end, but he carries on until my fear goes and all that's left is us.

16

Chapter Sixteen

Then
The second time I left my house after River died was when I wanted to steal some whiskey from the gas station. The first time had been to take my final exams. Somehow, I didn't fail them.

I had gone straight home after, thinking about how Riv would've aced his as I trudged through the heat.

Keith was working again that afternoon. I was glad he didn't try to talk to me, especially because I stood him up instead of going to that stupid dance. Luckily, he was preoccupied with Greta Stacy, who was leaning against the counter and flirting with him.

When I walked in, she crinkled her nose in disgust and turned to face him again. She'd gone from being nice to her usual mean self, but I didn't care which act she put on. I took advantage of his distracted state and easily smuggled some liquor. The chips I picked out were really just for show.

There were only a few of us there. Some locals were filling up their tanks, and a guy was browsing the drinks in the soda section. I slipped under the radar, eternally invisible, just a sixteen-year-old girl with a dead best friend.

When I approached the front of the store, I heard Greta say something that made my fingers curl into a fist. I was standing by a case full of ice cream, far enough away for her to act like I couldn't hear her.

"I wonder if she's just as crazy as he was," she sneered, sneaking a glance at me. "You know, people are saying he's going to hell for what he did. I'm not surprised. He deserves it. My mom says he was a basket case from the minute he was born."

I dropped my bag to the floor and shoved her against the counter as hard as I could. "You bitch!"

She yelped and narrowed her eyes at me. "What? I was only speaking the truth."

My nostrils flared. "Don't talk about River like that."

"I can talk about him however I want to," she challenged. "You're not gonna hit me, you psycho skank."

Before she could say anything else, I punched her as hard as I could, right in the teeth. Her blood got all over my hand as I hit her again in the nose. She tried to smack me, but I dodged it and socked her even harder. After she hit the floor, I jumped on top of her and kept hitting her. Keith tried to pull me off, but I elbowed him in the face and pushed him back. The wimp gave up after that and resorted to yelling.

One of the ladies outside watched me in utter horror, but I persisted, bloodying Greta as effectively as I could manage. Some sinister part of me snapped, so I kept going, my fists slamming into her face as I said through gritted teeth, "Don't. Talk. About. Him. Like. That."

She was crying, trying to shield herself with weak hands. I

144

would've felt bad for her if I wasn't so pissed.

All of a sudden, someone much stronger than me yanked me off of her. I pulled away immediately, wondering who had the nerve to break it up. While I fumed, Keith stared at me in shock and all but carried Greta as far away from me as they could get.

Whoever had stopped the fight pulled me by the arm right out the front door. I tugged back, but it was no use.

"Let me go!" I hollered.

"Hell no," a familiar voice said back. "Not until you calm down. If you do any more damage, you could get arrested."

He wasn't treating me like the pariah I had become, which was startling. Whoever it was must've known me well enough to care if I got thrown in jail, even though I didn't. At the moment, I couldn't give a damn about what might happen to me. All I cared about was defending the honor of a boy I loved.

It took a second to see his face, and once I did, recognition hit me.

"Funeral guy?" I gasped.

"Hi," he greeted, a grim expression on his face as he took in my bloody, bruising knuckles. "You know, River always said you were a firecracker, but *damn*. I've never seen a fight quite like that before."

I looked down at my messed up hands, repeated that name in my mind, and promptly burst into tears.

"Hey, please don't cry. I'm sorry."

"I just beat the shit out of Greta," I bawled.

"Yeah, you did," he said. "To be fair, she kind of deserved it. What she said wasn't right."

"You heard it?"

"Unfortunately," he replied. "I also wanted to punch her if

145

it's any consolation. Just take a deep breath, Emery."

I squeezed my eyes shut and willed the sobs to stop. He continued to tell me to breathe until I calmed enough to speak again. "I don't even know who you are."

"We've only met once or twice at family reunions. You and Riv were always together most of the time. He was so in love with you anyone could see it."

"You're not helping, funeral guy."

He winced. "Yeah. I'm not good at this stuff. I wish I could offer you more than just an apology, but it's the best I can do."

"God, you probably think I have zero class," I said, rubbing at my damp cheeks. "I should probably say it's nice to meet you, right?"

"It's a pleasure to make your acquaintance, darlin." He gave me an exaggerated bow. "I'm Silas."

Silas, I repeated in my mind. It suited him and was perfectly uncommon enough to be the first name of a Fields.

"I hate to ruin the moment here but I'm pretty sure the girl you pummeled won't leave until you do." He hiked his thumb at the door where, sure enough, Greta was standing and watching us.

"Do you have a ride?" I asked.

"I walked here, same as you," he replied. "Do you want to head back home?"

I thought of my empty house, the loneliness, and my head shook instantly. Another afternoon with no company was probably the last thing I needed, and definitely the last thing I wanted.

"We can go back to Aunt Carly's," he offered. "She's not home, though. I've just been fixing up her car all afternoon."

Car? I thought. *She walks everywhere. She used River's*

convertible when she needed to go anywhere far. She doesn't have a car. Not unless—

I stopped mid-thought. "Can I sit with you while you fix it?"

He shrugged. "Sure. Why not?"

We walked back to the trailer park in the summer heat, but since I'd dealt with this weather my whole life, it affected me less. I spent the trek analyzing him. He still had a southern accent, but it was different than mine. River had family in Texas, which explained Silas. Rob and his brother, Rich, were raised working in an auto shop, which would explain why both of them had a talent for working with cars. My chest ached thinking about how close Silas and River might've been if only they lived closer to one another. *If only.*

I held my breath as we approached the trailer. Part of me prayed that the convertible wouldn't be parked there, and part of me hoped it would, just so I could see it again. In the end, it wasn't. Instead, there was an old four-door Carly must've bought to fix up.

"You okay?" Silas nudged me. "You look pale."

"I'm fine," I said quickly. "Just thinking."

"Penny for your thoughts?"

"My thoughts are at least worth ten cents," I muttered dryly.

He laughed. "You're funny."

He knelt down and started sifting through the toolbox River had once used to restore the convertible. It was funny that he had been the one to destroy the very thing he had originally fixed. It was ironic in the worst way.

"Why are you talking to me?" I asked, hopping up into the hood.

"Is there a law against it?" Silas countered.

"No one has made an effort since... Well, you know." I

wondered how pathetic it was that I couldn't even think about describing the accident without my throat closing up.

"You're a person," he said. "And I'm a person too. You seem like you need a friend right now and I thought maybe I could be one to you."

"Is this about the funeral? I was just emotional then, it wasn't a big—"

"If you're going to try and downplay what happened to you, I'm going to smack some sense into you," he interjected. "But not literally because I'm not a fighter. Besides, you'd kick my ass."

He gave me a wry smile when he saw the one on my face. God, between the way his lips curled and his jawline speckled with stubble, I knew I was in trouble.

"How old are you?" I wondered aloud.

"Seventeen," he said. "I'm a senior, like you. I thought I should stay with Aunt Carly for a while. Mom wanted to make sure she got back into the swing of things and I figured she might need someone around."

When he turned back to the tools and crawled under the body of the car, I watched him with a newfound curiosity. He was honest, for sure, and genuinely kind.

Just like River.

River was the kid who shared his lunch with Tommy Phelps when his mom got hooked on meth and sold their food stamps. Every day he always gave Tommy the bigger half of his sandwich, even if it meant he went hungry. River was the kid who shook the hands of every veteran he met. River was the kid who washed my clothes when my period surprised me. Compassion was in their blood.

Oh yeah, this guy was definitely a Fields.

Silas called out to me from the ground. "Can I ask you something?"

"If you want to."

"Did you love him?" he asked.

"Of course I loved him," I said as if it should've been obvious.

"I mean the way he loved you," he clarified. "He was in love with you."

River and I had always been best friends, but I didn't think of him in a romantic way until recently. The question confused me because I never got the chance to sort out those feelings.

"It doesn't matter."

"Sure it does." He was still under the belly of the vehicle, so all I could see were his jeans and sneakers. His voice was muffled, and I wondered what face he was making. I wondered if he was screwing with me.

"Well, I don't know. He went and killed himself before I could figure out exactly what I felt," I said, bristling.

And then I was walking away. I knew Silas probably wanted to call after me and stop me from leaving, but it was a little late for that one. He let me go, knowing he couldn't say much to make me feel better. Maybe I wanted him to try. Maybe I didn't. I had no idea.

I went back home and played chess with myself for the next couple of hours. Per usual, I imagined what River might say with each move and tried to play the opposite side of the board as he would. The whole game was utterly depressing and melancholic, honestly.

Around seven-thirty, the smell of fresh casserole drifted under my bedroom door. I prepared myself for an awkward family dinner. My school counselor had told my mother that family time was supposed to help troubled teens like myself with grieving, but all we really did was awkwardly push food around our plates at meal time and avoid meaningful conversation.

Except tonight was different.

Tonight was different because when I came out of my room to set the table, Mom was answering a knock at the door. She opened it to reveal a crooked smile and a bouquet of flowers in the hands of Silas Fields. He was wearing a clean flannel, dark hair marked by comb tracks and damp from a shower.

Upon being prompted by Mom, Silas peered over at me and said, "I came by to drop these off. I thought Emery seemed down and I wanted to cheer her up."

Mom raised an eyebrow at me.

I ignored the obvious curiosity.

"How sweet," she cooed. "How about we invite him in for dinner, Em? Doesn't that sound like a great idea?"

I opened my mouth to protest, but Silas spoke first. "I'd like to, but I don't want to intrude."

I knew that this was the part where I could either send him away and go back to isolation, or play my part and let him stay for dinner.

For Mom's sake, knowing she would take this as a sign of me making progress, I said, "You should stay."

He looked wary but came inside all the same.

"I'm Miriam, by the way," Mom chirped happily. "My husband and I will be in the kitchen, so holler if you need something."

With that, she was gone, leaving just the two of us. I set the flowers in a vase full of water on the coffee table and avoided his eyes, fidgeting with one of the petals on a tulip. While we waited for the meal, I focused my best efforts on staring at the floor. We were as far apart as we could be on the couch, but I was still tempted to move to the floor.

Silas sighed. "Are you just going to avoid me all night?"

"If I can, yes," I replied.

"What did I do to you?" he asked. "My questions about River earlier were out of line, I get it, but I didn't mean to upset you."

"You didn't upset me," I said harshly, hoping my mom couldn't sense my agitation. "I'm fine."

He reached out to me but pulled away quickly, thinking better of it. "I don't know what to say."

"Let's just have dinner," I whispered. "I'm sorry for being a bitch. I promise I'm not normally like this."

"I know," he said, then changed the subject. "Do you think your parents will let you come back to Aunt Carly's after dinner? I want to show you something."

"Okay?" My tone held a question, but all he did was give me an enigmatic smirk. It was the kind of smirk I'd come to want more of.

Dad watched Silas like a hawk as he dug into his casserole, his eyes narrowed at him. River was a regular dinner guest, but Silas was a new boy, a foreign face, and my father wanted him as far away from me as he could get.

"Fields, you said?" Dad's mouth was full of food as he talked, and it was disgusting.

"Yeah," Silas confirmed.

"I didn't know River had a brother."

Mom must've pinched Dad under the table because he stopped speaking. It was like she thought me hearing about Riv could make me explode.

"Kellan," she said, a warning in her tone.

Dad shut his mouth promptly.

As emotionally charged as his name was, I'd started saying it more often in an attempt to get used to it. It was still hard, but I was adapting slowly but surely.

I swallowed a lump in my throat and pushed the noodles around my plate to make it look like I was eating.

"I'm his cousin," he explained, squeezing my knee under the table as if he knew I needed the comfort. "I'm spending my summer with Aunt Carly because I know how hard things have been for her."

"That kid of hers was so selfish," Dad started, but Mom interjected before he could continue.

"So, Silas, any idea where you want to go to school?" she asked.

He shrugged. "Anywhere, I guess, so long as I'm happy. I've still got time to choose during the next school year."

The idea of going off to college confused and terrified me all the same. River and I had planned to apply to universities far away from here together, but now I wasn't sure I even *wanted* to go to college in the first place. At least Silas didn't have a plan either.

He released my knee and my skin ached for his touch to return. I didn't know why, but he reminded me of the one person I needed more than anyone else in the world right now: River.

My parents chatted with Silas while I kept pushing my casserole around on the plate. It was probably delicious, but I merely picked at it. I never wanted to eat anymore. As they spoke, I tried to listen, but ultimately stopped paying attention.

After it was all said and done, Silas told Mom that Carly wanted me to come over and got her to agree to it. Frankly, I think she was grateful that I would be out of her hair for a night. She still hadn't heard about the fiasco with Greta, so I was free to leave. Once word reached my parents, I would probably be in trouble, but I wasn't worried about it.

I hugged both of them on the way out, surprised when my dad actually told me he loved me. He wasn't an affectionate man anyway, and our relationship had never been great, but hearing the words aloud was a nice change. Mom kissed my forehead and made sure I had my key, and then they let me leave.

"You didn't eat," Silas said when we got to the car.

He held my door open, waiting for me. I climbed in and stuffed my hands into my pockets sheepishly, surprised he had paid attention enough to notice. He got into the driver's seat shortly after, slipping the keys into the ignition.

"You fixed it," I observed, trying to change the subject.

"I did," he replied. "Now let's talk about the fact you weren't eating."

"Don't read too much into it. I just wasn't hungry." I hoped that my lie would be smooth enough for him to drop it, but he heard my stomach growl just seconds later.

"We're going to McDonald's," he decided, looking at me sidelong. "I'm getting you something and you're gonna eat it for me, okay, darlin?"

"I'm not hungry," I said.

"Tell that to your empty stomach," he shot back.

In the end, I relented and ordered a strawberry milkshake and fries. Silas even bought an order of chicken nuggets despite my protesting. He also offered to share his Coke with me, and his kindness was overwhelming enough to make me feel like crying all over again.

Back at the trailer, my throat closed when I realized that he

153

was staying in River's room. It felt wrong to go back inside with someone who wasn't River, like the space was tainted with the lingering essence of a dead boy.

Silas was oblivious, or maybe just ignoring the fact this room used to be so much more, and flicked the light switch on, already comfortable. He set the bag of food on the bed and kicked his sneakers off.

It was then that I started noticing the little differences. I inspected this space that used to be so familiar, watching as it marked the end of an age. River's stuff was boxed up in the closet, probably Carly's doing, and Silas's clothes now replaced what used to be in the dresser. The bed that River never made was now perfectly tidy and orderly.

Silas put his hand on my shoulder. "Emery?"

"Yeah?" I whispered.

"There's a box of stuff Carly left for you to go through if you want," he told me gently. "She packed a few of the things you left over here too. We can look after you eat."

My stomach churned in a way that indicated I probably didn't have the appetite for it, but since he paid for the food, the least I could do was choke it down. I finished my fries and even a few of the nuggets before I decided not to eat anymore.

My throat felt like it was closing as Silas pulled out the box marked *Emmy.* It was River's nickname for me, and it seemed Carly had taken to referring to me that way too.

I found his chessboard and the crossword puzzle books first, followed by forgotten clothes and pictures. All of these were odds and ends that were meaningless to anyone who wasn't River or me. It meant the world to me that Carly had thought to keep any of it, even if it wasn't meant to be mine in the first place.

I tugged the box into my lap and hugged my arms around it. The gesture probably looked strange, but it didn't stop me.

Silas didn't look at me judgmentally. Instead, he rested his palm on my back, right between my shoulder blades. I expected him to say something, but he didn't. He was reminding me that I had someone there if I needed it.

I don't know how long we sat there, but it had to have been a little while before I finally spoke. "Thank you."

"Don't mention it," he replied.

His eyes were fixated on my face, trying to gauge what headspace I was in. I wished I could vocalize exactly what I was feeling, but I wasn't sure if it would make any sense out loud. I was in between, caught in the middle of grief, moving on, and total acceptance.

In my gut, I knew Silas would play a part in it all— this process of healing. Sometimes, when someone enters your life, you know they're going to be important. It's the kind of thing you feel in your bones, even if you can't quite explain it.

I peeked over at the clock. "It's kind of late. Do you think you can take me home?"

"Yeah," he said, still looking at me. "I think I can do that."

17

Chapter Seventeen

Then

After getting a ride home from him, I decided Silas Fields probably wasn't a bad guy. I mean, considering he was related to Riv, it was no wonder he carried the same compassion and understanding. I'd had the same close friend for so long I'd fallen out of the practice of meeting new people. The only person I wanted to talk to about Silas was River and seeing as that wasn't really an option, I didn't know what to make of him. Whatever the verdict might be, it came down to my own judgment at this point.

I drifted back into the confines of my comfort zone. It wasn't like I could really show my face outside yet. Greta was probably holding a grudge, and she and her friends would definitely come after me if I didn't keep a low profile. I didn't really like them anyway, so I wasn't too bothered about it.

Summer was dull without anyone to spend it with. I wanted to be out on the curb, eating a melting popsicle while River made fun of my hair as it frizzed up. Our adventures weren't anything special, but they were a means of passing time.

Without him, I was bored.

Two days after meeting Silas, I was sitting in my room with an apartment to myself. My parents were working full time during the day and no longer had time to fuss over me. Now, I was back to being on my own. I'd always been pretty independent, but solitude was making me stir-crazy.

I was in the middle of playing another chess game with myself when I finally cracked.

I found myself holding my phone, which had been radio silent for several weeks and barely used, and considered calling Silas. It would be easy. He might not have plans anyway, and if I was going to be a homebody, I may as well have company. I tried not to make it a big deal, but for me, it was a huge step.

Before I'd left his car, he'd give me his number. I'd saved it, but I wasn't sure if I was going to use it. Plenty of people had contact information left untouched in my possession. I was awful at responding.

River would want me to talk to Silas. I knew that much to be true.

Emmy, he'd say. *You gotta talk to someone cool every once in a while. Nowhereland is boring all by yourself.*

It took a while to talk myself into it, but I found the courage to dial. A few rings in, he answered. "Hey."

"Hey," I echoed.

"I'm surprised you called," he admitted. "I was wondering if I scared you off."

I gripped my phone tighter. "I almost didn't."

"I'm glad you did. So what's up?"

"Do you know how to play chess?" I blurted.

He paused. "Um, yeah? I mean, it's been a while since I last played. Why do you ask?"

"Because I want to play chess with somebody."

I heard him chuckle on the other end of the line. "Are you asking me to play chess with you, Emery?"

"Yeah," I said. "I guess I am."

"You'll have to remind me of the rules, but I guess it could be fun. I'll be there in a few minutes."

After we hung up, I chewed on my lip nervously, looking down at my pajamas. If I was going to be friends with someone new, I really needed to get back to business as usual. The first step would probably be making myself presentable.

I changed in a pair of shorts and one of River's old t-shirts. I even dragged a comb through my curls, hoping to seem relatively put together.

When he knocked, I had to guide myself through a pep-talk before I opened the door. My nerves were eating away at me, which seemed silly because he was only a boy. I'd fallen out of the practice of hanging out with anyone and this was nerve-wracking.

The counselors were constantly emphasizing social interaction, and I'd have to get accustomed to it at some point.

Silas was on the other side of the door holding a greasy fast-food bag. "Have you eaten?"

I shrugged. "I had cereal earlier."

"Well, I brought extra fries just in case," he said. "Now, how about that game of chess?"

I felt weird about bringing him into my room, so I went to get my board.

We set up in the living room, sitting across from each other at the coffee table. I laid out the pieces for him because when he tried, he already mixed up the orientations for a few of them.

I let him take the first move. He pushed a pawn out, but I opted for a knight like I usually did.

"Who taught you how to play?" I questioned.

"My dad," he said. "You?"

"River. He was really good at it."

"I bet. He was a genius."

A few moves in, I captured one of his pieces. I wasn't sure if he'd let me do it on purpose, but after a few more times going back in forth, I realized it probably wasn't an accident. Silas wasn't bad at chess by any stretch, but he was definitely out of practice.

We split his fries, using the paper bag as a makeshift plate. I was hungry enough to actually have a snack, which was probably a good sign. I had to lick my fingers before moving anything, but I didn't mind. I forgot how good fast food could be, and how fun playing chess with someone else could be too.

About an hour after we started, I slid a rook across the board and trapped his king in place. My eyes skimmed over each piece, taking in every position, every scenario that could get him out of check. I found none. I'd actually won a game of chess, and it felt surreal to me.

"Checkmate," I breathed.

Silas held his hand out to me for a shake. "Good game."

I shook it, still fixated on the board. "Yeah."

"You're great at chess," he said.

"River was always better," I pointed out. "He won pretty much every time."

"You're a worthy opponent," he told me.

Snapping out of my haze, I started to put everything back into place for another round. "New game?"

"Sure."

159

He put up a better fight, but I still beat him at the next match too. It wasn't until our third game of chess that he finally won. It was nice having someone at the same caliber. It meant that the games were fairer and less repetitive. I loved playing with River, but I also liked playing with Silas. After our first rematch, I expected him to be bored and want to quit, but he was more than happy to go again.

"I never thought a board game could be so competitive," he said after beating me.

"Chess is super intense," I told him. "Like seriously. I actually smacked Riv once when we were in middle school. Obviously, we got more civilized after that, but it's always been a heated game."

"You hit hard. I'd rather not get on your bad side," he teased.

I raised my hand jokingly.

He shielded himself with his arms. "Have mercy, darlin. I'm fragile."

I giggled. "You are not."

"Maybe not," he conceded. "But I am definitely a wimp."

His phone buzzed in his back pocket, redirecting his attention. He slid it out and unlocked the screen, reading whatever the message said.

"Who is it?" I asked.

"Aunt Carly," said Silas. "She's just wondering when I'm gonna be home."

He'd been at my place for a couple of hours already, and I was a little disappointed to think about him leaving. I tried not to show it because I didn't want to ruin the mood.

"I can stay a little longer," he added. "If you want. Wanna do something else?"

"Like what?"

He thought for a second. "I'm honestly not sure. What do you people do here when it's summertime?"

"Nowhereland is pretty uneventful," I said. "You have to get creative."

"Nowhereland?" he repeated.

"It's our nickname for this place," I explained. "It came from a Beatles song."

"The Beatles, huh? My dad loves them."

"So did Riv's, it's where he got it from. I came around after a while."

"Nowhereland," Silas said again. "I kind of like it. It's a cool name."

"Most adults would think it's disrespectful."

"It's a good thing I'm not an adult because I think it's funny."

Despite the AC on and the fans I had rotating throughout the house, it was still pretty stuffy inside. It gave me a pretty decent idea of what we should do next, so I got to my feet and offered him a hand up.

"You like ice cream?" I asked.

"Who doesn't?"

We found ourselves in the kitchen seconds later, sitting on the counter with two spoons. Shoulders pressed together, we scooped rocky road straight out of the carton. It was a little freezer burnt from being in there so long, but it still tasted good after scraping the ice off the top. There was no better way to cool off than to eat ice cream, so that's exactly what we did.

"What's your favorite ice cream flavor?" I prompted, dragging my spoon out of my mouth slowly to make sure I didn't miss any.

"Probably mint chocolate chip," he said. "But this is good

too."

"Rocky road is the best, hands down, but I guess mint chip is okay."

"Just okay?"

"Don't push your luck, Silas."

We had nearly polished it off when my mom got home. She walked through the front door with plastic bags crinkling in her grip.

"Emery?" she called.

I hopped down. "Yeah?"

Since Silas was right on my heels, she saw him immediately. A small smile spread across her face. "I didn't realize you had company, honey."

"Well, I guess I do."

"Hi, Miriam," Silas said politely. "How are you?"

"I'm good," she said, glancing at me. "I'm glad to see you."

Normally, she would've asked me to unpack the groceries with her, but this time she didn't. I think she wanted me to keep spending time with Silas, and I wasn't complaining. It was one of the best afternoons I'd had in a while, which made up for all the grim, dark days I'd had lately.

Not too long after my mom came in, Silas went back to the trailer park. Before he left, he gave me a long, lingering hug. He gave great hugs, the kind that made you feel better even though it wasn't a big, extravagant gesture.

"So what's that about?" my mom asked, sitting down next to me on the couch.

"Nothing," I said. "We're friends."

"I know," she responded. "I'm glad to see you're making friends. He seems like a nice boy."

"He is," I agreed. "He's been staying with Carly to make sure she has a support system."

"I can't imagine what she must be going through," Mom said, tucking a strand of my hair behind my ear. "Losing a child, especially so young, is every mother's worst fear. I don't know what I'd do without you, Emery."

"You don't have to worry about me," I assured her.

"I'm very grateful for that," she murmured. "But I'm always going to worry for you. I'm your mom."

She and dad were both trying harder with me, which was a step in the right direction. We were more connected as a family, which made it easier to cope. I wasn't utterly alone. Even if they didn't spend nearly as much time with him as I did, my parents loved River. They cared about him, and his death had affected them too.

I thought about that box in my room, unsure of when I'd ever sort the things in it. It was far too soon to seriously consider it, but I owed it to River to get around to it. Everything was a game of baby steps, trying to work through little things until I could handle the bigger stuff.

18

Chapter Eighteen

Now
A few days after Caroline has finished moving into her apartment, I find myself getting back to the daily grind. After the messiness brought on by the lingering pain of my loss, it's nice to feel like who I am again.

Silas still isn't up yet, but I have to get ready for class, so I leave our warm, comfy bed to get dressed. I change quietly, brush my teeth, and leave him to hog all the blankets.

I'm flicking through flashcards as I make my coffee, trying to memorize some last-minute information. I only get a few minutes of studying in before he finally stumbles into the kitchen, half-naked and half-asleep. He wraps his arms around me from behind and burrows his face in my neck, kissing my skin to say good morning.

"Hey, sleepyhead," I chirp.

"Mornings are the devil," he grumbles.

"You can always go back to sleep," I remind him.

"Can't, I have work today. I've got a meeting today and I can't miss it." He sighs. "I want to take you back to bed with me."

"And I want you to put pants on," I reply. "And a shirt while you're at it, I don't think stuck-up attorneys take shirtless wonders like yourself seriously."

"Why the hell did I pick pre-law?" he whines.

"Because you're passionate and you want to help people," I tell him. "That's what you told me."

"How could I forget about that?" He presses another kiss to my neck, and I feel his smile against my skin when I shiver. "I figured that out after we got arrested."

"Nothing screams romantic like ending up in a cop car with the guy you're crushing on," I muse. "And I think it's funny that the reason you picked your career path because of that incident. You're such a troublemaker."

"Thank God they didn't press charges. I could never make it here if I had a record," he says.

"I think you're a bad influence."

"Yeah, yeah. You're the one prone to getting into fights. Maybe *you* corrupted me."

"It was one fight!" I exclaim indignantly.

"One fight for now. You could get into another one any day now," he teases.

"If you aren't careful, the next person I punch will be you." I raise my fist for emphasis, but I don't swing.

He closes his hand around my knuckles. "We all know you can kick my ass, darlin. No need to prove it."

He leans forward and presses his mouth to mine, ending the bickering. We kiss and drink coffee until it's time for me to leave.

As luck would have it, the studying I do on the bus to campus pays off, because I end up passing with a B. Silas sneaks a text to me sometime after, as I'm trekking across campus to buy one of my astrophysics books for next semester.

Silas: Nice job, darlin, I knew you could do it.

Before I can type out a reply, I hear a familiar voice call my name.

Rosemary jogs to catch up with me, clearly surprised. "I didn't know you went to school here. Physics major, right?"

I nod. "Yeah, what about you?"

"Biology," she replies. "Not too different from you, though physics has way too much math for my liking."

I shrug. "It's all formulas. Not so bad once you get used to it."

"Still," she says. "You must be wicked smart."

I try to be, but River was always better at this stuff. "Thank you. Give yourself some credit, girl, biology is pretty impressive too."

She shifts from foot to foot shyly. "Thanks, Em. Where are you headed?"

"Campus bookstore," I say, casting a look in its general direction. "What about you?"

"I'm done for the day, most of my classes are Wednesday and Thursday. I just have economics on Monday." She shifts her bag to her other shoulder. "Wanna grab lunch before your next class?"

I would normally be by myself, maybe sending a few messages to Silas, so this seems like a better option. My meltdown at Caroline's didn't scare her off, which means she's probably a good friend to have around.

"Sure!" I say.

We end up eating in a burger joint off campus, because even though the dining halls are good, they're super crowded around this time of day. As it would turn out, Rosemary has her own stories to tell. She's really laid back and candid, which makes her easy to talk to.

"So my Dad is super traditional. Catholic, actually," she explains. "And so in high school, when I got my first girlfriend, I think I nearly gave the poor man a heart attack. Thankfully, he got over it pretty quickly."

As she tells me about her parents, I wonder what it's like to have a family that is super involved in your love life. I'm also squealing internally at the mention of a girlfriend. I know one of Caroline's greatest concerns when it comes to dating is not knowing right away whether or not the person she's into is reciprocating.

Hopefully, Rosemary is.

I try to be subtle as I sip my iced tea. "So, what's the deal with you and Caroline?"

Rosemary takes a bite of her salad and says, "I'm not sure. She's great, don't get me wrong, but I'm no good with flirting and stuff like that. And she's got a nice ass. Don't tell her I said that, though."

It's crass coming from Rosemary, who is definitely someone I pegged for the sweet, quiet type. It just goes to show that surface-level appearances aren't what's really there. I can't help but find it amusing.

I laugh. "I won't. I'm straight, but even I can agree to that."

"Why do you ask?" she wonders.

"I don't know," I say smoothly. "I was just wondering if you two had anything going on."

"Why? Are you planning to leave Silas?" she jokes.

"Obviously. We've already established how great Caroline's ass is," I say, playing along. She nearly spits up her soda, and that makes it all the funnier. "In all seriousness though, you should go for it. I think she might be interested too."

I pick at my fries and try to keep my face neutral. Sometimes I can't help but hope for the universe to make something great happen for good people, and this is one of those times. My giddiness is probably so obvious.

"Maybe," Rosemary finally says. "We'll see how it goes."

In our hour-long conversation, I learn that she only listens to the country station in the car, and hates anything from the pop genre. I learn that she loves baseball and roots for the Dodgers (go figure, it is So-Cal, after all). It's funny what you can discover about a person just by spending time with them.

Afterward, she gives me a hug and tells me we should hang out again sometime.

"Absolutely!" I grin. "I'd love to. Hey, while you're at work, tell Caroline I said hi."

"I'll check her out for you too," Rosemary calls over her shoulder. "See you, Em."

"Bye," I say with a wave.

After I attend my second class of the day, a philosophy elective I need for my general ed requirements, I find that Silas has already texted me.

Silas: When are you going to be home?

Me: Leaving now. You'll probably beat me there.

Silas: Great!

Me: What are you hiding?

Silas: Nothing, darlin, I'll see you soon.

I roll my eyes at my phone and pocket it when I climb on the bus. On the way home, I force myself to listen to The Beatles, even though I want to skip *Eleanor Rigby* when I hear it start to play. I even bob my head a little, remembering how much

I've always liked this track. This music doesn't always have to bring sorrow. It's just easy to lose sight of that.

I roll through various scenarios in my mind while I'm climbing the stairs to the apartment. Silas is a romantic, even if he doesn't always act that way, and I know that he's definitely planning something. No matter what it is, I don't care. All I know for certain is that I'm so in love with him my heart might burst.

I open the door to candles all over the living room, which is cheesy as hell and lovely all the same. Silas is standing with his hands in his pockets, and the suit that he wears for his internship is still crisp and neat.

"Hey, darlin." His teeth make a slow appearance as his lips curl into a smile that makes my knees weak. I'm in his arms in an instant, my lips gently brushing his to say hello.

"Hi." I beam at him, and reach for the knot of his tie to loosen it. His fingers curl around my hips as I do so.

"By the way, Glenn says he hates that he hasn't been able to talk to you his last few shifts. He misses you," Silas says.

"I miss him too," I say earnestly. "He's honestly so great."

Since Silas is one of the interns for the firm, it was easy for him to put a good word in for me regarding the secretarial position. Si has such an easy time with everyone he meets; one look and he brightens the world up, one look and you want to be his friend. It's no wonder he's such a charmer.

He holds me tighter as I undo the top button of his collared shirt.

"I missed you today," he says.

"Is that why you're pulling out all the stops tonight?" I ask with an arched eyebrow.

"Partially," he admits. "But I also wanted to make sure

everything is perfect for this."

I'm not stupid, and between the five years we've been together, I have a pretty good guess as to what he's planning. For reasons I'm not entirely certain of, the idea scares me a bit.

Don't get me wrong, I love Silas more than anyone else in the entire world, and I want to be with him for the rest of my life, but sometimes I doubt him. Sometimes I fear he, like River, could be taken away from me.

That worry aside, he's here. He hasn't gone anywhere for a long time. That outweighs my confliction every day of the year.

"I'm excited. Does this night of yours involve me taking your suit off?"

He swallows hard. "Not until later, but if you keep talking like that, it might be a little sooner."

I stand on my tiptoes and kiss him deeply. "We can save that for a couple hours from now, then."

"You wearing that skirt makes it so difficult for me to exercise self-control," he says. "Em, are you trying to torture me?"

"I wasn't initially, but I suppose that's an added bonus of my wardrobe choice."

He groans. "I love you, even if you're a pain in my ass."

"Ditto, babe."

His big romantic gesture begins with glasses of wine. A few minutes later, I can smell the casserole baking in the oven and turn to him with a questioning look. "Is that what I think you're cooking?"

"The day we met, your mom made a casserole and I couldn't remember exactly what was in it, so I called her earlier today and got the recipe," he says nonchalantly. "I also got McDonald's, but it's all probably cold by now."

"Let me guess; you bought chicken nuggets, fries, and a strawberry milkshake."

"Shit, I thought it was vanilla," he mutters. "Sorry, darlin, I *almost* got it all right."

"You've failed me, Si," I drawl sarcastically. "How could you forget my favorite milkshake flavor?"

"I know, I'm a terrible boyfriend," he says, rolling his eyes. "Does it at least taste good?"

"Of course it does, it's a sugary milkshake," I say. "You know, you didn't have to go through all this trouble for one night."

He gives me a look that almost says I'm crazy for insinuating such a notion. "Of course I did. I needed you to know that I remember the little things. Except milkshake flavors. I've failed you there."

"You're sweet," I tell him. I extend the cup to him to offer him a sip, but he waves it away.

"It's yours," he says. "Anyway, I want to do this before dinner, because you look gorgeous and I love you so much and I'm an impatient bastard."

I giggle to hide how nervous I am and wipe my sweaty palms on my blouse.

Silas looks at me, searching my face with his eyes. He licks his lips, memorizing me for a second. "This is the easiest choice I've ever made, Em. I didn't have to think twice about it. Hell, you're the best choice I've ever made. When we crossed paths, my first thought was that I had to know you, because you were such a fighter and there was something in your eyes that made me wonder what else there was to you.

"The funeral wasn't the first time I noticed you though. The family barbecue back when you and River were only freshmen was the first time I noticed you. First, I saw how pretty you were, and then I got a glimpse of that stubbornness in you. You were dared by our cousin to try and skate up the ramp because he thought you couldn't do it."

I remember the afternoon vividly in my mind, down to the kid's scowl as he said, and I quote, "Chicks can't skateboard." I recall the event as humiliating, but Silas doesn't; he recalls it with nothing but admiration.

"I was sitting at the picnic table just watching you. You curled your hands into fists and told River to hand you the board. You skated anyway, even though you didn't know how, and you mostly succeeded. You also shredded your knees, but you refused to cry. I wanted to get up and help you, but River beat me to it. He carried you back to the lawn and bandaged your knees. The bond between the two of you was unbreakable, and I never thought I'd have a chance with you."

"You were wrong," I murmured.

"I'm so glad I was wrong," he said back. "I'd tell you more, but surely you know what came next. We become friends, we talked more, I fell in love with you, and I got lucky enough for you to love me too."

I'm the lucky one, Silas.

My breath catches in my throat, and I'm ninety percent sure I'm gonna cry happy tears at least once tonight.

He gets down on one knee and fishes the ring box out of his pocket. It's not fussy, and it's not a ridiculous diamond that makes me wonder how long it'll take to pay off. It's beautiful. It's perfect.

"I know we're young. I know the 'right' way to do this is to finish school and wait forever before I finally lock this down, but when have we ever done things the conventional way? Age doesn't matter. You're the love of my life and that's all there is to it. I think you know what I'm gonna ask you now, darlin. I'll say it anyway for the sake of formality. Will you marry me, Emery Leigh?"

Words have failed me. I've started to question whether or not I know how to talk anymore as I stand there looking baffled.

The greatest man in the world wants to marry me, I think, completely in disbelief. *This is my life?*

When I finally get control of my tongue, the word flows effortlessly. "Yes!"

19

Chapter Nineteen

Then Silas had started coming over to play chess with me more often. Every few days, I could count on him showing up to my front door with a snack, ready to spend the afternoon with me.

He never seemed to get bored, and with practice, got better and better at it. We started keeping score on an old McDonald's receipt. So far, I had won more games, but he was catching up.

One sweltering afternoon, we were sprawled out on my bedroom floor, nearing the end of a match. He had stolen more of my pieces, but I knew I was a few moves away from putting him in checkmate. I wondered if he would catch onto my play and stop me, but judging by how distracted he seemed, it was probably unlikely.

He glanced at me as he shifted a rook a few spaces over. "I think we should go out."

I frowned. "Um, Silas, you're really great but I don't think—"

"Not, like, on a date or anything," he clarified quickly. "I meant just in general. As friends. Friends go out."

"I guess they do," I agreed, scoping out the board.

"There's a new superhero movie playing at the cinema a few towns over," he told me. "I'll buy the popcorn."

"Your turn," I said, avoiding the offer.

"Come on, Em, when was the last time you left the house?"

The answer was a week ago, when I went to check the mail, but I'm sure that the answer would be both disappointing and pathetic.

"I don't know."

"That's all the more reason for us to go see it!"

I rubbed my dampening palms on the edge of my shirt. River was always the one who went places with me. I didn't want to get used to going anywhere without him. That's mostly why I stayed home. It made it easier to hide away.

We were still the talk of the town. I didn't have to hear the gossip to know. Whenever something big like a death happened, it was all people could chat about for months. I was the dead boy's friend, and carrying the weight of people's stares was maddening.

"We'll be out of Nowhereland," he added. "Chances are, there won't be anyone we know there."

I fidgeted with my queen.

"I won't make you do it if you don't want to," he said. "But if you change your mind, the offer is there."

Thank you, I thought.

"Your turn," I said instead.

He moved a random pawn, probably without thinking. I could tell he was disappointed, and I wasn't sure what to do.

I ended the game with a bishop. He wasn't paying attention anymore.

175

"Checkmate," I whispered.

I sat back, analyzing the board before reaching for the receipt to add a new tally to my side. The score was still in my favor after this round. One of us normally would've called for a rematch, but we were both done with chess by that point.

It took me a moment to muster up some bravery before I asked, "How long is the movie?"

He looked up, surprised. "A couple of hours. Why?"

"And you'll take me home right after?"

"Yeah," he replied. "If that's what you want."

"I'll go," I decided.

It wasn't a huge gesture, not outright, but both of us knew it was a challenge for me.

"I didn't think you would," he admitted.

"Neither did I." I chewed my lip. "Don't make me regret this."

"I won't," he promised, starting to grin. "The next show is in an hour. We better go soon if you want to see the previews."

"Who cares about the previews?"

"I do," he replied. "How else will you know what's coming to theaters soon?"

"The internet," I deadpanned.

"The old fashioned way is better."

"If you insist."

He pushed up from the carpet and offered me a hand. He pulled me onto my feet before he started to clean the chess pieces up. As he put the board away, I started to get nervous about the whole thing. Riv would encourage this, which reassured me a little bit.

I was still in my pajamas, which wasn't lost on either of us. He was in his typical flannel and jeans combo, but I definitely needed different attire.

"I'll let you change," he said, before I could ask him to step out. Like a gentleman, he shut the door behind him and left me to have some privacy.

I picked a pair of cutoff shorts and an old t-shirt, hoping that would be decent. Thankfully, I'd already brushed my hair and gotten it neat enough to be semi-presentable. That was good enough for me.

As I passed my jar full of change, I made sure to bring money for my ticket, shoving a few wadded bills into my pockets. I had to check for my keys and phone, since I'd become prone to forgetting things.

Silas was waiting for me on the couch, playing a game on his phone. He got up when I walked in and put his cell away.

"Ready?"

No. "As I'll ever be."

I texted my mom to let her know I was heading out, even though she probably wouldn't respond until later. We had been working on communicating more, so I was expected to hold up my end of the deal.

He rounded the car to my side first, opening the door for me. It was something he liked to do whenever we went somewhere, unless I beat him to it and got there before him. I flicked on the radio, searching for a decent station. The reception was spotty in Nowhereland, but sometimes I could find something.

I settled on pop music after a while, realizing it was the only thing coming in until we got further into civilization. I sat with my legs crisscrossed on the seat, the window down because Silas hadn't replaced the air conditioner yet. The warm air wasn't much better than the dry heat inside, but it was better than nothing.

"Aunt Carly is going to get me some parts this week," he

explained apologetically. "Then we'll have all the AC we want."

"It's fine, Si," I said.

It reminded me of riding in the convertible. Of course, a couple of open windows was nothing compared to the top down, but I still enjoyed it. It was reminiscent of better days, better times.

"It's cool that you're a mechanic," I continued.

"I could teach you a thing or two," he offered. "It's more of a hobby anyway, but I know my way around a car."

I tapped the dash with my palm. "I can tell."

I didn't leave town often. Not because I didn't want to, just because the opportunity never came up. I knew the highway pretty well though. It ran through endless dust and fields and swamps. That's Louisiana for you. The nice thing about it was the greenery from all the rain.

There weren't any clouds in the sky, and I took that as a good sign. There was plenty of downpours, even in the summertime, but nicer weather followed.

"So how are you liking Nowhereland?" I asked.

He lifted a shoulder lazily. "It's alright, not home or anything, but I don't hate it here."

"Do you miss Texas?"

"Sometimes. I suppose it's nice to change things up."

"I can't imagine living anywhere else," I said. "I want to move away, I always have, but it's hard to picture it. It's all I know."

I didn't want to get stuck; I was certain of that. But I was also horribly sheltered, and my lack of travel experience meant the only thing I had to reference other places was Google. I daydreamed a lot, but the pictures didn't compare to the real thing.

"Where would you want to go?"

"Maybe California?"

"SoCal is nice," said Silas. "I went to Disneyland a few years ago."

"I bet it's overrated," I said.

"And overpriced," he added.

"Let's never go to Disney."

"I can live without it."

It all rolled right off my tongue before the implications registered. I guess I'd already gotten so used to having Silas around that I never really considered it eventually wouldn't be the case anymore. He would go back to Texas, I would go back to being by myself. I didn't like that notion. I liked the one where we were still friends long enough to decide not to visit an expensive theme park.

I drummed my fingers on the armrest, on the lookout for road signs counting down the miles until we hit the next major city. I had lived in this state, this county, since the day I was born. It was hard not to marvel at Silas's ability to navigate the terrain so easily.

I looked for a GPS, but didn't find one. "Don't you need directions?"

"I've been to town a few times already," he replied.

"You've only been here for a month."

"You and I both know it's easy to run out of things to do."

"Good point."

River and I usually waited to rent movies, so we saw them when the excitement had fizzled out, well after their release dates. It meant there were no surprises within the plot, but that didn't ruin them. It had been a long time since I'd seen a film in theaters, and that made it all the more special. I wasn't about to give Silas the satisfaction of knowing he'd made my week, but he totally had.

He parked pretty close to the front entrance since it was a matinee and less crowded. It was only a short trek to the box office. Even though I was shorter than him and walked slower, he kept his pace with mine.

The line was short, so we only had to wait a few minutes before we were at the front. Behind us, a couple stood, kissing and laughing together. They seemed so happy, and it tugged at my heart for a fleeting moment. I never really had that, even with River, so it was hard to imagine being in their shoes. I found myself slightly jealous anyway.

"See? This isn't bad," he said.

"We've only been here a few minutes."

"Optimism is key."

"I'm stuck with Mr. Sunshine," I deadpanned. Secretly, I liked his positivity.

"Two, please," Silas told the cashier. He reached for his worn, leather wallet, but before he could pay, I slid my cash through the gap in the window.

"I have this one," I said.

"I could've paid," he protested.

The guy behind the counter handed us our ticket stubs, and I took mine before passing his over. "You basically buy everything as it is. I owe you a ton of money by now."

"No, you don't," he said. "I wasn't charging you and I never will."

"You're too generous."

"So they tell me."

We passed the snack stand, and he hiked his thumb over to the giant machine bursting with buttery popcorn. "Want something? I was planning on getting a giant bucket anyway."

"I guess we can share."

He ended up getting a large tub for us to snack on, but I wasn't sure we'd be able to finish it. That didn't seem to faze him. He was already helping himself before we'd even sat down.

"You're impatient," I said.

"Hungry," he corrected.

We ended up somewhere in the middle row, the best seats according to him. The view was pretty decent, and when paired with popcorn, it wasn't a bad experience at all. I munched on some as we waited for the lights to dim.

"Thanks for this," I mumbled as the first trailer started up.

"No problem. I'm glad to have changed your hermit ways."

"I'm still a hermit, just less so."

"I suppose that's true."

The previews weren't bad, and I actually found myself wanting to see a few of the films when they debuted in theaters. Silas probably wouldn't mind going to watch them with me, but I wasn't sure when I would bring it up.

When the opening scene began, I reached for some popcorn. As I chewed, I got lost in the plot. I watched intently, finally invested in something that wasn't River. This was what a normal experience felt like. A temporary suspension from grief was rare, but I had it. Sitting there, I was a girl, an audience member. That was it. That was all there was to it.

Midway through, I stopped grabbing popcorn and settled my arm against the rest between my seat and Silas's since I was too full for anymore. Without tearing his eyes from the screen, he seemed to notice I was done. Slowly, he set the bucket on the ground between our feet, presumably to save the rest for later.

I expected that to be his last movement. That is until his fingertips brushed mine.

I felt the touch through my whole body, aware of every inch of my skin. I froze, but I didn't pull away. I didn't know why, but I wanted him to do it again.

Because I didn't reject him, he continued until his fingers were sliding through mine. He held my hand firmly, but not too tight. The connection felt natural, right. Being intertwined with Silas was perfect. Being around him was too. For the next hour, we stayed like that, and it wasn't until the credits rolled that he finally let go.

The lights came up, breaking the spell. I checked my phone for the time, finding that my mother wanted me home for dinner soon. Obligations waited, but it wasn't unexpected. It's not like I could stay in a trance forever, only focused on what was in front of me.

"So what did you think?" Silas prompted.

"Of what?"

"The movie," he said, amused. "What else would I be referring to?"

The hand holding, for starters. "It was good, but not my favorite. You?"

"I think epic is a better word for it," he replied. "You're so hard to impress, Emery Leigh. I'll have to up my game."

"You can try."

He covered his chest. "You wound me."

"You poor thing."

We wandered out of the lobby into the heat waiting outside. I found myself missing the air conditioning immediately, which was commonplace for the summer season. It was more

182

bearable with the right people, or even just the right person. Walking alongside Silas, high on a good mood, definitely brightened the circumstances.

I settled into the passenger seat, clicking my seatbelt into place. He rolled the windows down as soon as the engine was on to rid the car of the stifling air. The breeze glided through my curls, and I pushed my hand through my hair to tame the mess.

"You had a good time, yeah?" he asked.

"Definitely." It was true. It was one of the truest things I'd said in a long time. I'd gotten good at feigning enjoyment, behaving as if I was really happy instead of just going through the motions. Today, it was all authentic.

I caught him glancing over at me while we're stopped at the first intersection.

"What?"

"Nothing," he said, looking away.

"No, seriously. What is it?"

"You're just…" he searched for the right words. "You're just so light right now. I like seeing you this way."

"I like being this way," I said honestly.

Silas wasn't River. I came to terms with that early on. They were different from the inside out. They were different people with different faces, demeanors, outlooks. The thing was, they came at their own perfect times, right when I needed somebody like that. Silas was Silas, and right in that car, I realized that I connected with him in our own way. I wasn't ready for the weight of my feelings yet, but I knew it was blooming. That eventual love for him, I mean.

Silas never asked for anything in return, but he gave so much without even knowing it.

183

He dropped me off back at my apartment minutes later. As I started up the path, he poked his head out of the open window on the passenger side.

"Have a good night, Emery," he called after me.

"You too."

I spent the rest of the evening grinning like a fool.

20

Chapter Twenty

Now

"Thank God," Silas says, sounding relieved. "You said yes! YOU HEAR THAT, WORLD? SHE SAID YES!"

His voice echoes, carrying through our little apartment. He's so giddy, so prepared for this moment. It only confirms what I've always known; he's the love of my life, and I'm the love of his.

"Of course I did, silly. I want to marry you," I say.

"Emery Fields! My girlfriend is gonna have my last name!" he exclaims, his entire face lit up with the biggest smile I've ever seen from him.

I giggle as he pushes the ring on my finger and lifts me off my feet into a firm hug. For a second, he's just squeezing me and being an excited goofball. It's so sweet and adorable that I close my eyes just to take it in. My heart feels like it's going to explode.

"You said yes," he murmurs when he pulls back.

"I did," I whisper. "Now are you going to kiss me?"

"Hell yeah."

His mouth collides with mine, hot and wet and passionate enough to make me delirious. His hands are bunching up the material of my skirt, pulling me up. I'm in his arms in seconds, legs wrapped around his hips as he carries me off to the bedroom.

His tongue parts my lips as he lays me down on the bed. Against my mouth, he whispers, "Can I take the skirt off now?"

I nod frantically.

He does.

Then, he shows me just how much he loves me, and I spend every minute of it trying to do the same.

* * *

An hour later, I'm trying to catch my breath and he's laughing against my neck as he rolls off of me. "I didn't plan for this, you know."

I would teasingly call him a liar if I could speak, but instead, I just shake my head.

He takes my sweaty jaw in his hands and smooths the loose strands of hair plastered to my cheeks away. He's so joyful. "I can't wait to marry you."

"Does it bother you that we're doing this as college students?" I question.

"Not in the slightest," he answers. "It doesn't matter if we wait until we're eighty. I'm gonna feel the same way I do right now, no matter how old we are."

I beam, hiding my expression by burying my face in his chest. "We're crazy."

"The craziest."

I used to wonder how it could last. Every adult used to tell me that first loves were full of infatuation that would melt away as soon as we hit adulthood, but that never happened for us. Every struggle brought us closer. Every challenge was something we handled together. I make mistakes all the time, but Si is never gonna be one of them.

"Can we just eat dinner naked?" he suggests. "I'll bring the food in and feed you and everything. I really like you being naked."

"I would feel weird eating cold casserole naked," I reply.

He juts his bottom lip out. "But I really want to look at you longer."

"Too bad, you can take it all off again after dinner."

I settle for panties and his shirt, only partially buttoned. The material swallows me whole since I'm so much smaller than he is, but he loves the way I look wearing his things.

We microwave the cold food and eat sitting on the kitchen counters. Afterward, Silas rinses the plates (naked, because he refused to put clothes on), and I twirl the gorgeous ring around on my finger, mesmerized by it. I keep blinking, wondering if I'll wake up back in Nowhereland without this amazing life, but I don't. I'm still here.

"Do you like it?" Silas asks hesitantly. "Look, I had to ask the sales lady what she thought you'd prefer. There's a warranty if you don't like it. We can return it and get a new one. Should I have picked a better diamond? Shit, darlin, I didn't think about the diamond. Do you want a higher karat?"

"Si, I love it," I interrupt.

"You do?" he murmurs. "You really do?"

"I really do," I assure him. "It's perfect."

His shoulders, once tense, relax. "Thank Christ. Okay.

187

Good. That thing was expensive as hell and my wallet is gonna cry for years to come."

"You didn't have to buy me an expensive ring. I would've liked any ring. Or even just marrying you would be enough."

His grip on my waist tightens as our foreheads touch.

"I want to marry you now," he admits. "I want to drive us to Vegas right now and just marry you. But you deserve a real wedding—"

"I don't want one," I interject. "The only people I'd want there are Caroline and Rosemary and you. My parents don't care about that sort of thing and I don't either. I just want to marry you."

He kisses the tip of my nose and asks the question as he does. "Would you marry me right now if you could?"

"I'd get dressed first," I say, looking him in the eyes so he knows I mean it. "But I would marry you. Right this second. And I wouldn't think twice."

"Let's go," he declares. "Let's go! I'll take the day off work and we're going to drive Caroline and Rosemary to Vegas with us and we're going to get married."

I'm smiling so big it hurts. "Silas, this is insane."

He takes my hands and tugs me off the counter. With no regard for the clock, prior engagements, or anything else, he excitedly says, "No, it's not. Not for us."

He's right. When we were younger, we went to New Orleans on our own. We moved across the country right after graduation. It wouldn't be our first impromptu trip. Honestly, there wouldn't be anything more fitting about this.

"We have to pack and then call the girls and get the keys and go!"

I laugh. "It's ten o'clock, Silas. And you're buck-ass naked."

"I don't care that I'm naked!" he exclaims. "I'm gonna marry the most beautiful girl in the world!"

"It's so short notice," I remind him. "I have that job interview for the academic journal Wednesday morning."

He's practically bouncing on the balls of his feet. "Do you want to marry me or not, woman?"

I nod. "Of course I do."

"So I'll make sure we're back by Wednesday," he promises. "Now let's go!"

"You better put clothes on, Silas Fields," I say. "I won't marry you naked."

He pouts. "You can get naked too."

"So you're cool with random men checking me out on the way to the chapel?" I raise an eyebrow at him.

"You're right, this ass is mine." He punctuates his statement by spanking me playfully. He chuckles when I yelp.

I start packing while he finds his boxers and a pair of jeans. After he's dressed, we trade off and I start to change into a more presentable outfit. As I'm pulling on my sweats, he comes up behind me and kisses my neck. "You promised I'd get to take it all off."

"We don't have time!" I giggle. "You're the idiot who wants to run off to the next state."

He sighs. "Fine. Touche."

I dress in one of his old sweatshirts and help him finish packing. The bag is surprisingly full considering all we have are a change of clothes and outfits for the ceremony. He shoves our toiletries in haphazardly and zips it as fast as he can. His urgency doesn't go unnoticed.

"You're really excited about this," I point out.

"Of course I am."

189

The rattle of the keys is what makes me start thinking. It's when he's dragging our luggage toward the door, on the phone with Caroline, about to drop everything and go, that my head catches up with my heart.

"Yeah, we'll come pick you both up," he's saying. "We're leaving right now."

My mouth suddenly feels really dry. I lose my speed, halting in the living room with my fingers closed around the strap of my purse.

This is real, I remind myself. *This is happening.*

"Alright, see you in a few. Bye." He hangs up the phone and turns around to say something. His words are lost when he sees the grim expression on my face. "What's wrong, darlin?"

"You want to marry me," I whisper. "You really want to marry me."

His brows furrow. "Yeah. I've had five years to think about it. I know that I want this."

"After everything?" I ask.

"After everything that's happened and everything that will," he says.

My gaze falls to my shoes. Part of me wonders if there's something wrong with me for not being as certain as he seems to be. Does that reflect poorly on my character? Does that make me a bad girlfriend?

Does that mean Silas deserves better?

"I'm scared too, Em," he admits. "This is gonna be a little different sure, but we already live together. We've known each other long enough for this to be okay. I'm ready to take this step with you because I want to spend the rest of my life with you. But I understand if you aren't in a hurry. It's okay not to be."

"I'm ready." I slide my fingers through his and hold on. "I'm ready to marry you."

"Good," he says. "Because if you're down for this, I'd like to get going."

We're almost running to the car. He drives so fast to Caroline's place that I have to remind him to slow down for a second. With a laugh, he obliges. "Sorry, darlin, I'll dial down the enthusiasm."

"No, it's fine," I say. "Just try not to kill us before we get there."

"You've got it."

I half-expect two stops to pick Caroline and Rosemary up individually, but they come out of Caroline's apartment together with flushed cheeks and messy hair. When Rosemary climbs into the backseat first, I catch sight of a small bruise on her collarbone. A hickey? *Oh.*

After she throws the bag in the trunk, Caroline shamelessly kisses Rosemary right in front of us, tongue and all. Both Silas and I are taken aback by it, watching it play out. All of us are on cloud nine, it seems.

"Well that's new." Silas looks genuinely surprised.

"Got a problem, Fields?" Caroline taunts.

He shakes his head. "Nope. You do you."

"I say it's about damn time," I chime in. "I was wondering if either of you would make a move."

"So was I, honestly," says Caroline.

"And we were wondering when you two would get married," Rosemary adds. "It seems like today is the day everything comes full circle. Now, do we get to see the ring?"

I blush and hold my hand up for them to see. The band catches the light and reminds me that it's there, that Silas loves me, and that going into that interview on Wednesday, I'll be a married woman.

I can't wait.

21

Chapter Twenty-One

hen

The smell of bacon was the first thing I noticed when I woke up a couple of mornings later. I was definitely confused by it, considering my parents never ate breakfast on a workday. If anything, they should've left by now.

I looked over at my alarm clock, frowning when I saw the time. Both of their shifts started around eight, and it was already eight-thirty. Last I checked, it was just another Thursday.

What's going on?

I reached my arms up and stretched before crawling out of bed. Since I slept in just a t-shirt, I tugged some shorts over my hips so I would be dressed when I stepped into the hallway.

Mom was in the kitchen, and she poked her head out when she heard my footsteps.

"Hey, Em," she chirped. "Sleep well?"

"Yeah," I replied, scanning the living room. I expected Dad to be on the couch, but he wasn't.

"Your father went to work already," she explained. "It's just us."

I sat down at the counter, fiddling with the cup of orange juice set out for me. "Don't you have to go in today?"

"I called in. I thought we could spend the day together," she said.

Mom fixed her attention back to the stove, pushing around some eggs with a spatula. I'd been eating cereal for weeks now, so an elaborate breakfast was practically a foreign concept. I watched as she hummed and danced through the kitchen, effortlessly putting it all together.

"Hey, Mom?" I asked.

"Yes?"

"Is this, like, a special occasion?"

She shook her head. "Not at all. It's just been so long since we hung out together. I decided I needed to do something about that."

Ever since River's death, Mom had made it her mission to turn our relationship around. When I got older, I definitely became more independent. It wasn't like we set out to be distant, but it seemed to happen as time passed. Lately, we ate dinner together and talked more often. I felt like I was getting somewhere with my parents, and that was fine with me.

She passed me a plate. "What do you want to do today?"

I nibbled on my toast, thinking. "Ummm, maybe we can get our nails done. My toenails are absolutely disgusting."

"That sounds lovely. I could use a mani-pedi myself." She held up her hands as proof, revealing chipped french tips. Mom cared more about her nails than I cared about mine, but it was the first thing that popped into my head. I figured I could accommodate.

After putting ketchup on my eggs, something River would've cringed at, I picked at those too. I still hadn't gotten my appetite back yet, but I was making progress in that regard.

"How was your date with Silas?" she prodded.

I'd been midway through drinking my orange juice and started coughing the second the words registered.

"What? No! We're not— it wasn't a *date*," I stammered.

"You went to the movies with him," she observed. "Your dad took me to the movies for our first date."

"That doesn't automatically mean every trip to the theater is a romantic thing," I argued.

"Emery, I've seen the way that boy looks at you."

My face was burning with embarrassment. "Mom, there's nothing to it. He just has eyes. That's how eyes work. They look at people. It's biology."

She seemed unconvinced. "Well, how was it anyway?"

"It was nice," I replied uncomfortably. "I had a good time."

"That's what I wanted to hear."

After we ate, I started on the dishes. I washed, she dried. We worked in harmony until everything was packed away in the drying rack. We moved easily together, as we always had. I missed time with my mom. I'd become so withdrawn, so disconnected that I'd forgotten how nice it was to be around her.

She drew me in for a hug when we were done, and I relaxed into her embrace. She smelled the same, carrying with her a familiar twinge of perfume and shampoo. Her arms tightened.

"You can talk to me about anything," she reminded me.

"I know."

"And I'm here no matter what."

"I know."

"How have you been? For real. I want to know everything."

I spoke into her shirt, a hesitant confession. "It's hard without him. It's really hard, Mom."

There were still mornings where I checked my phone for texts from him. There were afternoons where I started to call before I remembered his number had been disconnected. I looked at old photos and marveled at this new reality. For so long, I had always had River at my side, a constant. Now, I had a gap where he used to fill it.

Silas was changing that, but gradually. I was going to miss Riv forever, but that didn't mean I could never move on. When he was alive, he was always encouraging me to take steps forward, not back.

"He was a good kid," said Mom. "I couldn't have asked for a better friend for you."

The first time River met my parents was when we were two tiny elementary school students. They'd come to pick me up from school, and since Carly hadn't arrived yet, he was still next to me as I wandered out to the car.

I remember it so clearly. After my dad had scooped me up to say hello, River set his lunchbox on the ground and shook my mother's hand. He seriously shook her hand, as strange as it was at his age. Precocious River never ceased to surprise anyone.

"I'm River," he introduced himself.

"We've heard all about you," Mom said back. "It's nice to meet you."

He won both of them over, right then and there. River was like that with everybody he'd ever known.

A selfie we took a few weeks before he died was still my lock screen. I saw it every time I opened my phone, and this morning was no exception. I got a text from Silas after we were finished with breakfast, a few simple words. He always brought me back to Earth, no matter my headspace.

Silas: Want to hang out later?

I'll let you know when I'm free, I wrote back.

"Are you talking to Si?" Mom questioned, peering at me over the rim of her coffee mug.

"Maybe," I said sheepishly.

"You two will be absolutely adorable together," she declared.

"We're not together."

"Not right now, but you could be soon."

"Let's get to the nail salon," I said before she could keep teasing me. "It'll probably be busy soon."

Mom laughed. "Alright, alright."

Our usual pick was sandwiched between a liquor store and the one barbershop we had in Nowhereland. It wasn't the most glamorous place, but the people were nice and didn't charge too much. It had been a while since I last visited, but Mom was a regular.

She called her favorite technician on the way there to get us an appointment, chattering away about the latest gossip after logistics had been handled. Mom was easygoing, definitely more social than I'd ever been. She could make conversation with a total stranger if she wanted to. I admired that.

Upon arrival, we were ushered from the door to a row of chairs with steaming water at their feet. I peeled off my shoes and socks, leaving the worn garments in a messy heap on the floor. Mom set her sandals down beside her neatly, sliding into her chair with ease. I was less graceful, by all means, and she got a kick out of that.

Mom was (and still is) my role model. Yeah, it's a bit cliché and true for most girls. I'm no exception.

The seats were made out of worn leather and weren't much to look at between the peeling red detailing, but the massage fixtures seemed to work. As the mechanisms started moving, I let the tension in my back subside, falling into a nice groove with it.

The woman at my feet made sure we had a nice view of the TV, which was running some generic home improvement show my parents were into. I thought it was boring, but Mom seemed oddly invested in what kind of countertops they were going to pick. I passively liked marble, but she was in favor of granite.

As the pedicurist scrubbed at my heels, she clicked her tongue disapprovingly. "Granite compliments the kitchen best."

"Is it obvious I don't know the first thing about kitchens?" I questioned.

"Only a little," Mom assured me, trading a wink with the staff members.

When the commercials began to roll, advertising the latest season of a trashy reality show, Mom looked over at the blue polish the woman was painting my nails with.

"That's a nice color," she said.

Riv always liked blue, I thought.

I wiggled my toes. "Really? I think so too."

My mother did the same design each time she came in, sticking to her routine to keep things comfortable. Because I didn't want to hold us up, I'd grabbed the first bottle I saw. I rarely wore sandals anyway and figured I could just take it off if I hated it. In the end, it wasn't a bad choice by any stretch.

"It's nice," Mom said. "Hanging out with you, I mean."

"Yeah," I agreed.

After our toenails had dried, small slices of cotton were woven in between each of them. It meant we were walking a little funny, but that was fine. It was something to laugh about.

Mom passed her credit card to the cashier as we stood by the doors. In between getting rung up and leaving, the bell behind us chimed, indicating another customer had arrived. I lost my footing when I turned and nearly ran into Carly Fields.

"Oh!" I sputtered. "Hi! I'm so sorry!"

"Nice to see you, Carly," Mom said, at the same time.

She was standing there, in the flesh. Her work uniform was still on, painted with the logo for the local grocery store over the pocket. Her hair was pulled back, streaked with a little more grey than it had before River died. Her face was worn, but happy. She was smiling, which surprised me.

It wasn't like I expected her to be utterly devastated for the rest of her life, but she seemed to be in a better place.

"I thought that might be you, Emery," said Carly. "I haven't spoken to you in a while. How have you been?"

"Good," I managed. "Really good."

"Silas mentioned you two have been hanging out. Seems like you two are getting along well." She didn't mention Riv, but I felt his name unspoken. I knew there would always be that comparison for her, having another boy in the house. A boy who may have been the same age, but never would be her son. There was no way he could ever replace Riv, even if he fit into the mold of the life he left behind.

"He's great," I said.

"I've met him," Mom chimed in, sparing me from the full impact of the awkwardness. "He's such a sweet boy."

"Definitely," Carly said, holding up a voucher for us to see.

"He picked this up for me a few days ago. I thought I should spend it soon."

"That's lovely," Mom replied.

"He's thoughtful. He's been such a help through this difficult time for me. I don't know what I'd do without him. He's a pretty great nephew."

He was a pretty great person in general. I knew that much to be true.

Silas was progressively working his way into Nowhereland, meeting people, laying down roots. It was rare that someone new ever showed up, so most everyone knew him, or knew of him. The smallest alteration made a ripple in the fabric of this town.

"You know, I heard your nephew moved in," one of the salon workers chimed in as she walked by. "He seems like a nice boy."

I didn't even know her name, but it wasn't a shock that she knew about Silas. Word traveled fast around here.

"I have the night off," Carly said, shifting gears. "Would you like to join us for dinner, Emery?"

I wasn't in a rush to be back at the trailer since the last visit was emotionally draining enough. The hopeful look on Carly's face made it impossible for me to refuse. I was a huge part of her life because of my friendship with River, and that mattered. I knew I was like a daughter to her, and I couldn't cut her out.

"Yeah," I said. "Thanks."

It wasn't long before we parted ways. Carly went off to get her nails done and Mom and I headed back home. I still had some time to kill before supper, so I settled into a comfortable seat on the couch and watched an old black and white movie. It was one of the only film channels that came in for free on our old, clunky TV, but aside from the grainy quality, it was alright.

Mom joined me a few scenes in, and we laughed at the outdated humor together. It was a simple day, but I felt closer to her somehow. I wasn't as alone as I'd felt right after I lost Riv. My circle was growing, just a little, and it was nice.

I ended up walking to Carly's place, even though Mom offered to give me a ride. It was a familiar route, and returning back to the things I knew was helpful for me. The dust clung to the sweat beading on my legs, but I'd gotten so used to it that it didn't make much of a difference to me one way or the other.

My sneakers clomped down the dirt path, kicking it up in the process and creating clouds in the slight breeze breaking through the dense, sweltering sunshine. Riv and I used to pick up heaps of it and pitch it at each other when we were much younger, coming back to his house with grubby hands and faces for Carly to wash with old rags in the kitchen.

Despite it being juvenile, I bent down and scooped up a handful of dirt and gravel, turning it over in my grip. Before all of it could slide through the cracks in my hands, I let it go in a puff. It looked ridiculous, but I could almost feel Riv there with me.

He would throw it back at me if he could. I knew he would. *"You'll pay for that, Emmy!"*

Silas was out front when I arrived, sitting with a cold can of soda pressed to his forehead in an attempt to cool off. He didn't rise from the porch, but he waved at me.

"Why are you outside?" I questioned.

"I was waiting for you," he answered matter-of-factly. "Did you walk here?"

"Duh," I replied. "It's not too far."

"Out here, it must feel like forever. It's so damn hot."

"Doesn't Texas have heat?" I teased.

"Not like this. This humidity is insane."

"Be grateful you're not here year-round," I said. "It's always swampy and absolutely disgusting."

"I imagine so."

I lowered myself on the wooden step beside him, looking out at the rows of mobile homes lining this street. It was the same sight through different eyes. Very little evolved in Nowhereland aside from the people. We changed, but this town went on.

"June's almost over," he observed.

It had been a while since I checked the date, but when I unlocked my phone, it was proven true. "Yeah, guess it is. When do you go back home?"

"August, maybe?" he guessed. "Haven't planned it yet."

"It's gonna be weird when you leave," I said.

"Are you gonna miss me?"

Is that even a question? Yes.

"No," I lied. "Not even a little."

He didn't buy it, but he also didn't call me out. "Well, I'm gonna miss you."

I raised my eyebrows. "For real?"

"Don't look so surprised," he said bluntly. "I'm with you all the time. I'd be stupid not to."

We sat facing each other, fingertips brushing from where our hands met in the middle of the long piece of plywood under us. I thought about how we'd held hands at the movie and got flustered replaying it. I wanted to do it again. I didn't know how to interpret that desire, but I knew it existed.

"I don't know who else I'll play chess with," I said.

"You could start a club at your school. I bet you'll get lots of people," he suggested.

"None of them will be as good as you."

"I'm not that great at chess."

"Well, no, but you're the best to play with."

Silas glanced down sheepishly. "I guess I'll just have to visit more often then."

"You wanna come back to Nowhereland for chess?"

Suddenly, his fingers were squeezing mine. My breath hitched as our eyes met.

"I can think of a few other reasons," he murmured.

The screen door swung open, breaking our intense eye contact.

"You made it!" Carly called out. "You two better get washed up, dinner's almost ready."

"We're coming," Silas hollered back.

The moment was over, and we were back to our fun-loving selves. We raced each other to the sink, and even though he beat me to the bathroom, he let me use it first.

We sat side by side at the cramped little table they used for dining. Carly was across from us, dishing out grilled cheese sandwiches to go with our tomato soup. It was one of River's favorites and mine too. Of all the things she made, it was always a hit.

Both Silas and I respectfully let her pray over the food. It was a newer habit, but it had seemed to stick for her and that was okay. Whatever helped her cope was something I could get behind. Still, I peeked when my eyes were supposed to be shut.

Miraculously, I was at ease all through dinner. We made

small-talk, enjoying a home-cooked meal. The loss was kept at bay, the weight of life held back with it. The three of us cracked jokes and talked about the daily grind. I laughed, I laughed so hard my belly ached. All of us did.

None of us said it, but this was probably what closure felt like. It felt like making peace with the unfair and reconnecting with the better parts of oneself.

And we did it together.

22

Chapter Twenty-Two

Then

When Silas woke me up in the middle of the night with a phone call, my mind immediately flooded with worst-case scenarios. I reached for my cell with a shaking hand, hoping with everything I had that no one else was dead, that Carly was safe, that this was just good news he couldn't wait to share.

My voice was small and shaky as I whispered, "What's up, Si?"

"Are you okay, darlin?" he asked immediately. "You sound upset. What's wrong?"

"Nothing," I replied. "I don't know why you're calling me. I guess I assumed something bad happened."

"Shit," he swore. "I'm sorry. I should've thought about that before I went and got you worked up."

"I'm okay."

"I know that, but you're also hurting enough without me adding to your stress."

"Silas—"

"Emery—"

"It's two o'clock in the morning," I pointed out. "What's going on?"

He sighed, obviously reluctant. "Look, there's no easy way to say this."

"Say what?"

"I couldn't sleep knowing you had no idea. I have to tell you because I feel guilty about keeping this from you."

"Spit it out," I pressed.

A pause. A too-long pause.

"I found the driver," he said.

The air flooded out of my room suddenly, leaving me to choke on my shock. "What?"

I didn't have to ask him what he meant. I immediately knew who he was referring to.

"I spoke to the driver who was involved in the accident," he said after a few seconds. "He's trucker named Don Randall, and he's gonna be in New Orleans tomorrow. I radioed him earlier."

"Why does it matter that he's coming to New Orleans?" I snapped. "He killed my best friend, you know. I'm not gonna send him a greeting card anytime soon."

It wasn't right, getting upset with Si. I knew the sharpness of my tone probably made him feel guilty for bringing it up. It wasn't like he did anything wrong, so it was hardly warranted.

"I guess I wanted to help you find closure with it," he admitted. "I tracked him down hoping, well, I don't really know what I was hoping. I don't know how to help you sometimes, Em, and I wanted to do something good. I've probably had better ideas, though."

I felt myself softening, wishing I could reach out and hug

him through the phone. He only meant well, which made it impossible to get defensive.

"That's sweet, Si," I told him.

"That was the goal."

"What did he say? When you talked to him, I mean."

"He said he was sorry for my loss," Silas said. "He was surprised I contacted him. He didn't think any of us would want to see him after what happened to Riv. He feels so bad. You can tell he does."

I considered this, trying not to imagine Riv in his final moments. The truck driver was the last person to see Riv alive, and that really hurt. A total stranger was the only face around when my best friend died. That was gonna make me feel guilty forever.

"So what's your big idea?" I asked.

"I wanted us to meet with him, face to face," he said. "But if you aren't up for it, I understand."

"I'm up for it," I cut in.

"Really?"

"I have to know what happened. I read the statements from the police but I need to hear it for myself."

Silas said nothing.

"I can't believe you did all this for me," I finished.

"It's what you do for a friend," he said nonchalantly.

"You still didn't have to."

"I know."

I pinched the bridge of my nose. "God, I don't know if my parents are gonna be okay with this."

"We won't know until we ask."

"My mom has been so concerned. It's like she thinks the littlest thing will set me off or something."

"I don't blame her," said Silas. "River was a huge part of your life. I remember when we first met, you weren't okay. You were volatile and I think all of us are worried that you'll be that girl again."

"I don't want to be," I insisted.

"I don't want that either," he said. "I want this to be good for you. So if you aren't absolutely sure—"

"I'm sure."

I tried to convince both of us of this fact. I wanted it to be true. I wanted to be certain that this would be my next big leap going forward. It would take a lot to overcome the doubt, but I could. I would have to.

"I'll talk to my mom tomorrow," I said, shifting to lie back down.

"Want me to come?"

"I can do it," I replied. "I'll let you know if you can come get me."

"Alright. See you then."

"See you then."

He hung up and I held my phone there still, processing and in a daze.

* * *

It took a hell of a lot of begging before Mom finally let up. The moment I brought the idea to her, she rejected it, afraid of what it might do to me to have a conversation with the guy involved in River's death. After plenty of pleading, though, she seemed to see just how desperate I was.

Her face relaxed, hard lines disappearing. With a reluctant look, she'd finally said, "Alright, Emery. Alright."

After she and Dad left for work, I found myself too worked up to go back to sleep. I'd gotten up early so I could meet them before they headed out. Silas probably wouldn't be awake yet.

I shot him a text, letting him know whatever plan he came up with would be fine for me.

He arrived around noon, holding a milkshake when I opened the door. I grinned immediately, taking the cup from him.

"Thanks, Si!"

"No prob," he said, leaning against the frame. "Milkshakes are good for nerves. How are you feeling?"

"I'm okay," I responded, fiddling with the edge of the lid. "I don't know what to expect."

"Neither do I," he admitted.

I started to reach for the duffel bag I packed ahead of time, in case we needed to stay in a motel or something. New Orleans, while not far, was still a decent drive away, and I didn't know how long we'd be in the city. Silas beat me to it, lifting the bag off the floor before I had the chance.

As we walked downstairs, he reached for my hand with his free one. I let our fingers latch, despite myself. It was the second time he held my hand, and I loved it, every second of it.

I was grateful the AC was working when we sat down in the car. Road trips in Louisiana heat were awful without one. I was also grateful for the music he had drifting from the stereo. An awkward silence wasn't ideal.

As he drove, he gestured to the shoebox in the backseat and told me, "You can pick one if you want. Aunt Carly offered a good selection."

As I flicked through them, I realized that all of the CDs were from one person, one collection now passed along without a care for how many memories were made with them playing in the background. *River*. From The Beatles to Green Day, all of them were River's.

The ache from missing him grew stronger as I pulled out a Beatles CD and skipped ahead to *Hey Jude*. It was one of the better tracks because I could still feel closer to Riv without imagining his voice as he sang along. He didn't like the song nearly as much, which certainly helped. It made it so it wasn't as heavy for me.

Silas was a better driver than Riv. He kept his eyes on the road and his hands on the wheel and didn't try to multitask. His phone sat idly in the backseat, only occasionally flashing with a notification. He ignored it.

"We should talk," I decided after twenty minutes of quiet. "We should get to know each other if we're gonna be stuck together for the next twenty-four hours. What's Texas like?"

"It's Texas," he drawled with extra emphasis. "Lots of farms and stuff. I grew up on a ranch and had a horse named Ferris growing up."

"As in Bueller?" I laughed.

"The one and only," he replied.

I giggled into my hands and his face flushed again. I thought it was funny that I could make him blush so much. Because he was someone who usually stayed smooth and confident, it was amusing to watch him get uncomfortable.

"Mom named him, I promise. I'm not that lame."

"I'm gonna call you Bueller from here on out," I declared. "And you're gonna deal with it."

"I already regret telling you that story," he muttered, shaking his head.

"What was that, Bueller?"

He reached over and turned up the music. "Sorry. Can't hear you and your obnoxious teasing anymore."

I listened to a few more songs, letting the lyrics flood right through me. If I turned away, I could pretend River was driving instead of Silas. I wasn't sure I wanted to. It seemed a bit counterproductive to compare the two of them.

"You sure you want to do this?" Silas asked, sensing a shift in my demeanor.

"Yeah," I said. "I know that it's a little morbid talking to the guy who watched my best friend off himself, but part of me feels like there's stuff that's missing. I think that if I get the whole story, I'll be able to move on."

"I'm here if you want to talk about it," he replied. "What else is a random guy from out of town good for?"

"Impromptu road trips to New Orleans?"

He rolled his eyes. "Touche."

"Have you ever been?"

"No, but I've always wanted to go. I don't think we'll have much time. I want to get you back before tomorrow so your father doesn't kill me. He's a scary guy. I'm pretty sure he doesn't like me."

"I think he likes you just fine," I argued.

"Maybe, maybe not."

"Let me take you around the city," I offered. "You can't go to New Orleans and not see everything. The nightlife is awesome."

"How could I say no to that?" he said.

After a few minutes, I impulsively asked, "Can I drive?"

"Hell no," he said immediately. "This is Aunt Carly's, I have no idea if you're a decent driver, and I didn't fix it up for you to destroy it."

I pouted, jutting out my bottom lip and all, but he ignored me and kept moving with no regard for it.

I flicked through the CDs again in my boredom and found that one, in particular, caught my eye. "You know what we should do?"

He raised an eyebrow as if to say *go on*.

"We should sing." I reached over and took the current Beatles album out, replacing it with one of River's custom mixes he burned on his old PC. The first song was *I'm Gonna Be (500 Miles)* by The Proclaimers, and judging by the chuckle that escaped from Silas, he recognized it.

"I'm an awful singer," he protested.

"Just do it," I pleaded. "Please?"

He took a breath and belted out, terribly off-key, *"When I wake up, well I know I'm gonna be, I'm gonna be the man who wakes up next you."*

I sang just as loud as he did, and probably just as poorly. We sang everything from *Don't Stop Believing* and *Shake It Off*. I screamed words to songs I hadn't heard in forever, and for once my mind wasn't caught in the past. It was in the here and now, as it should've been all this time.

We sang until we ran out of songs on the CD. My throat was raw as I said, "Thanks, Si."

"Don't mention it… And, what's with Si? I've been meaning to ask why you started calling me that."

"Am I not allowed to nickname you? Do you prefer Bueller?"

"I'm fine with it, darlin."

We were a few miles out from city limits by now, so I seized the chance to ask him a question that had been gnawing at me. "How'd you find this guy?"

"I went down to the station and asked," he said. "He was in

the police report, so I searched him up online and contacted him."

"Why go through all that trouble? Does it even matter that much to you?"

"Not really, but it matters more to you."

It was then that I realized he cared a lot more than I gave him credit for.

Silas Fields, I wondered. *What else is there to you?*

"Where are we meeting him?" I glanced around, trying to recognize what street we were on. It had been a while since I visited the city. The last time was for River's sixteenth birthday when Carly took us for an impromptu vacation.

"Just a diner in the middle of town," he said. "Nothing special, but I'll buy lunch."

As we drove, I couldn't help but wish I'd grown up here instead of Nowhereland. Between the culture and history, I knew that this is the sort of place River and I deserved to make memories in. I intended to make the most of my day with Silas because it was nice to be away from my problems for a while.

The gravity of what we were about to do hit me when I got out of the truck outside the restaurant. The second my sneakers met the asphalt, the realization that I was going to confront the truth resonated in me.

Silas came up behind me, voice soft as he spoke. "Hey, Emery?"

"Yeah?"

"You can do this, darlin," he said, tucking one of his hands under my chin so my face was tilted upward. Dark eyes met mine, and for once, I didn't wish they were green. I was glad they were Si's.

"What if I can't?"

213

"You can," he insisted. "All you have to do is breathe, and get in there with your chin up."

I swallowed and looked at the door, wondering if I was ready to face what waited behind it. After a breath or two, I walked forward with Silas in tow.

Be brave, Emmy, River would say.

I'm trying, Riv. I'm trying.

The man was sitting at the end of the counter with a coffee and a somber demeanor. I knew it was him by the guilt that marked his face. He wore a ratty ball cap, a plaid shirt similar to mine, and looked like he hadn't slept in days. He probably hadn't, much like myself.

He turned when he heard the door open, and his eyes fell on us.

Don Randall. The last man who ever saw River Fields breathing.

23

Chapter Twenty-Three

Now
Adjusting to the weight of a ring on my finger is a lot more complicated than I initially believed. When I grab the handrail on the bus, my fingers fall differently on the metal. When I grip my thermos to take a sip of my coffee, the ring causes me to shift my fingers. Knowing that I'll sign the papers in this interview *Emery Fields* is enough to make me over the moon with joy.

The change in my life, as new as it is, is still wonderful and welcomed.

I've practiced for a number of questions, but I'm still nervous. The big one I know they'll ask is still one that I have no answer for. No matter how hard I try, I can't come up with the right words.

Why physics?

The truth of my major is that I picked it drunk one night. I didn't think it through. It was a whim, something that hit me in between shots at the bar with Caroline. All I could think was that I was directionless and that River always said I'd be good at physics. I made that my major, my focus by default.

I kept going with it out of habit, but now that I'm sitting here actually thinking about it, I'm doubting whether or not I want this to be my career. The question is— do I want this to be what I do for the rest of my life?

If you have to think about it, the answer is no.

An epiphany is a rare thing in life. It's not like every day is bursting with life-changing revelations for most people. I feel off-kilter, my mind racing as I consider this. All I've ever seemed to do is complain about physics, about the workload. I hated the endless slew of science classes. It never made me happy, but I refused to be a quitter. Being stubborn is my worst flaw.

I picked this for Riv. I picked it for Riv, and now that I've finally let myself come to terms with it, I can't go through with this job. It's not what I really want. It's never been what I really want.

This is the final step of grief. This is me truly letting go.

Before I can stop myself, I'm getting off the bus at the law firm I work at with Silas instead of continuing on to the interview. My hands are texting the appointment office to cancel. My body is racing through the doors, and I'm running toward my husband at a dead sprint.

"Si!"

He nearly drops the papers in his hands, a case he's probably making copies of. "Darlin, what are you doing here? What about the interview?"

I shake my head. "I don't want to go to the interview. I don't like physics, Si. I never did."

Silas sets the file down and frames my face, inspecting me with concern. "Are you okay? Did you hit your head, darlin?

Are you sick?"

"I'm not sick, Si," I tell him. "I just realized on the bus that I picked physics because I didn't know what else to do. It hit me that I don't want to find another dimension, or do endless formulas for the rest of my life. I hate math, Si. I don't like physics. I wanted to be close to Riv so I made the choice. I want to change this. I want to be happy. Living my life to fulfill River's dreams is pointless. I want to live for *me*."

He looks stunned. "Wow. I don't know what to say to that."

Glenn pokes his head out into the hallway from his office. "I do. Congrats, Emery. You deserve to find what you love most and do it."

I blush. "Thanks, Glenn."

"Don't mention it, kiddo," he says affectionately. "It's nice to see you again, by the way. How come I wasn't invited to the wedding?"

Silas laughs. "If we'd had a traditional ceremony we would've invited you. It was a spur of the moment sort of thing."

"My wife and I eloped too," Glenn says. "I remember that I just wanted to marry her. It doesn't have to be anything more than that unless you want it to be."

"Definitely," I agree. "Though my mother isn't going to like the fact we ran off to Vegas. I have no idea how I'm going to tell her."

"Maybe tell her on Thanksgiving?" Silas suggests.

I turn to face him, confused. "What do you mean?"

"I mean that she called me this morning after I left to invite us down to Louisiana for the holiday weekend. It's been a while."

He isn't wrong there. My parents and I talk on the phone a couple of times a month, but neither of us visits often. The

217

last time they came to California was two years ago, and I have no intention of going back to Nowhereland. Since I left that place behind me, I vowed that I wouldn't go back. It stemmed from a promise made to River long ago, and I want to keep it.

Glenn went back into his office, calling over his shoulder, "I'll let you two chat for a bit, but I expect you to be back to work soon, Fields."

"You got it, boss," Silas says before turning back to me. "Anyway, I know you don't want to go, but I think we ought to. I want to tell them about us in person, and it'll give you time to think about changing your major before you do it."

I want to say no, but he's right. For all these years, I avoided coming home because I thought I would get sucked back in. My escape didn't feel permanent, and my fears and unresolved moments were haunting me. Now that I find myself here, I know what I have to do.

It's not like I'm moving back to town. It won't hurt to face my past, just a little. Besides, I miss Mom and Dad and Carly.

I nod. "Alright. You better get back to work, babe. We can talk later."

He gives me a chaste kiss. "I love you, Em."

"Love you more," I reply.

After I leave, I spend the afternoon on my college's website, searching for a new major. It's impractical to change it so late in the game, but necessary in the long run as much as I don't want to admit it. I spend hours pouring over every program, lost and doubting myself.

Jesus, tuition is going to suck.

I'm still searching when Silas gets home hours later. He comes up behind me and rests his chin on top of my head, his eyes scanning over the screen. "Hmmm... what is my beautiful wife thinking about majoring in?"

"She has no idea," I say, flustered. "Am I being stupid for changing it?"

"Your major? Not at all. You should prioritize what makes you happy, darlin. It's inconvenient, but it sure as hell isn't stupid." After a few seconds, he sighs and closes my laptop for me. "Alright, we're going to take a break from that."

"And do what?" I ask. "I need to pick a major."

"Not right now, you don't," he replies. "We need to book a flight to Louisiana for this weekend. And as for what we're going to do during your break, I have a few ideas."

"Marriage has made you a sex-crazed pervert," I say with a scoff.

"That's not true!"

"Mmhmm, sure."

"You have a dirty mind, Emery Fields."

"That's because I spend too much time with you."

He thinks for a second, trying to find something to occupy ourselves with.

"Well, how about we play chess?" he suggests.

"Out of all the games we've played, you've only won a few of them," I remind him.

"That's not true and you know it!" he says indignantly.

I shrug. "Have it your way then. You're on."

Our game ends in a stalemate an hour later, but Silas is perfectly content with that. He teases me about how close he was to victory while I figure out what I'm cooking for the night.

He books our flight. I make dinner. I'm dicing tomatoes for spaghetti sauce with one of our new kitchen knives when he suddenly asks a question that startles me.

"How do you feel about kids?"

I'm shocked, genuinely and totally. The blade slips and slides down the side of the fruit, effectively cutting my thumb open. Instantly, I swear loudly and drop the bloody knife.

"Shit, Em," Silas curses.

Immediately, he's at my side, leading me over to the kitchen sink. He holds my hand under the water for a few minutes and wraps my finger in a paper towel. I keep it there while he fetches the first aid kit. We don't speak until after he's bandaged my finger and even kissed it better.

"I probably shouldn't have popped that question," he says apologetically. "I'll be the first to admit I have terrible timing."

"I'll say." I frown as I throw the ruined tomato into the trash. "So why do you ask?"

"I don't mean that I want one *now*," he clarifies. "We haven't finished school yet, so I don't expect that for a long time. It's just that we're married now and I want to talk to you about that. I want to know what you think."

I haven't thought about it. Not really. His question has definitely thrown a wrench into my plans because now I can't *not* think about it.

"I don't know, Si. I haven't considered it."

"Kelley from work is pregnant," he says. "I guess it got me thinking. If our kids are anything like you, I'd love to have ten. You're pretty amazing."

"And so are you," I reply. "But I don't really want to talk about a baby until after I get my career settled."

He almost looks disappointed. "Oh. Well, yeah. I get that."

I walk over to him and loop my arms around his neck. "Something wrong?"

"No. I guess I just expected a different answer," he admits.

"You're right, though. You've got more important things to worry about. Besides, your parents don't need too much new information at once."

I laugh. "Exactly."

He smoothly changes the subject, as though we weren't discussing something important. "How about I cut the rest of the tomatoes? I owe you for the finger."

I gesture to the cutting board. "By all means, take it away."

For the rest of the night, everything goes without a hitch. We're still Silas and Emery, still madly in love, still in a great, happy marriage, but the reality remains. I've got a million things on my mind, and all I can hope for is figuring it out.

As we're falling asleep, Silas pulls me closer and murmurs, "Relax, darlin, you'll find the perfect major. You're okay. We're going to be okay."

I don't have to tell him I'm stressed, or that I'm feeling unsure. He's always been attuned to my needs like that.

But as I'm falling asleep, I realize that I'm unconvinced, even with his reassurance.

24

Chapter Twenty-Four

Then I had to remind myself to chill out. Over and over, I had to remind myself to take in a breath, release it, and do it again. The weight on my chest didn't seem to be letting up. I was gonna have to work with that.

Silas touched the small of my back, coaxing me forward, onward.

"You must be Silas," Don said, extending his hand politely.

Silas shook without hesitation. "That would be me."

Don turned to me, cocking his head. "And who is this?"

I was gawking at him wordlessly.

"Emery," Silas supplied. "This is Emery."

He wisely didn't try to shake my hand, probably because he could tell just how standoffish I was. I didn't want anything to do with him, and I hoped he could pick that up on his own. The whole situation was making me nauseous, but I tried to look composed on the surface.

"Is she your girlfriend?" he asked.

We both shook our heads at the same time.

"No, I—" I started.

"We're just friends—" Silas began.

"Sorry for assuming," Don apologized. "I guess I just don't really know what to say. You seem like good kids. I'd rather not leave a bad impression, you know?"

It was a little late for that. He left a bad impression when he killed my best friend. A small part of me knew he wasn't responsible. Not really. Or rather, not entirely. He didn't set out to kill Riv. River made a lot of choices that night, and yeah, things could've played out differently, but they didn't.

There we were. I was looking for someone to blame, and after a month of assigning responsibility to myself, I pinned it on Don instead.

"How about we sit down?" he suggested. "I'll buy you kids some lunch and we'll talk."

"That's generous of you," Silas said graciously.

"It's the least I can do," Don replied. "He must've been important to you, huh?"

"I was River's best friend," I corrected him. "Important doesn't even scratch the surface."

Silas, bless him, acted as a buffer and took the stool between Don and me at the counter. Sitting next to him would make my skin crawl, and the proximity would undoubtedly be unbearable. He seemed like a nice guy, but I couldn't find mercy in me to forgive him. My forgiveness wasn't something I could ever dole out so easily.

"What was he like? If you don't mind," Don prompted. "See, I don't know anything about him. I'd like to get a clearer picture, if that's alright with you."

"Emery knew him best," said Silas. "He was my cousin but I'm from out of town. I wish I'd spent more time with him."

"Sometimes we miss out on important stuff in life," Don reasoned.

"Too often," Silas agreed.

Both of them looked to me, waiting for my answer.

For years, River was untouchable. He was my rock.

How was I supposed to explain a boy who was unexplainable? How was I supposed to explain the greatest person I ever knew? He was impossible to describe because he was so much more than a few words. He was a combination of endless memories and sentences; I couldn't find the most important ones to share.

I picked up my phone, found a picture of us, one of the few more recent ones I had, and slid it over to Don.

"That's River," I said, pointing at his smile. "That's *my* River."

That was all anyone was going to get out of me, so he didn't press for more.

I was a bundle of nerves, my curiosity gnawing at my insides. Shortly after we ordered sodas, my self-control crumbled. I looked to the broken man beside me and made a demand. "Tell me all of it."

"Darlin," Silas hissed. *Calm down,* he didn't say.

Don waved his hand dismissively. "It's okay. I don't blame her for being angry. I would be too."

"I wanna know about that night," I said.

"I know," Don muttered. "I'll try my best. It's sort of hazy. Before you ask, I wasn't drunk or high. I'd never mess up my job on purpose."

Yet you did.

"You get used to a calm, consistent drive after a while. The traffic is all the same— there's no changes really. You just continue down the expanse of road until you reach your destination, and that's it. That's all I thought it would be."

You were wrong.

A waitress handed me my diet Coke and I practically started chugging to keep myself from speaking.

A shudder rolled through Don. It was such a subtle thing, but I saw it. I watched him as the horror the memories brought flashed through his eyes. "He was driving so fast, that kid. And I know they were telling you it was a suicide, but it sure as hell wasn't."

I coughed up my gulp of soda in shock, the sticky mess spraying across my lap. "What did you just say?"

"But the police—" Silas started.

"The police didn't get my side of things because I was in the ER," he cut us off. "He swerved. He had been barrelling down the road going at least eighty. I watched his car swerve and plow right through the fence. He was trying to stop. I could see the panic in his eyes as he lost control of the car and darted right in front of the truck. He didn't want to die. It was in his face, but I couldn't stop in time."

River didn't want to die. *River didn't want to die.* This new information was enough to make the world tip. I could believe the notion that he took his own life because it fit so well into the puzzle. River was sick and upset and it made sense that he wouldn't be thinking clearly.

But if he didn't want to die, if it was truly an accident, then there may have been hope.

There could have been hope.

There could have been hope, but he was gone anyway.

"It all happened so fast and the next thing I knew I was being carried to an ambulance and he was slumped in the driver's seat—"

225

"I think that's enough," Silas interjected.

It was then that I realized that somewhere in the middle of the story, I'd grabbed onto Silas's hand and was holding onto it for dear life. He wasn't letting go, and when our eyes met, he squeezed my fingers.

"You don't think it was a suicide?" I clarified slowly.

Don shook his head. "I don't. And that's what makes it feel worse."

"He was having one of his bad days that night," I told him. "Sometimes he got these episodes where he was really depressed. And he was in the middle of one when he drove off."

Remembering the details of that night was different. This time, vocalizing everything that happened was cathartic. A flood of all the hurt was coming out of me like word vomit.

"I thought he was going to be back. When they told me what happened, I thought he killed himself on purpose because we had a fight and he wasn't right in the head when it happened."

Even though the waitress serving Don more coffee pretended she wasn't eavesdropping, I knew she was. The pity was radiating off of her. I saw it everywhere I went in my hometown, and it seemed like it followed me here too.

"I can't speak for him," said Don. "But I know what I saw, and I can only hope that maybe that brings you some comfort."

I was tempted to make a scene. I wanted to pound my fists against the wall and holler until my vocal cords ripped. I wanted to be so loud that the heavens would open up and turn back time, but I didn't act on my impulses.

I just sat there and told him, "Thank you for your time."

I started to get up, but Silas held on tight. "Emery, we should get something to eat."

"I'm not hungry right now," I said, my voice shockingly calm. "No thanks."

"Really," Don chimed in. "It's my treat. It's the least I could do."

"Please stay," Silas added.

I caved, relenting. "Sure. Let me go to the bathroom first."

I locked myself in the first stall I could find and found some semblance of privacy. In my distress, I cried a lot. I didn't want to do that again, so I took a few calming breaths until I felt like I could face those two again.

"Why, Riv?" I whispered to no one.

Why did you have to go?

I knew Don wanted forgiveness. He needed to clear his conscience. Since I felt the same way, I decided I would try to find it in me to give him mercy. So, I sat back down and ordered a fruit salad because I knew I needed to eat anyway.

Silas got a turkey sandwich and insisted on sharing with me, even though I told him I didn't want any. He even talked with Don about his job as if making awkward conversation could smooth everything over. I was still trying to process the revelation, trying to understand how everything I thought was true could just be changed in an instant.

It doesn't matter, I told myself. *It doesn't matter because either way, Riv is still dead.*

Somewhere between infrequent bites and slow chewing, I stole a glance at Don's worn face, wondering if him being here did anything for him. Probably not, as evidenced by the defeated way his shoulders slouched. My gut twisted because even with my blinding grief, I could acknowledge that neither of us were really at fault. He needed to hear it.

My lips parted and the words escaped before I could really

think. Something inside me, a rational voice I'd suppressed in my mourning, seized control of my mouth and spoke up. "It was an accident, sir, and it's really easy to get caught up in wondering what you could've done differently to save him. But the truth of it is, thinking isn't gonna bring him back. You can't turn back time, and you can't change what happened that night. I know you probably want us to forgive you, but we don't have to. You don't need it. You need to forgive yourself."

I'd been completely lifeless and quiet for the entire meal, which explained why Don was so surprised by me. He smiled, just barely, and said, "You know, kid, maybe you should take your own advice."

"Yeah," Silas agreed. "Maybe you should."

They were right, but could I? Could I try to forgive myself?

It wasn't long before we were done eating, and the check was paid. I thanked Don for the food, trying to pretend I wasn't anxiously waiting for a chance to leave. I didn't rush away, as much as I wanted to.

After we left the diner, Silas stopped me before I get in the car. It was oppressively hot and the air hung thick around us. The humidity was an unrelenting force, but even though I hated it, I barely noticed. I had a feeling I could handle the weather for something important.

I shoved my sweaty fists into the pockets of my shorts and squinted at him through the bright sun in my eyes.

He leaned against the passenger door and cocked his head at me. "You know what you said in there really helped him. Anyone can see it."

"That's good, I guess," I said. "It just came out."

"I meant what I said about forgiving yourself."

"I know. I'm trying."

I wasn't sure if it was true. I wanted it to be, but all I could think as I stared down at my ratty shoes was that I wasn't certain I'd never be able to.

I wanted to let go of everything because lingering in the memories and hypotheticals wasn't doing anything for me.

"Tell me what you're thinking," Silas pleaded. "Talk to me."

"What good will that do?" I asked.

"It'll help you vocalize what you're feeling," he said. "My mom's a social worker, I know this stuff."

Listening to Silas describe his family was always amusing because I could hear all the fondness he had for them in his voice. He had a point and I started babbling because I reached the point where I was desperate to do anything to make me feel better.

"He was my first kiss. And he was going to be my first everything if things had gone differently. Riv was probably bipolar or something, and if he'd gotten proper treatment, he would still be here. I used to wish I could rewind it all and bring him back. It's why I hated you at first, why I wanted nothing to do with you. You reminded me that he wasn't coming back."

I wondered if that made Silas feel guilty, but if it did, he didn't let on.

"But now I'm not sure I would change how it all went. I'm not sure this didn't happen for a reason. Yeah, it sucks and it hurts, and if he were still alive, it would be him holding my hand and not you. I'm not sure that's what I want anymore because I don't regret meeting you."

I'm not sure if I said too much there. All I'm doing is humiliating myself.

I looked up at him, studying his dark eyes. "Hey, Si?"

229

He squeezed back. "Yeah?"

"Why are you holding my hand?"

I wasn't sure when he reached for me. Even though this wasn't the first time it happened, it probably wouldn't ever get old.

He looked down at our intertwined fingers as if realizing what he was doing for the first time. His head perked up again, a blush spreading across his face. "I wanted to."

I wanted him to do it too, at least subconsciously.

"You know, darlin, the circumstances aren't great, I'll admit, but I don't regret meeting you for a second."

Ditto.

When he took his hand away from mine, I resisted the urge to whimper from the loss. Even though it was summer and it wasn't glamorous or anything, I longed for the closeness of his touch, the comfort of it.

He pulled me in for a hug next, tucking his chin on top of my head because I was petite enough for him to do so. He held me for a few seconds, and all I could think was that I wanted to stay like that forever because Silas Fields felt like home.

"So what do you say we get past the sad part of today and paint New Orleans red?" he proposed.

The corners of my mouth lifted when I saw the hopeful look he wore. "I'm a Rolling Stones fan, so I prefer painting things black, but I'd love to show you around."

"And I'd love to accompany you," he replied. "Even if your jokes are terrible."

"You can deal with my humor. We've got bigger things to do. Ready for your next adventure, Bueller?"

He tugged on the handle of the passenger door and gestured at the seat. "After you, m'lady."

I felt lighter as he started the car. For once, I could just live in the moment and the freedom that came with a big city to explore. New Orleans was about as exciting as things got in Louisiana, and I'd forgotten how much I liked the vast opportunities places outside of Nowhereland city limits brought. It was strange not having River to sit beside me and lead the adventure, but I liked the newness of this.

And I also liked Silas Fields sitting beside me.

Or, maybe, I just liked him in general.

25

Chapter Twenty-Five

Then Silas parked near Bourbon Street, which was basically the center for tourists in New Orleans. He climbed out of the car and raised his arms over his head to stretch as he looked around. "Where to, Em?"

I shrugged. "Honestly, there are so many options. It depends on what you want to do."

Silas glanced at his surroundings with a newfound fascination. Bourbon street was still crowded during the day, but it lacked the typical lights and chaos of the nightlife. We walked past a guitarist as he strummed a low key cover of a sappy love song. Silas nudged my shoulder with his. "You okay?"

I frowned. "Why wouldn't I be?"

He cocked his head at me as if to say *really?*

I sighed and stole a glance at him. "I'm fine. Just distracted."

"That's understandable," he said. "What do you want to do first?"

I pointed at a small building at the end of the block. "There's a cool antique shop around here, and there's also a cafe that lets independent artists play during dinner hours."

"Sounds like a plan," Silas affirmed.

From there, we wandered aimlessly. There was no purpose in the fall of our shoes against the pavement, no purpose as we ventured streets amid crowds of people who would never know our names. Big cities are humbling; sometimes you need to be reminded of how small you are.

The antique shop glittered with knickknacks, some so old I was scared to touch them. I stared at endless glass figurines, studied the dusty paintings that hung on the walls. I knew Silas was behind me without looking. That might be crazy, but I swore I could feel his presence, knowing there wasn't even a foot between us as we wove in and out of the aisles.

It wasn't until I saw our reflection in a jewelry box mirror that I realized he wasn't looking at any of it.

He was looking at me.

Those dark eyes were following me around like he couldn't take his gaze off me. It was almost out of fear that I might disappear into thin air. I felt my breath catch and hoped I could keep my voice even.

I reached for a floppy hat off a mannequin, pulling it over my head even though I was certain I looked ridiculous.

"What do you think?" I asked. "Does it suit me?"

His lips twitched, fighting a smile. "I think it's a bit oversized."

I considered this. "Oh well. Maybe I'll never be a hat girl."

I set it back down and pivoted on my heel to face him again. I was going to suggest we look at books or something, but the words died when he caught me around the wrist and pulled me closer. My shoes squeaked as the gap between us closed, and I pressed my hands on his chest to keep my balance.

"Si?" I murmured.

He hesitated. "What would you say if I told you that hat was adorable?"

"I'd say thank you," I said slowly. "I also would accuse you of lying."

"It's the truth. The hat *was* adorable."

"We'll have to agree to disagree on that one."

I felt his forehead fall forward against mine. Our noses touched. My face became scorching hot in anticipation, but I was ready for it. I wanted him to kiss me. I knew the proximity was a sign it was bound to happen, and I could feel myself growing impatient.

"Darlin, I want to kiss you really bad right now, and I don't know what to do about it."

"There's only one thing you can do," I answered. "So are you going to do it or what?"

And gently, he kissed me. His lips were feather-light against mine, soft and slow as if taking his time to memorize me. I gasped against his mouth, and then his teeth gently nibbled my lower lip. The kiss deepened, and our surroundings melted away.

I was kissing Silas. I was kissing Silas Fields and it was *incredible*.

If someone else hadn't opened the door to the shop, we would've started making out in public. I almost felt a little embarrassed, but the expression on Si's face extinguished that feeling.

He looked excited, a little bit shaken up, and in total disbelief. "What?"

"I got to kiss you," he said. "I don't know if there's anything better than that."

I took his hand sheepishly.

We wandered around the streets like that, thoughtless and blissfully unaware of everything. I'd been to New Orleans a few times before, but seeing it with him was a new experience. I welcomed it. Holding his hand, the ghost of his mouth on my lips, felt so right. Everything with Si felt right.

The worst part was, I wanted to tell Riv about it. Maybe at another time, one where we weren't anything more than friends, I would've been able to. Somehow, I wasn't too sad. Instead, I wasn't stuck in the past. My grief was dwindling. Right then, everything was okay.

Hours passed like this. We found ourselves navigating through brutal humidity and the muggy Louisiana sunshine before settling down for dinner at the cafe I'd mentioned earlier. Silas made a point to pull my chair out from the table for me. A laugh escaped me.

"Chivalry isn't dead," he reminded me.

"It's not the end of the world for me to pull my own chair out," I said, leaning against my palm. I propped my elbow on the table and turned to watch the band play a cover of a song I'd never heard onstage. I couldn't recognize it for the life of me. Then again, River and I never really listened to anything modern anyway. Whatever it was, it sounded nice. The notes from the piano drifted and settled softly over the room, like the perfect close for a day like this.

It was as I sat there nudging Silas's feet with my own under the table that I realized how strange moving on after death was. For so long everything moved like molasses, dragging on endlessly, and then all of a sudden life was okay. It's almost as if I woke up one day and realized it was better now, easier to keep going than it was before.

For the first time in what felt like an eternity, breathing didn't hurt. Thinking didn't hurt. Life didn't hurt.

"What's this song called?" I asked Silas, snapping out of my reverie.

"I'll look it up." He listened for a few seconds, thumbing the lyrics into his phone until he came up with an answer. "It's called *Flowers In Your Hair*, originally by The Lumineers. Ever heard of it?"

I shook my head. "No, but I kinda like it."

A waiter came by and took our drink orders, sliding a couple menus onto the table for us. When my fingers brushed Silas's as I took one, my heart slammed against my ribs.

Why am I like this right now? I wondered. *It's just Silas.*

I tried to pick something to order, but I didn't feel hungry. I looked up at him, our eyes met, and my mouth went dry.

He said my name. Once.

"I want to get out of here," I managed to say suddenly. "Can we just get out of here?"

He nodded slowly, wondering what I meant by that.

"I want to get a pizza and find somewhere cool to eat it," I said. "I know that probably sounds so weird, but this place is so boring."

Silas's brows raised and he chuckled. "I was wondering if I was the only one who felt that way."

I felt my shoulders relax in relief. "This is why we're friends."

"This is why I like you," he added. "I like you a lot."

It was so straight to the point, but sweet all the same. The way Silas said the words held so much hesitance. It was so perfectly teenaged, so unsure and wonderful at the same time. This was the guy who had brought me out of my shell again. I could listen to him say he liked me on repeat.

"I like you too," I said shyly.

"Glad we cleared that up."

We left in a hurry, only paying for the sodas we never touched. Silas found the nearest pizza joint quickly, and we ordered a large pepperoni to go. I carried the greasy cardboard box in my lap, the warmth of it pressing into my legs. It was hard not to be giddy as we drove without any idea where we were going. Between the grumbling in my stomach and the butterflies, I was feeling so much all at once.

Our destination ended up being a small park next to the Mississippi, right where we could sit on the lawn and hear the water as it crashed and moved along. Shoulder to shoulder, we faced the view and set the pizza down, half on his lap and half on mine. Since neither of us thought to bring plates, I was eating sloppily over the box, trying not to spill.

"When I take you on a real date, I promise I'll do a better job than this," Silas said. "Spontaneity is not my thing."

I rolled my eyes. "This is perfect."

"You're easy to please."

"Sure am."

I took another bite, shifting as he watched. "Don't look at me while I'm eating. It's weird."

"I can't help it," he said. "Where else am I supposed to look?"

"I don't know. Not at me?"

He covered his eyes jokingly with his hand. "There. Better?"

"Much."

I finished my slice and wiped my fingers on a cheap napkin. "I still can't believe we're here. I always forget the world outside of Nowhereland exists. Sometimes it's so isolated it seems like there's nothing else."

"I get what you mean. It's suffocating. I'm not sure how you

237

survived for so many years."

"It's all I know," I said. "I'm used to it."

"I wasn't sure if you'd want to come with me," he admitted. "Is that crazy? I can't read you sometimes and I couldn't breathe for pretty much the entire phone call."

"I can't be *that* hard to figure out!" I protested. "You know me pretty well."

"Are you kidding? You're not exactly an open book. You're like a book that's been glued shut."

"I didn't realize I was so enigmatic."

He groaned. "You have no idea. Getting to know you has been impossible."

"You're doing fine."

"That's because I've been trying as hard as I possibly can," he said earnestly. "Seriously, darlin. From the moment we met, I was hellbent on learning everything there is to know about you. You're the most interesting, complicated person I've ever known."

I was stunned into silence.

"And you're also probably the funniest. You genuinely make me laugh without much effort. You also have a big heart. You're so loyal. I can't help but miss you whenever I'm not around you. You can kick my ass at chess all you want if it means I get to see you smile."

I searched for a reason to believe he was flattering me. After being hit with some of the worst luck I've ever had, he seemed so out of reach. Yet, this cute guy was so enamored with me that it was like I was the only person in the world when he spoke to me.

The corners of my mouth tilted up. "I do kick your ass at chess a lot, don't I?"

"I'll get better," he said. "And when I do, you'll have to give me more credit. You've just been playing longer. I put up a good fight."

"You do, but that doesn't stop me from winning."

"Sometimes I win!"

"Sometimes," I agreed.

He reached out a tucked a strand of my hair behind my ear. "I'll even the score."

"You can try," I teased. He probably would, but I didn't have it in me to give in so easily.

The food was long forgotten. He moved the half-eaten box, and I realized it was because he wanted to kiss me without it getting in the way. I felt his breath fanning across my mouth before our lips met in the middle.

The kiss was gentle and slow, without a rush. He could tell he would have plenty of time to kiss me after, so he didn't hurry this one. I could've kissed him forever, if that were possible. I was convinced that this was as close as I could get to cloud nine.

When we broke apart, I felt incomplete. I wanted more. How much more, I wasn't sure.

He framed my face with his fingertips. "About that real date… are you in?"

"Yes," I said easily. "Is that even a question?"

"It is if I asked it."

"Well, you have your response. Yes, I'm in."

"Cool," he said. "I have no idea what I was going to say if you told me no."

He was so unapologetic about it and it was amusing.

I ruffled his hair, pushing it out of his eyes to get a better look at him. He wasn't River. I didn't mean to compare them, but it was impossible not to. It's only natural to find similarities and differences in the people who turn your world upside-down.

"What are you thinking?"

"I'm thinking that you're not Riv," I replied.

He swallowed hard, probably afraid of what I was going to say.

"I'm glad you're not," I reassured him. "He was like family to me and that bond is never going away. The memories won't either if I can do anything about it. That doesn't mean that I can't move on with you.

"I like that what we have is its own thing. I like the way I feel with you because it's not the same. I would be trapped and unable to grow if it was the same story unfolding again. I think the way you treat me and the things you've done for me outweigh all my doubts. This summer saved my life. *You* changed me."

I don't know who moved first, but within seconds we were kissing again. His hands slid up under my shirt and grabbed my waist. He pushed me closer to him until we were flush against each other. His jaw scratched my chin, our noses brushed every couple seconds, and my heart was slow, steady. I wasn't nervous. I felt safe.

We didn't get to kiss long before the siren blared behind us. Blue and red lights flashed, bringing me out of the Silas-induced haze. Suddenly, the reality was there, nagging me.

"This is great. Just fantastic," Silas muttered.

The cop coming out of the cruiser was a short, beady-eyed man. His gaze narrowed on Silas immediately. He definitely didn't seem like he was feeling patient, and I swallowed hard as he approached us.

"Can I help you?" Silas deadpanned, probably with a bit too

much annoyance.

"I think you can," the cop said. "Care to tell me what you're doing on private property?"

We exchanged glances.

"What do you mean?" I asked.

"I mean you're on private property. The owner called to report two teenagers loitering. Didn't you see the sign?"

Both of us shook our heads.

The officer jabbed a finger at a small fixture on a light post, several feet over. That must've been the sign, and it was just our luck that we missed it.

"We'll clear out," I began. "Let us get our stuff—"

"There's a penalty for trespassing," the cop interrupted. "What world do you think you live in, girl? Do you think you can just get away with everything?"

"There's no need to be rude," Silas cut in.

"You ought to shut your mouth. Didn't your mother ever tell you not to talk back? Where is she anyway?"

"I'm from out of town," Silas replied.

"Don't take a tone with me," the officer warned. "This won't be pretty for you if you don't learn how to address me."

I wanted to talk Silas down, but I didn't know what to say. I was scared shitless.

I mean, come on, the looming threat of arrest was a good deterrent. Besides, I was never one for confrontation with authority. Other kids, like Greta, were one thing, but this was another.

"Do they teach you to be a dick in cop school, or is that just your style?" Silas snapped.

"Silas!" I gasped.

"Alright, that's it!" the cop growled.

The man had Si on the hood in thirty seconds flat, snapping a pair of cuffs around his wrists. Next thing I knew, I had a set of my own. We were in the back of the cruiser, watching the officer talk on the radio to some guy at the station, letting him know we were being brought in for trespassing.

I just got arrested, I realized. *Oh my God.*

"I'm sorry, Em," Silas apologized quietly, so the cop wouldn't hear. "I didn't mean to get us into trouble. I lost my cool there."

"It's not like you can do much about it now," I said, trying not to freak out.

"I'm still sorry."

"We'll call my parents when we're there," I decided. "They'll come to get us. It'll be fine."

"I hope so." He threw his head back and sighed. "Your dad is going to kill me."

"He'll be killing me too. We'll face the wrath together."

"This isn't going to help me win points with him. How am I going to earn his approval?"

"I have no clue."

"That's not comforting!"

"It's true, though."

"Would you two shut up?" the cop quipped. "Keep it silent back there."

Silas's lips pursed, and I could see he was trying to bite his tongue.

This would be a long night.

26

Chapter Twenty-Six

Then

There was a lot going through my mind as I sat in a holding cell, several feet from Silas, rubbing my wrists where the cuffs once held them. He was slouched against the wall, head back with his jaw wound tight. I kept sneaking looks at him, wondering if he was ever going to say anything.

"This sucks," I managed.

He peered over at me. "That's an understatement."

Hearing his voice gave me a sense of relief. At least he wasn't totally pissed.

"I'm sorry," he continued. "This really wasn't my plan for tonight. I shouldn't have mouthed off."

"I get why you did it," I said.

"That doesn't mean it's right."

They gave us our obligatory phone calls when we were first brought into the station. As promised, I called my parents, he called Carly. They were on their way, but since New Orleans was a bit of a drive, we would be sitting for a while. My mother was disappointed, and my dad was pissed, but at least they were going to bail us out instead of letting us rot here.

"So how are we going to pass the time?" I asked.

"You tell me," he said. "I have no idea."

I chewed my lip nervously. "Is this your first time getting arrested?"

He stared at me, frowning. "Do I look like a criminal to you?"

"Well, no, but—" I started to get defensive, but I cut myself off when he started to laugh.

"I'm messing with you," he told me. "I'm sorry but the face you just made was adorable. You seemed so worried about offending me."

"Well, are you? Offended, I mean."

"Nah," he replied. "To answer your question, I've never been arrested before. I really hope they don't charge us or anything. This will be hard to explain if it goes on my record."

"Here's hoping."

He scooted a little closer to me, taking my hand. "You know, I think you might be a bad influence."

I gaped at him. "Me? *I'm* a bad influence?"

"Oh yeah," he teased. "It was your idea to leave the cafe."

"It was your idea to go to that damn park!" I exclaimed.

"Well, I still blame you."

"I think you corrupted me," I said.

He leaned in and kissed me, keeping me from arguing any further.

When we broke apart, I felt my cheeks flush. "I like it when you do that."

"Good," he said. "Because I like doing it."

We kept our fingers laced together as we sat there. The waiting was awful, and stewing in silence with no privacy or space to stretch wasn't fun either. I had to pee, but I wasn't about to use the nasty toilet a few feet over. I felt weird even considering the idea and crossed my legs like that would make my discomfort lessen.

I rested my head on Silas's shoulder and he mirrored the motion, letting out a small yawn.

"I can't wait to be back in my own bed," he declared. "This is so uncomfortable."

"I don't think holding cells are supposed to be comfortable," I pointed out.

He examined the clock hanging on the wall. "There's still probably a good two hours before they'll be here to take us home."

"Wonderful," I grumbled.

"At least we're together," he said. "I'd be bored without company."

"Aren't we still bored anyway?"

"Less bored," he corrected me. "We're less bored than we'd be separated."

"That's fair."

I didn't say it out loud, but I always thought if there was anyone I'd be arrested with, it would be River. Most of our time was spent with me trying to keep him out of trouble. A stunt like this was right up his alley. But, with the way things had panned out, it didn't appear that we would ever get a chance to share an incident like this one.

I was glad it was Silas, or at least I tried to be. I didn't know what we would use to describe our relationship, at least where it stood now, but I didn't care about the labels. I cared about him and about what we had. All of this, in the end, was because he wanted to help me move on. It meant so much to me that there weren't even words for it.

"I should become a lawyer," he announced suddenly.

"Why?" I questioned.

"Because then I can work cases for teenagers who get arrested for stupid reasons," he replied. "Sort of like us."

I giggled. "This is a strange way to pick your job."

"Doesn't matter. You'll probably be the only one who ever hears the story."

"I don't think telling everyone we got arrested together would go over well."

He paused. "How grounded do you think we are?"

"Very," I answered. "So grounded I probably won't be free for a good month."

"I'll miss you," he said earnestly.

"I'll miss you too," I said, and meant it. "We'll play chess as soon as I'm able to."

"I look forward to winning."

"Ha," I said dryly.

Somehow, the remaining time passed quickly. I was happy when I heard the sound of a door opening and several voices coming closer. An officer we hadn't seen yet stood beside my parents, holding the keys to the cell.

Freedom was too sweet. I was so excited I could cry.

"Mom!" I rushed forward and immediately began sobbing into her shirt. "Momma, I'm so sorry!"

She ran a hand through my hair. "I'm just glad you're okay. You scared the hell out of us."

My dad, the man of few words he was, nodded his head to affirm her sentiment. His eyes fell on mine, softening.

"You're so grounded," she told me. "And you are never doing this again, do you hear me?"

"I'm sorry," I whispered as I started crying again. She smelled like cheap detergent and nervous sweat and a fresh casserole, but she was still my mom, and sometimes all you need is your mom.

She kissed the top of my head. "We're going to take you home, lovebug."

My childhood nickname was enough to bring me comfort. I squeezed her tighter and smiled. "I love you."

"We love you too," my father chimed in.

"You really worried us," Mom went on. "I got a call in the middle of the night and I was so worried. After Riv—"

She stopped, noticing her mistake.

"It's fine, Mom," I assured her. "I get it."

Silas came up behind me, his fists in his pockets. "Look, this whole thing was my fault. I'm really sorry for all the inconvenience I caused."

My mother put her hand on his shoulder. "We're not happy with either of you, but this whole mess has been tiring and all I can hope is that you've learned from this mistake."

"Believe me, I have," Silas said.

"Good," my father added. "As much as I'd like to smack you upside the head, Miriam and I agreed to let this one go. Life's short, kid."

"I appreciate it, sir," Silas said sincerely.

"Sir?" Dad echoed. "I could get used to that."

As we walked out to the parking lot, Mom told Silas that Carly would be picking up the car and "dealing with him when he got home" or something. He didn't look excited about that, but I knew Carly wouldn't be too hard on him. It wasn't her style.

In the backseat, Si and I kept a respectable distance between us, but our fingers still brushed where they met in the middle.

Honestly, I was surprised that my dad was making conversation with him.

"Are you going back to Texas at the end of summer?" he asked Silas.

"I actually think I might stick around longer," Silas answered. "I can think of a few reasons why."

I didn't miss the small glance he cast at me when he said it. He didn't miss the way I beamed a little afterward.

Chapter Twenty-Seven

Then I ended up serving the entire grounding for the rest of the summer, much to my dismay. Even though I didn't really have anywhere to go, I knew that there was so much left to be resolved between Silas and me. It bothered me to no end, lingering in the back of my mind for what seemed like forever. I wanted to see him, but I wouldn't be able to. It royally sucked.

The morning of the first day of senior year, Mom made me breakfast, bacon and eggs, and sat with me at the table while I ate.

"I think you should talk to Silas at school today," she said suddenly.

"I was planning on it," I admitted through a bite of eggs. I was also probably going to kiss him again, but I kept that to myself.

"Good, because you two seem to really like each other."

I nearly died from embarrassment.

"Let me know when you'll be home, okay?" she added.

I nodded. "Alright."

She looked at the clock. "Well, I better get to work. Good luck, Em!"

Mom ruffled my hair on the way out, and just like that, I was alone again.

I finished my breakfast in silence, unable to stop wondering what Silas was up to. Ever since that night, I had been thinking about him. How could I not?

The only problem was, I had no idea if he was thinking about me too.

The halls were buzzing with life, holding onto the thrill of summer.

I stopped fixating on him when I got to school, other matters stealing my attention.

My schedule was lighter as a senior, and I was especially excited that I got to leave a period early because I didn't need more units than what I signed up for. It was the stuff of dreams.

My day was mostly teachers telling us their expectations for the year and some AP assignments. It went quickly enough, and most everyone had long forgotten about River.

Greta even let me sit with her and her friends at lunch. Even though I felt awkward about it (considering I had punched her in the face a few times months before), it was nice. Still, it was strange having the first day without Riv there.

I didn't see Silas until one of my last classes since both of us had statistics together. I was so happy his registration for school worked out. Knowing I would have him around another year made my punishment more bearable. Carly had stopped by to tell me herself, and I was over the moon about it. I knew she was too. He was helping all of us heal.

Outside the door, he pulled me into a giant hug and nearly

knocked me over.

"Hi," I breathed.

"Hey," he said. "God, I missed the hell out of you, darlin."

"It's good to see you," I told him.

"Meet me after school today," he pleaded. "We have to catch up."

"Yeah, we do," I agreed.

Before the bell rang, he snuck in a quick kiss, and we went to take our seats.

* * *

I walked to the trailer park like I had hundreds of times, but I knew this was different. I kept my fingers crossed as I went, one set of fingers for luck with Silas, and one set for the weather. I was wearing a flannel and a pair of shorts, which weren't going to hold up if I got caught outside in the rain.

When I knocked on the door, Silas was the one who opened it. He lit up when he saw me, which set the butterflies in my stomach off instantly.

"Are you going to invite me in?" I asked playfully.

He pushed the door open further and stepped away to let me inside. The trailer itself hadn't changed, but it still felt different. I looked around, taking it in as if I needed to commit the space to memory again. "Is Carly home?"

He shook his head. "She's at work."

"Oh," I said.

"Why? Did you need her?"

"No."

He rubbed the back of his neck, fingers tangling in the messy hair at the nape of his neck. "Why are we being so awkward?"

"It could be because we got arrested and haven't spoken in weeks," I offered.

"It's been terrible without you," he said. "I don't know how to manage without my Emery."

My *Emery*, I thought. *I like it.*

Then he was kissing me. For real, this time.

He moved so fast I couldn't say anything else. His lips silenced me, catching the words before they slipped out. He held me tightly, like he was scared he'd lose me if he let go. I kissed him back, melting beneath his touch.

Before it could go any further, he broke away. "I like you so much. I like you so much I don't know what to do with myself."

"I like you too. It's scary for me, but I do."

He let out a breath. "You have no idea how good that is to hear."

"Why?" I wondered.

"I was scared you lost interest in me," he said. "We were apart for a long time and couldn't really see each other. I didn't want to lose my shot with you."

"You didn't," I said softly. "Are you crazy? That wasn't ever going to happen."

"You never know."

I pressed my lips to his once more. "I'm pretty sure this isn't going away anytime soon."

I was being totally honest. I couldn't imagine things between us being different. He was such an amazing guy and our connection was important to me. I adored him, and somehow, he adored me. He was a miracle. If there ever was a miracle in my life, in Nowhereland, he was it.

My eyebrows furrowed. "Why me? What drew you to me?"

"Why not you?" he countered.

"I guess I just don't get what you see in me," I confessed. "You brought me out of a bad place and reminded me that there are amazing people waiting even at the worst times. I don't know how it happened, how *we* happened. What made you decide to stick around with me?"

He paused for a second, thinking, then got to his feet and tugged me toward his room by my hands. He closed the door first, then lowered me onto the bed.

"Silas—"

"I'm gonna tell you what I see in you," he whispered. "And I need you to pay attention. Don't talk. Just listen."

He kissed my forehead first, tracing his way to my temple. "You're smart."

He found the corner of my mouth next. "You're also funny. Your laugh is beautiful."

After kissing me on the lips, he whispered, "And you're a really good kisser."

My toes curled inside my high-tops when he kissed my neck slowly. "You're loyal."

Another kiss, this time to my shoulder as he pulled my shirt to the side. "You're gorgeous. Kind. Honest."

He kissed my hand, running his mouth across my knuckles. "You throw a good punch."

After that, he laced our fingers together and pulled me up so that we were face to face. "And Em, I enjoy the time I spend with you. I enjoy your teasing. The stories you have. The fact that you admit your faults. I like that you forgive people, even when they hurt you. I like that it doesn't take much to make you happy. I like that you listen. All of that is what I see in you."

"I don't deserve you," I told him.

"You're right, you deserve better than me," he said. "Which is why I'm going to try to be a better man. I'm gonna do everything I can to be what you deserve and more."

My eyes welled with tears at his sincerity, his tenderness.

"Please don't cry," he pleaded, kissing my forehead and holding me close. "There's one more, very important thing I need to tell you."

I looked up at him with curiosity. "What is it?"

His brown eyes locked on mine, and he spoke the words slowly so that I would hear each of them. "I think I'm falling in love with you."

A second passed. Then another.

"Do you mean that?" I asked, afraid the statement was ingenuine, afraid he didn't know what he was saying.

Silas kissed the tip of my nose gently. "I do."

Words didn't just fail me— they *abandoned* me entirely. I sat there stupidly, staring at him. After a second, he realized that I probably wouldn't be able to say anything, and reached for the chessboard that sat beside the bed. He scooted backward, bunching the blanket up as he did, and handed me both queens, white and black alike, giving me the choice.

I mentally thanked him for the distraction, picked the latter, and played a silent game of chess with him. After a few minutes, I gathered the courage to ask what CD he wanted to listen to. He picked The Rolling Stones, which meant I got to bypass every Beatles album for one that I hadn't listened to very often.

"What time do you have to be home later?" he asked, breaking our silence as he captured one of my pawns.

"Probably before dinner," I informed him.

I hesitantly moved a knight, squinting down at the board in an attempt to decide what my strategy was going to be. When I played River, the only thing I did was try to stay alive as long as possible, but Silas was different. He was someone I could beat, and admittedly that was fun for me.

"Checkmate," Silas said seconds later.

I glared at him. "You're distracting me."

"That's the idea." He wiggled his eyebrows at me. "Did it work?"

"You just like to screw with my head."

"I've been nothing but honest," he replied. "Now, do you want a ride home? It's raining, and I can't just let you walk."

"You can, but you don't want to."

"It violates my moral code."

"You are so weird."

"Yeah, but you picked me."

He had me there, and the cheeky smirk he wore only confirmed that he knew it. I glared at him and he smiled back at me all the same. I leaned over the chessboard, my knees tipping a few of the pieces over, and gave him a kiss because he looked so damn adorable that I couldn't help myself.

His hands reached out, sliding into the back pockets of my shorts. A rook poked the inside of my thigh but I didn't care. I kissed him anyway.

"This is weird," I announced when I pulled back.

"Why?" His forehead crinkled.

"I've never really had a boyfriend, and now I'm kissing a boy in his room and there are chess pieces where chess pieces should not be and I couldn't care less."

He threw his head back. I noticed then that Silas laughed with his whole body. His shoulders shook, his face lit up, and his eyes closed. It was a detail I intended to commit to memory. There are just some things you never want to let yourself forget. You just can't.

"How many girlfriends have you had?" I asked.

He shrugged. "A couple."

"What was the last one like?"

He thought for a second. "Uh, her name was Lana. We dated for a year or so. She was… cool? Why do you ask?"

I chewed my lip and looked down at my lap, at the fuzz that was growing back because I was too lazy to shave. I absently wondered if Lana shaved her legs all the time. I wondered if she was tall and blonde. I wondered about her until I almost went insane. I probably would've obsessed over it more, but Silas interrupted me.

"Stop that," he said. "My ex-girlfriend doesn't matter. You're the only one who matters to me right now. Besides, we broke up because she wasn't right for me. I never felt anything strong for her. You're the first of all of that for me."

"I didn't mean it like that," I said, feeling a need to clarify. "The thing is, you grew up in Texas, in a place with more people than a small town like this. You have all of these experiences that I don't, and I'm curious about it. I've never known anything other than this, but I want to more than anything. It's why I plan to get the hell out of here. Out of Nowhereland."

"I bet you can make that happen," he said.

I pushed the chessboard away. "Anywhere is better than here."

He took me in his arms and we lay back against the pillows. I rested my face against his chest, feeling the low rumble of his voice as he told me, "That's not always true, but we'll figure it out. I wouldn't mind seeing somewhere else too."

"You sure you want to stick around that long?" I teased.

He trailed his fingers up my bicep, leaving goosebumps in his wake. "I'm positively sure, Em."

28

Chapter Twenty-Eight

Now

We fly into New Orleans the Wednesday before Thanksgiving. I'm so nervous I can hardly relax into my seat, but Silas spends the entire flight with his head on my shoulder asleep. He can pass out anywhere, but I've never had that luxury. I wake him up when we're supposed to leave the plane, and the sleepy look on his face is so cute I feel my worries subside momentarily.

He yawns as we head for the baggage claim. "Why'd you have to wake me up?"

"Would you rather it be an angry flight attendant?" I asked.

"No, but—"

"Don't complain."

"Someone's feeling bossy," he remarks.

"And someone else is feeling grumpy," I say.

He heaves his suitcase off the conveyor belt, sighing. "You're lucky I love you."

"I love you too," I respond. "Now, let's go meet my father."

Dad drove in to pick us up, and even though he's getting

older, he still runs to hug me. He nearly crushes my spine doing it, his smile downright infectious. "God, Emery, you're so grown-up now."

"I look the same, Dad," I say with a laugh.

"You're making me feel old," he replies. "Now let me have a look at the boyfriend. Or is it fiance now? I saw the ring from a mile away."

"Husband," Silas informs him. "We got married a few days ago. It was a lowkey thing. Nothing major."

"Miriam ain't gonna like that you didn't invite her to the wedding," Dad says. "But, hey, I was wondering when y'all would do it. Congratulations. Just a head's up, son, I better not get any grandkids until both of you have degrees in hand."

"Yes, sir," Silas says.

I've noticed that even after years, he's still a little intimidated by my dad. For the first few months of our relationship, he was so worried the arrest would dampen his chances of getting my dad to like him. He had nothing to be scared of. Si is so likable that Dad couldn't be angry too long.

I stifle a giggle as they load our bags in the trunk, struggling, but working together. It's a good thing they get along because this would be extremely awkward otherwise. On the way back to Nowhereland, Dad and Si talk about football among other things I don't know much about. I don't mind.

I want the drive to last forever, dreading the moment I have to face the past again.

The town hasn't changed one bit. The ghosts of memories haunt me as we head home. To occupy myself with something other than a thought spiral, I look to my father and ask if Carly is coming to dinner tomorrow night.

He nods. "Of course. She and your mother are very close

now. They went and got their nails done the other night."

"That's funny," I say. "Mom never liked having girlfriends."

"She does now," he told me. "She even does yoga too."

"So does Em," Silas chimes in. "She looks like a small pretzel curled up on our carpet. I'm worried she'll break something."

"Miriam is the same way," Dad says. "That woman is bendy considering she's almost fifty years old, but she's timeless. She's gorgeous even now. Women are like wine. They get better with age. Only don't quote me on that, because she hates being reminded that we aren't kids anymore."

Silas chuckles. "I'll keep that in mind."

The apartment smells like a casserole, as always, and I can hear my mother chattering loudly on the phone from the moment I walk through the door. Her voice helps me relax.

"I'm telling you, Car, the last thing I expected was the third kid from Greta and Keith. You'd think two would be enough when they're barely twenty-two. Jesus Christ, they're like rabbits. I'll say it again, *freakin rabbits*—"

She stops mid-sentence, her phone pressed between her shoulder and chin.

"Hey, momma," I say with a wave.

"I'll call you back, Carly, my baby girl is home."

She hangs up and all but drops her phone to hug me immediately. Silas gets one almost immediately after, and then a swat on the back of the head when she sees our rings. "You didn't invite me to the wedding?"

Told you, Dad mouths at me.

Before either of us can explain, she waves a hand dismissively. "You know what? I don't care. I love you two and I'm glad you're happy. That's all I want."

"Thanks, Miriam," Silas says cheerfully. "I'm just glad this girl gets my last name. I love her to death."

Mom smiles. "I know. If you didn't, I'd beat your ass."

Dad laughs. I do too. Even Silas smiles, knowing she's teasing.

"I've got a dinner to finish," she says, shooing us away. "You two should get settled in. I'll holler when it's ready."

It's a short walk to the bedroom we'll be staying in. I know this place well, and even though I've been away for a long time, it still feels like a second home. Our apartment is where I feel most at peace, but the place I grew up comes close.

"Your parents are amazing people," Si tells me. "This should be a fun weekend."

"I'll drink to that," I say. "They love you."

"I hope so," he says. "I've been around long enough."

We cuddle on my old, tiny bed, just like we did on countless other days right at the beginning. There's something wonderful about coming back to this, back to the old habits we left behind.

"Did you ever think we'd be here?" I ask him.

"I hoped for a long time. And then I knew this was where I wanted to be. I was certain I'd spend the rest of my life with you."

"You're so charming, don't you ever get tired of it?"

He shakes his head. "Never."

As the jet-lag catches up with us, we head out to the kitchen table for dinner. Silas even sets the table for my mom before I can. If she doesn't already adore him, he only makes it better.

Countless minutes of happiness later, we are happily eating a new lasagna and mac and cheese hybrid. No matter how bizarre it sounds, it's phenomenal.

"So how is college going, lovebug?" Mom asks between bites.

"Good," I say. "I'm changing my major though."

"Really?" Dad raises his eyebrows. "I always thought physics was an odd choice. You hated that class in school."

"True," I admit. "I picked it on impulse. Honestly, I picked it for River. For the longest time, I wanted to be passionate and excited about it, but I wasn't. The other day on the way to a job interview, I figured it out, told Silas, and am now sitting here with no idea what to change it to."

"English?" Mom suggests.

I crinkle my nose. "Too many classic books. So boring."

"Bioengineering?" Dad jokes.

"More math and science? Count me out."

"What do you think, Silas?" Mom glances over at him.

He pauses before saying, "All I want is for her to be happy. I don't care if she picks Russian language as her major. I just want her to love what she does every day of her life."

I reach over and squeeze his hand, telling him how much that means to me without words.

"What about psychology?" Mom says after a second. "You loved that class last semester."

I think about it. She isn't wrong. The course, while mandatory, ended up being fascinating and fun. I learned a lot and loved every second, but since I was focused on physics, I never gave it too much thought.

She definitely has me wondering about the things I could do if I pursued it. There are kids like River I could help before their lives ended too short or something horrible happened to them. I don't want to jump to a new major hastily, but the idea is worth considering.

"I think we have a winner," Silas says. "You're a genius, Miriam."

"That she is," Dad chimes in. "What do you think, Em?"

"I think I'll sleep on it," I decide. "Maybe I'll give it a shot."

The answer is enough for my parents, who turn their attention to Si.

"So what about you, son?" Dad asks. "How's law school going?"

Silas considers his answer for a second before speaking up. "I really love it. I love the idea of giving a voice to the innocent and helping people. I remember that night we got arrested, I decided that I would go into law and make sure that I was a good attorney. The story used to be embarrassing to me, but I think it makes for a fun thing to talk about."

Mom and Dad exchange glances.

"You know, there's nothing like looking back at how your daughter and the love of her life got arrested together," says Mom.

"Romantic," Dad muses.

I scoff. "I'll say."

"At least we never did that," Mom remarks.

Dad jumps in. "Well, there was that one time—"

"Kellan!" she exclaims. "Not now."

My mom never blushes, but she's scarlet now.

Silas nudges me with his elbow. "We need to hear this story someday."

"I'll say," I reply.

The rest of our night is calm and bright. I win a long round Monopoly and fall asleep in Silas's arms. It's a perfect conclusion to a long day, a moment of calm in my life when it feels like it's never going to stop shifting and changing.

We spend Thanksgiving catching up with all the people we left behind, hearing stories about Carly's puppy and her new boyfriend, who brings a bottle of wine to dinner and wins my dad's good graces instantly. I run into Greta at the grocery store when I'm picking up a pie on Saturday after the holidays, and even give Keith a hug.

On our last day before we fly out, I go for a morning run past the cemetery where River is buried. I find myself relearning the streets of Nowhereland, taking in the way the infrequent cars sound on the old roads.

I end up running longer than I initially meant to, just as an excuse to look at all the sights I forgot were there. The newer things, like a flower shop on the main street, or Keith's convenience store, are proof that things move on even if I'm not there to move with them.

I memorize the details, old and new, because a small part of me knows that I'll dread leaving, even if I love California a lot more.

I run until I reach the end of the road that meets the highway. I watch trucks rush by, cars in a hurry to get somewhere, but never stopping here. Nowhereland may as well be invisible, judging by the way people speed past it.

I stay there and catch my breath, thinking of all the times River and I sped down that highway, to sit by it and dream of what it might feel like to leave. This time, I'm not in a convertible. I'm not with him. I'm by myself, hunched over, sweaty, and nearly delirious.

A few feet from where I'm stopped, he took his last breath, trapped in a cage of illness and struggle and the shattered remains of that damned car he loved so much. I don't want to remember this highway as a death sentence. I'd rather think of my birthday when we drove too fast and the other times we came this way.

"Riv," I murmur, despite him not being there to listen. "It's me."

I get no reply, but it doesn't matter. Ever since he died, I've been taking moments like this to throw my thoughts out there. Admittedly, it feels a little pointless sometimes, but other times, it makes me feel better. I knew him well enough to imagine what he would say back, if he could say anything back.

"I know I talk to you sometimes, even though it's weird to be having a one-sided conversation."

I know, he might joke. *Doesn't talking to a dead guy get old?*

"I don't know if you ever get my messages, if you can even call them that. I never wanted to come back here. You and I never did, actually. That was always the plan, but I'm changing it up a bit as I go."

You're such a bad listener, Emmy, he would probably say. *Haven't you heard a word I've said?*

"Mom and Dad are great and I can't stay away from them for too long. Plus, seeing Carly brightens my day. She's so happy, Riv. I wish you could see how great she's doing. She's even got a new boyfriend now, and even though she misses you and Rob, she's feeling whole again. We all are. You left us so much heartache, but we're finding ways to fill it with each other."

I'm glad. Mom deserves it. You all do.

"I'm married now if you can believe that. It's crazy to think I actually got married."

Lucky bastard. He better take care of you.

"I feel like a real adult now, even though I have no idea what I'm doing. I could use your advice, if you're willing to give it. I saw a creepy movie with a ouija board, so that's out of the question, but we can come up with something else. You're a genius, not me."

You seem to be fine, Emmy. Trust yourself a little more.

"I wish you were here," I say, swiping at my eyes to keep from crying. "I love you so much. I don't really know how to do this without my best friend."

I love you too. I'm always going to be your best friend.

"River Fields, you left a hole in me that I'll never really know how to fill. I don't intend to. I'll always have a piece of me that belongs to you. I won't forget you, and one day, I'll be telling so many stories about you that people will get bored."

How could they? I'm a legend.

"I might have to stop talking to you, though," I go on. "I don't want to, but I think it might be good for me to take a break. One day, I might feel differently about it, but for now, I'm working on letting go."

I understand. You don't have to wait around for me.

"I love you, Riv. Forever and ever."

I love you more than I love The Beatles.

"I'll be seeing you," I finish. "One of these days."

And that's it. I put my earbuds back in and start running back to my parents' place. The next song on shuffle is *I Will* and somehow, I just know that it's Riv. It's from him. The words stick with me the whole way there.

"Love you forever and forever. Love you with all my heart. Love you whenever we're together. Love you when we're apart. You know I will. I will."

* * *

The nostalgia is fierce within me as my parents take us to the airport later that day. I want to stay longer, even though I know I can't. Besides, I don't fit there anymore. I'm making my home somewhere else, and there isn't anything wrong with that. I'm gonna miss this place, the people in it too.

As I'm getting on the plane with Si, I stare out the window below us and say goodbye to my hometown. But I don't call it Nowhereland this time. Instead, I give a small wave at the tiny town somewhere below us, a town with one big road running through it and only a handful of people.

Goodbye, Lauton, Louisiana.

This moment is a closing page, a goodbye to the girl and boy who grew up here. Goodbye to the girl who lived and loved and got her heart broken and put back together. She's a woman now, a strong one at that. This is a goodbye to more than a place, a goodbye to something so much bigger than coordinates on a map.

Even though I'd like to think we both got out of Nowhereland, I realize that River and I were wrong to think like that. Where I'm from isn't a trap. It's a part of me, whether I like it or not.

That's the thing about hometowns— you can go other places, but you never quite leave.

The End.

About the Author

Maddie Kopecki is a California native, avid reader, and a proud Ravenclaw. When she's not writing, she can usually be found with her nose in a book, jittery from her last cup of coffee.

You can connect with me on:
- https://www.wattpad.com/user/epicmishamigo
- https://www.facebook.com/maddiewritesthings
- https://www.instagram.com/maddiefaith_

Made in the USA
Columbia, SC
11 February 2020

87664690R00167